EYES OF THE WICKED

ADAM J. WRIGHT

THE MURDER FORCE SERIES

Book 1: EYES OF THE WICKED

Book 2: SILENCE OF THE BONES

Book 3: REMAINS OF THE NIGHT

CHAPTER ONE

December 21st

"WE'RE NOT LOST," Melissa Wood said to her husband. "The SatNav knows exactly where we're going." She glanced at the illuminated map on the car's dashboard. Their Volvo was shown as a red arrow following a twisting blue line. The display showed nothing on either side of the car other than solid blocks of green pixels.

Melissa turned her attention to the windscreen. Other than the section of road illuminated in the Volvo's headlights, everything else was lost to the night. She knew they were driving through moors and woodland and might have liked to see the barren landscape that was such a contrast to their hometown of Birmingham but the thin sliver of moon high above them did nothing to illuminate their surroundings. It was as if they were driving through ink.

"She's been quiet for too long," Jeff said, looking at the map. In the glow from the dashboard, his features seemed ghostly, an effect heightened by the blackness of the window behind his profile. He tapped the digital map and said, "Speak to me. Where are we?"

"She's not saying anything because we need to follow this road for another nine miles before she gives us the next direction. She won't have a chat with you on the way. She'll speak when she needs to." Melissa smiled at her husband's lack of distrust where technology was concerned.

Even she had to admit, though, that the computerised female voice—which had talked incessantly when they were driving through Birmingham—would be a welcome sound out here in the middle of nowhere.

She looked at the map again. The red arrow was following the blue line. That was all there was to it. They were on the right route. And this pitch-black road was probably a lot less creepy during the daytime.

It had been Jeff's idea to travel at night. The Christmas holidays started tomorrow so the traffic on the motorways would be horrendous. Cars packed with families and their belongings would be bumper to bumper. There would be accidents. Traffic jams

Jeff's idea to avoid all that had been a good one. They'd arrive at the house his parents had rented in Whitby later tonight, get a good night's sleep, and wake up refreshed tomorrow when the rest of the extended family arrived for the annual festivities.

Jeff's parents rented a different house every year for the family gathering and it was usually somewhere posh. Last year, it had been in Devon. The travelling had been a bit much—another reason for their nocturnal journey this year—but the place had been stunning and they'd spent Christmas afternoon on the beach.

Melissa always enjoyed the Wood family get-togethers. Her own parents had been killed in a car crash over a decade ago and she'd been an only child, so it wasn't like she had anywhere else to go at this time of year.

She was distant from her few living relations, so she'd been glad when Jeff's folks had accepted her as one of their own. And now that she was expecting a baby to extend the Wood dynasty—a girl due to arrive next year—they'd taken her even more under their wing.

"I don't like this," Jeff said. "It's too bloody dark. What if someone was standing in the road? I'd never see them until it was too late."

"Why would someone be standing in the road in the middle of nowhere at this hour? I haven't seen a house since we passed those cottages half an hour ago. There's no one out here so stop worrying."

"I'm not worrying, I just don't want to kill someone."

"I'd be more worried about the wildlife. They have

deer out here, don't they?" She felt a sudden irrational fear that they might hit a large animal and crash into the trees at the side of the road. They'd be stuck out here all night. Her phone, which was sitting on the dashboard, had lost its signal at about the same time they'd left the cottages behind. She hadn't seen any other vehicles since then either, so the chances of them flagging down another motorist were slim.

"I don't know if there are deer here or not," he said.

"Just drive carefully," she told him.

"I am driving bloody carefully."

Melissa looked out of the windscreen at that moment and saw a pale figure standing in the pool of light cast by the headlights. "Jeff!" she screamed.

He slammed his foot on the brakes. The car shuddered and the squeal of the tyres against the road sounded like a banshee proclaiming a tragedy.

The figure caught in the headlights wasn't a deer. Melissa's fear of hitting one and crashing into the trees suddenly seemed silly because what was about to happen was worse than that. Much, much worse.

A young girl stood in the middle of the road. She couldn't have been more than thirteen or fourteen years old. She wore a white nightgown that seemed old-fashioned and made Melissa wonder—hope might be a better word—that the girl was a ghost or a figment of her imagination.

The sudden flash of hope disappeared as suddenly as it had arrived; Melissa didn't believe in ghosts and the fact that Jeff had hit the brakes meant he saw the girl too, so she wasn't imagining her.

Not only had he hit the brakes, Jeff was shouting, "No, no, no!" and pulling back on the steering wheel as if doing so could stop the car.

The girl's face was partly hidden by her long dark hair, but Melissa clearly saw her eyes widen in terror and her mouth form an "O" of surprise.

She closed her own eyes, desperate not to see that face disappear under the front bumper of the Volvo. She waited for the telltale thump that would signal the impact of steel on flesh, but it never came. Instead, the car juddered to a halt and stalled.

"Are you all right?" Jeff asked.

"Yes," she said, opening her eyes.

He looked down at her belly. "The baby?"

"We're fine." She struggled out of her seatbelt, which had locked around her. "We need to see if that girl is okay."

"I didn't hit her," he said. Then he repeated the words under his breath, as if reciting a mantra. "I didn't hit her."

Melissa opened her door and got out. The chiming of the car's open door warning system seemed unusually loud. The smell of burnt rubber rose from the tyres and the road.

"Is she okay?" Jeff asked, getting out on his side.

"I don't know," she said. There was no sign of the girl. The headlights shone on an empty section of road.

Melissa shivered. The night air held a sharp chill.

She wasn't a ghost. She was real. She has to be somewhere.

A rustling by the side of the road caught her attention. The girl appeared, fleeing from the darkness. She sprinted towards the Volvo, pulled open the back door, and clambered inside.

"Hey!" Jeff shouted. "What are you doing?" He leaned against the window and peered in at the girl. Then he looked at Melissa, his face as white as a sheet. "Oh my God, she's covered in blood."

Melissa went to the rear of the Volvo and opened the door. The girl cowered away from her, pressing herself against the opposite door. For a moment, Melissa wondered if she was going to open that door and run but the girl seemed to be terrified of something other than Melissa and Jeff. Something on the moors?

"We're not going to hurt you," she said gently.

"I didn't hit her," Jeff said. "I stopped in time. There shouldn't be blood."

The girl's nightgown was stained with deep red blots. Melissa cast her mind back to when she'd first seen the girl in the headlights. Had she been bloody then? Yes, she was sure of it. The girl had been covered in blood when she'd first appeared on the road.

"Were you in an accident?" she asked, wondering if some poor family had experienced the accident she'd been dreading further along the road. Maybe this girl was the only survivor and she'd been wandering around in a daze.

She didn't look like she'd been in an accident,

though. Other than the blood on her nightgown, she seemed unhurt. There were no wounds on her arms and legs other than a multitude of thin scratches that were probably the result of running through the woods.

"I don't think it's her blood," Melissa said. The small scratches wouldn't make the large stains of red that she could see on the nightgown.

"Thank God for that!" Jeff said. He frowned and leaned closer to the open door, inspecting the girl. "So whose blood is it?"

"That's not important at the moment," Melissa told him. "We've got to get her to a hospital. She seems to be in shock. I think she was in an accident."

"I'll call an ambulance," he said, fishing his phone out of his pocket. He looked at the screen and his face fell. "Have you got a signal? Mine's dead."

"No, I haven't." She turned her attention to the girl. "Listen, we're going to get you to a hospital. Everything will be all right." She attempted a reassuring smile but was sure the girl would see through it.

She didn't feel she had any right to try and reassure the girl of anything; something bad had obviously happened. If this poor girl's family had been killed in a car crash, her life would never be the same again. Melissa knew that from experience and her heart went out to the cowering, blood-covered girl in the back seat.

"Where's the nearest hospital?" she asked Jeff. She knew the question was futile—her husband had no more idea about hospitals in this area than she did—but she asked it anyway.

"How should I know?" He was jabbing at his phone's screen, as if doing so would miraculously resurrect the dead signal.

Melissa scanned the darkness around them for some sign that they might be near a village or even a house that had a landline with which they could call an ambulance. A cold wind blew across the moors, chilling her. The sky was choked with thick clouds and small flakes of snow danced in the air.

She spotted lights in the distance, perhaps half a mile away, although she couldn't judge the distance with any certainty due to the almost impenetrable blackness of the night.

"Over there," she said to Jeff, pointing at the lights. "We need to get over there."

He threw up his arms in a helpless gesture. "And how do you propose we do that? We can't tell the SatNav to take us to the lights in the distance. It doesn't work that way."

"There must be a road up ahead," she said, getting back into the car. "It looks like a village so there'll be a road."

Jeff got back in behind the wheel. "Shouldn't we continue to Whitby? We can get help there."

"Those lights are closer," she told him.

With a sigh of resignation, he put the Volvo into gear and set off along the road again. "Keep an eye out for that road."

"I will," Melissa said. She turned in her seat to look

at the girl who was cowering in the back. "Don't you worry. We're going to get help for you."

The girl looked at her with terrified eyes and said nothing.

Melissa turned back to face the windscreen, remembering that she had to look out for a road that would take them to the nearby village. Another memory forced its way into her head. An image on a TV screen.

"Oh my God," she said, when she realized where the memory had come from.

Jeff looked at her from the corner of his eye as he navigated the winding road. "What's the matter?"

"She's that girl from the News," she said, lowering her voice. "The one who went missing."

Jeff glanced up at the rearview mirror to look at the girl. "Are you sure?"

The more she thought about it, the more certain she was. There had been photos of the girl on every channel and in the papers. And now, she was here in the back of their car. Melissa was sure the girl had gone missing almost a month ago. Where had she been all that time?

"How did we get ourselves involved in this?" Jeff asked under his breath.

"We're helping someone in trouble," she said. "If it was our daughter who needed help"—she touched her swollen stomach almost unconsciously—"we'd want someone to do the same."

Jeff pointed at the windscreen. "This must be the road."

Melissa looked out. It was snowing more heavily now, the fat flakes tumbling in the headlight beams. The road ahead snaked away from the one they were currently on towards the lights in the distance.

"Take it," she told him.

They turned onto the road, which was barely wide enough for the car, and followed it. Jeff kept their speed at barely more than ten miles an hour; he was probably still shook up after almost hitting the girl and also wary of sudden bends in the road lurking unseen in the darkness ahead.

When they finally reached the village, which was barely more than half a dozen buildings huddled together against the weather, Melissa said, "Stop here. There are lights on in that house."

She waited for the car to come to a complete stop and got out, blinking against the falling snow as she trudged to the house's front door. She knocked and waited, shivering as the biting wind cut through her clothes and chilled her skin.

If they hadn't found the girl, she would have quickly frozen to death out there on the moors.

The door opened and an elderly gentleman in a dark blue jumper and baggy trousers looked at her expectantly. "Hello?"

"I'm sorry to bother you," Melissa said, "but do you have a phone? I need to call an ambulance."

"An ambulance?" He looked past her to the Volvo. "Has there been an accident?"

A voice came from somewhere inside the house. "Dad? Who is it?" A dark-haired woman in her forties appeared. She wore an apron and looked like she'd been cooking. Melissa realised she could smell something delicious on the air that reached her on the porch; something like warm scones or biscuits.

"There's been an accident," the old man said to his daughter. "This lady needs an ambulance."

The woman's eyes widened. "Oh my God, what happened?"

"There's no accident," Melissa said. "We found a girl wandering on the moors."

"A girl?"

Melissa nodded. "I think it's the girl who went missing some time ago. Do you have a phone?"

"Yes, of course, come in."

The old man stepped aside, and Melissa went into the house, thankful to be out of the wind.

The woman picked up the receiver of a phone that was attached to the wall and handed it to Melissa.

"While you're on to them, I'll fetch Mrs Summers," she said. "An ambulance will take a while to get here. She only lives half a mile away." She pulled a pair of walking boots from behind the door and took a heavy coat from a peg on the wall.

"Mrs Summers?" Melissa asked.

"She's a police detective," the woman said. "If the girl is the one who went missing, she'll know what to do. Bring her into the house where it's warm. Dad, make them a cup of tea." She pointed a key fob out into the night and the headlights of a Land Rover illuminated briefly. "I'll be back shortly," the woman said before going out to the vehicle.

"I'll put the kettle on," the old man said, making his way to the kitchen.

Melissa dialled 999 and realised she didn't know where she was. She didn't know where they should send the ambulance. "Where are we?" she shouted after the man.

"Rosemoor House. Tollby village," he said.

When the operator answered, she told him she'd found a girl wandering on the moors and that she was in shock and might have hypothermia. He told her he was sending an ambulance right away and she gave him the address the old man had given her.

After hanging up, she went out to the car and opened the rear door. The girl shrank away from her and pressed herself against the opposite door.

"Do you want to come inside?" Melissa asked in as gentle a voice as she could muster. "It's nice and warm and they've even got scones. I'm sure they'd let you have one."

She got no response other than a frightened stare.

Reaching out her hand to the girl, she said, "Come on. No one is going to hurt you."

The girl whimpered and tried to press herself even further into the opposite door.

Melissa sighed and shut the door before climbing

into the front. "I've rung an ambulance and the Land Rover that just pulled away was someone going to get a policewoman who lives nearby," she told Jeff. "We'll just have to wait in here."

He nodded. "Well at least I've got a signal on my phone now, even if it's a weak one. I can call my parents and let them know we've been delayed."

Melissa took out her phone and saw that she also had a weak signal. She brought up the Internet and typed *Missing Girl UK* into the search box.

A photo of a dark-haired girl appeared on the screen with a headline beneath it that read, *Abigail Newton Still Missing*.

Turning in her seat, she looked closely at the cowering girl's face and then at the picture on her phone. There was no doubt about it; this girl was Abigail Newton. She was no longer missing; she was in their car.

But where had she been all this time? What had she been through?

Someone would find the answers to those questions. Seeing the look on the girl's face, Melissa realised that she didn't envy the person who would eventually discover this poor girl's story.

CHAPTER TWO

Detective Inspector Danica Summers hated the winter-time. For too many years, the arrival of the season had heralded the discovery of dead bodies on the moors, all victims of a murderer the media had dubbed the Snow Killer.

This was the first year when there would be no such discoveries--the Snow Killer had been dealt with and wouldn't strike again--but her mind still seemed to be on edge, waiting for a call that would take her out into the snow to find a dead girl encased in ice.

Even now, when she should be relaxing in front of the telly or reading a book, she was sitting in the window seat and watching the snow fall over the bleak landscape. Barney and Jack, her German Shepherds, were stretched out in front of the fireplace, basking in the warmth there. They had the right idea, but Dani couldn't hope to achieve that level of relaxation while her thoughts whirled like snowflakes in a storm.

This was the first Christmas she'd be spending alone. Her daughter Charlotte was spending the day with her boyfriend's parents. She'd assured Dani that she'd come to the cottage if Dani really wanted her to but Dani didn't need to be a Detective Inspector to see that Charlie wanted to spend the holidays with the boyfriend she'd met at Birmingham Uni so she'd said she was working over Christmas anyway. That had been a lie. She'd booked Christmas day off ages ago when she'd thought Charlie would be visiting.

She couldn't blame Charlie for not wanting to come to North Yorkshire for the holidays; the last time she'd been here, there had been reporters everywhere, all of them trying to get an exclusive story with the woman who'd caught the Snow Killer, or the Red Ribbon Killer as some of them had called him. They'd followed Dani everywhere as she went about her job, rung her in the middle of the night, and called at the cottage at all hours, although Barney and Jack had put a stop to that when they'd gone berserk every time someone came to the door. The dogs had detected Dani's frustration with the media and acted accordingly.

The number of reporters had eventually dwindled as more exciting stories had grabbed their attention and drawn them away like flies attracted to a cow pat. Dani still got the odd call but other than that, her life had settled down and become quiet again.

Then the damn snow had arrived.

The weather had brought with it memories of

death and tragedy. When Dani closed her eyes, she could clearly see the faces of the girls she'd been called to on the moors. She remembered them all year round--their faces would never leave her--but the snow made the memories more vivid. It reminded her of the cold-ness she'd felt while walking across the frozen ground to each girl's final resting place, a coldness that was just as much internal as it was external as she steeled herself against the scene she was about to witness.

"It won't happen again," she told herself. "It's over."

Lights in the distance caught her attention, almost indistinguishable from the white landscape at first but getting brighter as they approached.

Barney lifted his head, ears pricked. Jack did the same and made a light chuffing sound through his teeth.

"Calm down," Dani told them. "I don't think any reporter would brave this weather just to get a story."

But if not a reporter, then who?

When the Land Rover pulled up outside the cottage, she realised she knew the vehicle. It belonged to someone in Tollby , didn't it? She searched her mind for the name of the owner. It was a woman, wasn't it? Deborah? No, Deirdre. Deirdre Murray.

She went to the front door and opened it as Deirdre climbed out of the vehicle. Barney and Jack, realising the visitor was friendly and not one of those pesky reporters, stood by Dani's legs with their tails wagging.

Deirdre approached the door and now Dani could see a worried look on her face.

"What is it? What's wrong?"

"Someone found a girl wandering on the moors. They've called an ambulance, but I thought we should get you." She paused and then added, "It's that girl who went missing."

Abigail Newton. The name came to Dani immediately. Abigail's name and photo had been on the News and in the papers almost every day since she'd gone missing. The latest reports had simply said that since she hadn't been found, the police feared the worst. But now Deirdre was saying she was here?

"Are you sure it's Abigail?" she said as she grabbed her coat and boots. "She went missing over a hundred miles away from here, in Derbyshire."

"I'm not sure," Deirdre admitted. "But they've found someone. She was wandering on the moors alone."

Once she'd laced her boots, Dani stepped out into the cold night air with her coat under her arm. She could put it on later. She locked the front door of the cottage and asked Deirdre, "Where is she now?"

"At my house."

"I'll follow you." Dani climbed into her silver Land Rover Discovery and gunned the engine. She dialled the heating up to full blast and turned on the windscreen wipers.

Deirdre climbed back into her own vehicle and pulled out onto the road. Dani followed, reminding herself that the road was treacherous in this weather and she had to keep her speed down and stay a good distance from the vehicle in front, even though she was anxious to attend to the girl who'd been found on the moors.

Found alive on the moors. That was a hell of a lot better than winters past.

The village of Tollby wasn't far from her cottage and when they arrived, she noticed a Volvo parked outside Deirdre Murrays' house with its lights on. As she got out of the Discovery, the Volvo's passenger door opened and a woman got out, pointing Dani to the backseat of the vehicle.

She grabbed her coat and hurried over to the Volvo. "Are you the person who found her?" she asked the woman.

"Me and my husband."

"And what were you doing on the moors?"

"We were going to see my husband's parents. I'm Melissa Wood. My husband's name is Jeff."

Dani could check all this later. Right now, she had to see the girl. She opened the Volvo's rear door and peered inside.

The girl was dressed in a bloodstained white nightgown. She had nothing on her feet and even though the air in the Volvo felt like the heaters had been turned to Tropical, she was shivering. That was probably shock. Dani offered the girl a gentle smile and placed her coat over her bare feet.

In return, the girl regarded her with eyes full of fear.

There was no doubt about it; this was the face Dani

had seen on the News and in the tabloids. This was Abigail Newton.

"Do you mind if I sit next to you?" Dani asked. "It's cold out here."

The girl didn't say anything, but she moved her legs slightly, tucking them tighter to her chest, leaving room for Dani to get into the car.

"Thanks," she said, getting into the Volvo. "Sir," she said to the man in the driver's seat, "Would you leave the vehicle, please?"

"Okay," the man said before getting out and closing the door.

"There," Dani said, turning to the girl. "Now it's just us. Your name's Abigail, isn't it? I'm Dani. "

Abigail simply stared at her.

Dani cast her mind back to the News reports she'd seen about Abigail and remembered the girl's parents putting out a heartfelt appeal for their daughter's safe return.

"Abigail, your mum and dad are going to be so happy to know that you're okay. Shall we see what we can do about letting them know you're here?"

The girl looked into Dani's eyes for the briefest of moments and gave the tiniest of nods.

"Okay. I'm going to use the phone in the house just there." She pointed at the Murray residence. "Because my mobile doesn't work that great in the village and I want to make sure I have a good, clear line when I talk to someone who can help us get in contact with your parents." She made to open the door, but Abigail grabbed her arm.

"Do you want to come with me?"

Abigail nodded decisively.

"Okay. Why don't you put my coat on first? It's cold out there." She pressed the button to open the window and it buzzed down slowly. Deirdre was standing no more than a couple of feet away with Melissa Wood and her husband. "Do you have a spare pair of boots?" Dani asked.

Deirdre nodded and rushed into the house.

Dani closed the window again and turned to Abigail. "We want to keep your feet nice and warm." The girl had put on the coat. It swamped her, making her appear even more vulnerable and fragile.

Deirdre knocked on the window and Dani opened the door to accept the pair of Karrimoor boots that were passed to her. She held them up so Abigail could see them. "Do you want to put these on?"

Abigail took them from her and slipped her feet into them.

"There," Dani said. "Now let's get to that phone and let your mum and dad know you're okay." She climbed out of the Volvo and Abigail followed, sliding across the backseat and getting out of the same door. To Dani's surprise, the girl reached out and held her hand as they walked towards the house.

Once they were inside, along with Deirdre, Melissa, and Jeff, Dani closed the front door.

Trevor Murray, Deirdre's dad, emerged from the

kitchen. He looked at the group of people gathered in the hallway. "Is everything all right?"

"Everything's fine, Mr Murray," Dani said. "If you could take everyone into the living room while I make a phone call, that would be great."

Deidre took him by the arm. "Come on, Dad, let's put the kettle on." She pointed out the living room to the Woods and they went through, leaving Dani and Abigail in the hallway.

Dani picked up the phone and dialled the head-quarters of the North Yorkshire Police--her own force-- at Northallerton. She got through to the automated menu and keyed in the extension for DS Matt Flowers, her work colleague who she knew was on a late shift tonight. Matt answered after a couple of rings.

"Detective Sergeant Matt Flowers."

"Matt, it's Dani."

His tone became serious when he realised it was his boss on the line. "Everything all right, guv?"

"Yeah, I need you to do me a favour. Find out who's in charge of the Abigail Newton case in Derbyshire. I need a phone number."

"No problem. I think there's an incident room number."

"No, not the incident room. I want the person in charge."

"Okay, just a second."

She heard him typing on his keyboard. There was a pause and then he said, "That would be DCI Stewart Battle." He read out a phone number.

"That's his work number. His mobile is also listed here."

"Give me his mobile."

He read out the digits and Dani committed them to memory. "Thanks, Matt."

"Has something happened, guv?"

"I'll tell you all about it later." She hung up and dialled the number Matt had given her.

The man who answered sounded gruff. "Hello?"

"DCI Battle?"

"Yes."

"This is DI Danica Summers of the North Yorkshire Police. I'm calling you because I believe you're in charge of the Abigail Newton missing person case."

"That's right. If you have some information, there's an incident room--"

"I have Abigail Newton here with me, sir."

"What?"

"She was found earlier tonight on the North Yorkshire moors."

"Do you mean...she's alive?"

"Yes, she is, sir. Very much so."

His tone brightened. "North Yorkshire, you say? I'll get up there immediately. Which station are you based at?"

"There's an ambulance on the way," Dani told him. "We'll be at the Whitby hospital."

"Is she hurt?" he asked.

That was a question Dani couldn't truly answer if it included mental damage as well as physical. God only knew what Abigail had endured for the past three weeks. It was obvious that the blood on the nightgown wasn't hers, but it was someone's. What had this poor girl witnessed?

"She's in shock," she said to Battle.

"Of course she is. I'll let her parents know she's alive and get them up to Whitby along with my team. They'll be as surprised as I am. They'd given up all hope of seeing her alive again."

"Well they needn't worry," Dani assured him. She heard a vehicle in the street outside and saw flashing lights through the frosted glass in the door. "The ambulance is here. I have to go. I'll see you when you get to Whitby, sir."

"Yes, and thank you, DI Summers." He hung up.

Dani did the same and rang DS Flowers again. When he answered, she said, "Matt, I need a couple of uniforms at Rosemoor House in Tollby. There's a couple here who found Abigail Newton on the moors tonight. We need to get statements."

"Abigail Newton? The missing girl from Derbyshire?"

"That's her. Get these people's statements so they can be on their way. We can hand the paperwork over to the Derbyshire police later."

"Of course. I'm on it."

"Thanks. I'll be at the Whitby hospital if anyone needs me."

The hospital? Is she...?"

"She's all right," Dani told him. "Just in shock."

Remembering how long it was going to take Battle and his team to get here, she added, "And get a SOCO to the hospital. There's some blood we need analysed. Might as well do it in our lab to save time."

"Okay, guv. One Scenes of Crime Officer will be at the hospital shortly."

"Thanks, Matt." She hung up and turned to Abigail. "The policeman I just spoke to is going to tell your parents that you're okay and bring them up here to see you. Now, we just need to go to the hospital to get you checked over while they're on their way. Is that okay with you?"

Abigail nodded.

Dani popped her head into the living room where Melissa and Jeff Wood were sitting together on the settee. "There's an officer on the way to take a statement from you and then you can continue on to your destination."

They looked at her and nodded. Dani wondered if they were suffering from mild shock themselves. It wasn't every day a missing girl in bloodied clothes ran in front of your car. But they'd soon get over whatever negative effects they were experiencing and the story of this night and how they'd found Abigail Newton would eventually become one they told to anyone who would listen, including the press most likely.

Deirdre appeared at the kitchen doorway. "The ambulance is here."

"I know," Dani said. "I've asked for officers to come

and interview the Woods. They'll want to get a statement from you as well."

"That's fine," Deirdre said.

"Thanks for coming to get me. You did the right thing."

Deirdre smiled. "I know."

Dani took Abigail's hand. "Okay, let's go." She led the girl outside, where the ambulance waited. The rear doors were open, and a female paramedic stood in the light spilling from the vehicle's interior. The snow was falling thick and fast now, covering the village in a thick white blanket.

It would also be covering any evidence on the moors that might have told them exactly where Abigail had come from.

Dani looked up at the snow-laden night sky and silently cursed the weather.

CHAPTER THREE

Battle ended the call with DI Summers and looked across the table at Rowena. "I've got to go."

Her face fell as she regarded him and the dinner he'd hardly touched. They were eating late because he'd been held up at work and she'd waited for him to arrive home before cooking a spaghetti bolognese. "Right now?" she asked. "This moment?"

He nodded. "I'm afraid so. They've found her."

Her disappointed expression became one of surprise. "Abigail Newton? Where?"

"North Yorkshire, of all places," he said, pushing back his chair and getting up. "I've got to go up there."

"I'll make you a sandwich to take with you. You can't drive all that way and not eat anything." She got up from the table and disappeared into the kitchen.

Battle went upstairs and splashed some cold water on his face in the bathroom before changing into a fresh shirt and tie, trousers, and tweed jacket. He'd already worked a full shift and he didn't fancy driving all the way to Whitby but if that was where Abigail was, then that was where he had to go. How she'd travelled more than a hundred miles since being abducted from a country lane here in Derbyshire, he had no idea but hopefully that question would be answered by Abigail herself.

She'd obviously escaped her captor or been released. Either way, she could more than likely give the police some information which would help them catch the bastard.

"She's alive," he told himself. All through the investigation, which had basically come up with nothing but dead ends, he'd held out hope that Abigail was alive. It was the only way to conduct a missing persons investigation as far as he was concerned. But that hope had been wearing a bit thin lately. Now she'd been found, and his investigation would have a new focus; that of finding her abductor.

He went back downstairs and found Rowena waiting by the front door with a paper bag and a Thermos flask. "Sandwiches and coffee," she said as she handed them to him. "And please be careful."

"I'm always careful." He took his heavy winter coat from the stand by the door, kissed his wife, and stepped out into the wintry evening.

"See if you can find us a house by the sea while you're there," Rowena called after him as he unlocked his Range Rover.

He smiled. They'd talked about a house by the sea

for years. Living in landlocked Derbyshire made that dream seem very far away but they'd vaguely promised each other that they'd retire to the coast eventually. That sounded fine to Battle but he had no intention of retiring yet and had a few years to go before the force kicked him out. He intended to use those years to do as much good police work as he could. The sea could wait a little longer. It wasn't going anywhere.

He climbed into his Range Rover and switched on the SatNav. When he typed Whitby Hospital into the destination field and saw that it was almost a four-hour drive, he groaned. Before he could embark on the trek north, he had to drive to Abigail's house and tell her parents that she'd been found. They lived in Matlock, which was half an hour's drive from here. He wouldn't get to Whitby until the early hours of tomorrow morning at this rate.

He used his mobile to call Lorna Morgan, his DS. When she answered, he said, "Lorna, meet me at the Newton's house as soon as you can. And bring whatever you need for a trip to Whitby."

"I'm assuming you're not taking me on holiday, guv," she said. Then her tone darkened, and she asked, "Has something happened?"

"They've found her, Lorna. The North Yorkshire Police have found Abigail." Before she could ask the inevitable question, he added, "She's alive."

He heard her sigh on the other end of the line. "Thank God for that. How is she?"

"Not sure yet. In shock, apparently. She was

wandering over the moors. We'll know more when we get to the hospital in Whitby."

"Right, I'll meet you at the Newton house. They'll be so relieved to know she's alive."

"They will," he agreed before ending the call.

He supposed he should call the Superintendent and let him know what was happening. If the press got wind of this, they'd be hounding the Derbyshire force for information and in Battle's absence, it would be up to the Super to make a statement to the media. He didn't have the Super's home number so he dialled his work number instead. He could leave a voicemail explaining where he'd gone, and that Abigail had been found.

He was surprised when his call was answered by Jean King, Superintendent Powers' secretary.

"Jean," he said. "It's Stewart Battle. I didn't expect you to be working so late."

"The superintendent has a late meeting," she said curtly. Battle had known Jean for years and had never known her to be anything but curt and to the point.

"Must be important if he's in the office at this hour. So I take it he's not available for a chat."

"He isn't," she said.

"Well could you ask him to ring me when he's done?"

"When he's done, he'll be going home to get ready for an evening dinner at the Police Association."

"Still, I think he's going to want to speak to me,

Jean. What I've got to say is more important than hobnobbing with the high-ups."

She sighed. "All right. What shall I tell him you want to discuss that is so important?"

"Tell him we've found Abigail Newton, please. Thanks."

She started to say something, but Battle ended the call.

He put the Range Rover in reverse and backed out of the drive and onto the road. Turning the SatNav off for now, he set off for Matlock and the Newton residence. Like Lorna had said, Eric and Sarah Newton would be over the moon to discover that their daughter was still alive. Over the course of the three-week investigation, he'd seen the spark of hope gradually fade from their eyes. He couldn't blame them for fearing the worst; finding an abducted child alive after three weeks was rare.

After that amount of time, if they were found at all it was usually in a shallow grave that some dog walker stumbled across in the woods or washed up in a canal somewhere. Abigail had been lucky to beat the odds.

Or had she? What horrors had she endured at the hands of her captor during the time she'd been missing? Three weeks was a long time to be at the mercy of an abductor.

His mobile, which was synced with the hands-free system in the Range Rover, rang. Battle answered it by pressing a button on the steering wheel. "DCI Battle."

Superintendent Powers' voice filled the car. "Battle, what the hell do you mean they've found her?"

"Abigail Newton, sir. She's been found in North Yorkshire."

"North Yorkshire? What the bloody hell is she doing in North Yorkshire?"

"I don't know, sir. I'll hopefully find that out when I get there. I'm on my way there now."

"Oh," Powers said. He sounded surprised. "Can't someone else handle it?"

Now it was Battle's turn to be surprised. Was his boss trying to take him off the case? "I'm in charge of the Abigail Newton case, sir," he said, in case Powers had somehow forgotten.

"I know that," his superior said, "but something's come up. Something important. I need you here first thing in the morning."

Battle had no idea what could be so important that Powers was willing to take him off the Abigail Newton case at the moment the girl had been found but he knew that he wasn't going to abandon Abigail now.

"Sir, this is a critical moment in the case. I need to see this through."

"Listen, Battle." Powers voice had risen in tone, betraying his frustration. "You're off the case. I can't tell you why over the phone, but you'll thank me tomorrow. I put in a good word for you this evening so don't let me down now."

"What was that? I can't hear you," Battle said, even

though the superintendent's voice was booming loud and clear in the car. "You're breaking up, sir."

"I said don't let me down, Battle. Be in my office tomorrow morning at nine sharp."

Battle hung up. He had no idea what Powers was talking about and at this moment, he didn't care. He had far more important things demanding his attention. Eric and Sarah needed to be told that their daughter was alive. Abigail needed to be reunited with her parents and brought home. In an ideal world, she'd be able to put the events of the past three weeks behind her but in Battle's experience working with victims of abduction, that rarely happened.

It was more likely that Abigail would carry emotional scars with her for the rest of her life.

The first flakes of snow hit the windscreen and melted on the glass. The windscreen wipers swept them away.

Battle groaned. This was all he needed. Bad weather and a four-hour drive north. He might as well add an extra hour on that estimate if the roads were going to be bad.

When he arrived at the Newton residence in Matlock, the snow was coming down faster. He could only hope the gritters had been out to keep the main roads clear.

DS Morgan's cherry red Toyota Yaris was parked outside the Newton house and Morgan was inside the car, waiting for him.

He got out and waved to her. She waved back and

climbed out of the Yaris, bundled up in a long woollen coat and scarf. Her face was framed by her long black hair and a blue knitted hat that sat on her head.

"Right, let's deliver the good news," Battle said. "Then we need to get up to Whitby and see what Abigail can tell us that will help us catch the bastard that did this." He didn't mention his conversation with Powers or the fact that the superintendent had told him he was off the case. Powers might have been a good policeman at one time but too much time sitting behind a desk and attending swanky dinners had caused him to put political motivations over good honest police work. He'd never have tried to pull Battle off the Abigail Newton case at the very moment she'd been found otherwise.

They trudged through the deepening snow along the path that led to the unremarkable stone cottage that was Abigail's home. Battle knocked sharply on the door. They only had to wait a few seconds before it was opened by Eric Newton. His wife stood behind him, a look of horror on her face as she realised the police were calling at this late hour and that could only mean one thing.

Unwilling to prolong their agony a second longer than he had to, Battle simply said, "Abigail has been found. She's alive."

Sarah Newton collapsed. Her legs gave way and she slid down the wall until she was sitting on the hallway floor, sobbing. Her husband went to her and put his arms around her.

"Where?" he asked, looking at Battle through tear-filled eyes. "Where is she?"

"She's in Whitby. She was found wandering on the moors near there."

"Is she all right? What happened to her?" His voice was becoming desperate.

Battle understood that they wanted answers, but he couldn't give them any at the moment. "The police have taken her to the hospital because she may be suffering from shock but that's all I know at the moment. I'll arrange for a couple of uniformed officers to drive you up there."

Eric nodded. His wife was still crying, her head buried against her husband's chest.

"I suggest you pack a bag with some of Abigail's things," Battle said. "The police car will be along shortly to take you to her." He closed the door and walked back along the path with DS Morgan in tow.

"Can you call in and arrange that car?" he asked her.

"Of course, guv."

He didn't tell her that he couldn't do it himself because he was officially off the case.

CHAPTER FOUR

December 22nd

DANI WOKE UP WITH A START. At first, she didn't know where she was as her bleary eyes picked out an assortment of high-backed chairs --one of which she was sitting on--and a television bolted to the wall with the volume turned down. Then she remembered she was in the Day Room of the ward where Abigail Newton had been taken.

She checked her watch. Almost 2 a.m. Battle should have been here by now, unless the weather was holding him up. She got out of the chair, ignoring an ache in her lower back, and went to the window. The hospital car park and the paths below the window were shrouded with snow. Dani stretched painfully and went in search of Abigail.

A SOCO had been here earlier and had taken

away the bloodied nightgown as well as samples from Abigail's skin and body that a female doctor had collected using a SAFE kit. The process was undignified, but Abigail had taken it all in her stride and Dani had been proud of the girl.

Abigail still wasn't talking but seemed to have calmed down since Dani first met her in the back of the Volvo in Tollby. She'd been given her own room, a fresh hospital gown, and a sedative before being put to bed with a saline drip in her arm.

Dani had rung Matt Flowers and asked him to arrange for a uniform to be posted outside Abigail's room. The girl was a witness and her abductor was still at large. Her safety was paramount. But it wasn't a uniformed officer she found outside Abigail's room; it was Matt himself.

"Guv," he said, getting up from a plastic chair he'd placed outside the room.

"Everything okay?" she asked.

"Everything's quiet. She's out like a light."

"Hopefully she'll stay that way until morning. After what she's been through, she needs to rest."

"Do we know what she's been through?"

"No, not exactly. She isn't talking." One thing they did know was that Abigail hadn't been sexually assaulted. The doctor who'd used the Sexual Assault Forensic Evidence kit and examined Abigail had confirmed that. Abigail would probably suffer emotional damage from her ordeal but at least she hadn't been physically damaged as well.

"And this bloody weather isn't helping either," Dani said. "Any clues we might have found on the moors are probably buried under a foot of snow by now."

"Probably still worth taking a look, though."

"Of course it is. But we have to remember that this isn't our case, no matter how much we might want to solve it. The Derbyshire police are on their way here and when they arrive, we have to hand everything over to them."

The thought of letting someone else handle this rankled her. She wanted to investigate, needed to find out who had put that fearful look in Abigail's eyes and make sure they paid. But that wasn't going to happen. The best she could hope for was that the Derbyshire police asked for assistance in running the Yorkshire end of the investigation. But they might not even do that and could decide to do everything themselves.

She hated inter-force politics.

Still, if it meant catching Abigail's abductor, she was willing to do anything she could to help.

The sound of voices coming from the nurse's station up the hall caught her attention. She turned in that direction to see a couple she recognised as Abigail's parents. She'd seen them on the News pleading for their daughter's safe return. Miraculously, their wish had been granted and they were about to see Abigail again, alive and well. It was probably more than they ever realistically expected, especially in those moments when they were being pragmatic. This was not how abduction cases usually ended.

Abigail's parents were accompanied by two female uniformed officers, presumably from Derbyshire. After a brief word with one of the nurses, they were led towards their daughter's room. Dani and Matt stepped aside and said nothing as the couple walked past them and into the room. This was a time for them to be with Abigail without interruption from outside agencies.

A stocky man with a twee hat and bushy salt and pepper moustache appeared at the nurse's station, accompanied by a dark-haired woman wearing a blue knitted hat. The nurse they spoke to pointed at Dani and Matt.

The stocky man and dark-haired woman approached the Yorkshire detectives.

"DCI Battle?" Dani asked.

The man nodded and held out his right hand. "DI Summers, I presume."

"Yes, and this is my colleague, DS Matt Flowers."

Battle shook their hands and introduced his companion as DS Lorna Morgan.

"How is she doing?" he asked, nodding his head towards Abigail's room.

"She was traumatised when she came off the moors, but she's been sedated and she's sleeping now. According to the doctor, she hasn't been sexually assaulted. We've sent DNA samples to our lab to be analysed. The nightgown she was wearing was covered with blood, but it wasn't Abigail's."

Battle pursed his lips. "Do we know whose it is?"

"Not yet, sir."

"I like to be a bit more informal with colleagues," he said, referring to the title by which Dani had addressed him.

"No problem, guv," she said. "Do you have any plans about how you're going to progress the investigation now that Abigail's been found?"

He sighed. "I suppose a search of the moors is in order, but this weather isn't going to be any help. Could we use some uniforms from your force? It's going to take a lot of resources."

"You'd have to speak to my guv'nor. Superintendent Brian Holloway."

"Thanks. I'll do that." He took a small black notepad out of his jacket and made a quick note in it. Then he turned to DS Morgan. "There isn't much more we can do here at the moment, so I suggest we find somewhere to bed down and start fresh in the morning."

Morgan nodded. "Yes, guv."

Battle turned back to Dani. "I'll check in with you tomorrow. Are you headquartered here in Whitby?"

"No, the HQ is at Northallerton. An hour's drive from here."

He nodded. "And is that where I'll find..." He consulted the notepad. "Superintendent Holloway?"

"It is."

"Good. I'll see you tomorrow, then." He nodded to

Dani and Matt and then turned and left with DS Morgan.

"What do you think?" Matt asked when the two Derbyshire detectives had left the ward.

"I think they'll do a fine job," she said. "I just wish we could see this case through."

He nodded thoughtfully. "Don't you think DCI Battle looks...I don't know...familiar?"

Now that Matt mentioned it, she did think she'd seen Battle's face somewhere before. In the papers, perhaps? "Maybe," she said.

He was typing something into his phone. "Ah," he said. "He was involved in the Blackden Edge Murderer case a couple of years ago."

Dani remembered the case but only vaguely. Something about murders stretching back forty years in a remote part of Derbyshire. She hadn't paid much attention at the time because she'd been in the process of moving house. Shaun had been gone a couple of years and she and Charlie were making a fresh start. Or running away from the memories that were locked in their old house.

"Two celebrity cops in one place," Matt mused.

"What are you talking about?"

He shrugged and his eyes fell to the floor. He looked like a schoolboy who'd just sworn in front of his mother and was about to experience the consequences. "Just that you're famous for catching the Snow Killer and DCI Battle is famous for catching the Blackden Edge Murderer."

His eyes returned to hers and she held him in a gaze that she hoped would tell him she didn't want to hear anything like that again.

"Sorry," he said. "I know you don't like that kind of talk. About celebrity coppers, I mean."

"No, I don't." As far as she was concerned, she'd simply been doing her job when she'd caught the Snow Killer and Battle had no doubt simply been doing his in Derbyshire. The raising of certain detectives to celebrity status rankled her because every one of those detectives was supported by a team who put in hours of work that made catching the killer possible. No arrest was the result of a detective acting alone but rather the end result of hours and hours of teamwork.

"Come on," she said to Matt. "We might as well go home and see what tomorrow brings."

They left the hospital and went outside, where the cold wind was whipping snow across the car park.

"Oh, shit!" Dani said.

Matt looked at her quizzically. "Guv?"

"My car is in Tollby," she said. "I came here in the ambulance."

"No problem," he said. "I'll give you a lift."

"Thanks, Matt." She got into the passenger side of his Kodiaq and waited while he brushed snow off the windscreen before getting in behind the wheel.

The drive to Tollby was slow and tedious, thanks to the weather. The view beyond the windows was nothing more than flurries of snow that made the world beyond the car looked like a TV screen that wasn't tuned in properly.

Dani took the opportunity to lean her head against the window and close her eyes, but she couldn't sleep. Her mind was whirring. Would Holloway make sure her team stayed involved in the Abigail Newton case?

She doubted it. She'd learned from past experience that it wasn't a good idea to rely on Holloway for anything. He didn't like her for some reason and seemed to like her even less after the conclusion of the Snow Killer case and the media attention that followed it.

She reckoned that Holloway--a social climber-- didn't share her views on celebrity and would have liked to grab the limelight regarding the Snow Killer. But the reporters had focused on Dani and that had probably made him jealous of her, even though she hadn't wanted the attention.

If she went to his office tomorrow and told him she wanted to stay on the Newton case, he'd probably say no just to spite her. Maybe she should use reverse psychology and tell him she definitely didn't want to be involved in the case. Then he'd probably make sure she was.

"Here we are," Matt said at last. "Tollby."

"Thanks, Matt." She opened the car door and got out into the wind and snow. "Go home and get some sleep. We may have a busy day tomorrow searching those moors."

"I will," he said. "Night, Guv."

She trudged through the deepening snow to her own car and started the engine, letting the vehicle warm up while she brushed snow off the windscreen and windows. When that was done, she got in and carefully drove the short distance to her cottage.

Barney and Jack were waiting by the front door and shuffled around her, tails banging against the floor when she got inside.

Dani fed them and ruffled the fur on the backs of their necks before opening the back door and taking them out to the garden. She didn't have to take them out; the dogs had access to the large garden whenever they needed it via a dog door that had been built into the cottage's rear wall. But after what she'd seen today —namely the fear in Abigail Newton's eyes—Dani needed to spend time with the animals and watch them play in the snow.

The world could be a terrible place and her line of work meant she only saw its dark side. She needed to be reminded that there was light as well. Watching Barney and Jack romp in the garden, shaking snow off their faces and play fighting, lifted her spirits. She threw snowballs for them to chase and laughed when they shook the snow off their fur and covered her with it.

Eventually, she went back inside the cottage, had a quick shower, and headed to the bedroom. She left the light off and slipped into her pyjamas in the dark before climbing wearily into bed.

She closed her eyes and tried to get to sleep.

After a few minutes, she heard the *tick tick* of the dogs' claws on the wooden floor as they came into the room and settled down next to the bed.

Dani fell asleep listening to the snow falling against the window, wondering what secrets it was burying out on the moors.

CHAPTER FIVE

Andy Clifton didn't appreciate the fact that his wife was nudging his shoulder, trying to wake him up. Had she forgotten he was off work for Christmas? He intended to sleep in for as long as he liked and had told her as much last night when they went to bed.

"Andy," she whispered. "I heard a noise."

He half-opened his eyes and groaned inwardly when he saw that it was still pitch black outside. What time was it? His bleary eyes had trouble seeing the alarm clock on his bedside table. Then the illuminated hands came into focus. 6:30. Way too early to be getting up when he was on holiday.

"What noise?" he grumbled.

"Outside. In the barn."

The barn. Why did Sheila insist on calling it that? They'd agreed that now it was being done up for the tourist trade, they were going to call it *The Annexe*. That would be much more appealing to potential guests than *The Barn*, even if the latter title was more accurate.

They'd bought Brambleberry Farm and the land attached to it on the edge of the North Yorkshire Moors National Park last year, using money Andy had made as a trader in London. The barn, which was situated almost a quarter of a mile from the house—so Andy had no idea how Sheila could possible hear a noise that far away—had been just that; an old cow shed that was now defunct since Brambleberry Farm had ceased to be a working farm some years ago.

They'd brought in builders to convert the building into a living accommodation for tourists. Sheila planned to cook breakfast for the guests in the rustic kitchen downstairs. It wasn't Andy's cup of tea—he preferred the city and spent almost all of his time there, staying in a flat in Chelsea during the week and only returning here on weekends and holidays.

So he was eager to let Sheila run a little business here. It was what she wanted and would keep her content.

"Andy!" she said.

He'd drifted off. "What?"

"I think someone's in the barn."

"It's probably a fox." He pulled the duvet over his head, hoping it would indicate to her that he wanted no more disturbances.

"No, I heard hammering."

"Hammering? You must be dreaming."

"I'm not."

"I thought the builders were done until after Christmas."

"They are. And they wouldn't come this early anyway. Please go and check."

He sighed. He wasn't going to get any peace until he did as she asked, that much was certain. "All right." He regretfully pushed the duvet off his body, feeling cold air on his feet. "Bloody hell, it's freezing!"

"The heating hasn't come on yet," she explained.

He padded across the cold wooden floor to his chest of drawers and dressed as quickly as he could in a pair of Tom Ford jeans and a John Smedley jumper. He might be in the middle of nowhere but that didn't mean he was going to wear any old tat.

Sheila was sitting up in bed, looking at the window with concern in her eyes. "I can't hear anything now."

He nodded sagely. "You probably didn't hear anything before either. You're used to hearing building sounds coming from the barn so now you're dreaming about them."

She pursed her lips, seemingly considering if what he was saying could be true. "All right, perhaps it was just a dream. Come back to bed."

"No, no," he said. He was up and dressed now and he was going to be a martyr to it. "I'll check the barn for your peace of mind. Even though it looks like there's five feet of snow out there."

"Andy, don't be ridiculous. I'm sorry I said anything now. Just forget about it."

"No, my love," he said as he put on an extra pair of

socks. "I'm going out there. You won't be able to rest until you know there's no phantom builder hammering in the barn."

He left the room and went downstairs to the kitchen. His Le Chameau boots and Moncler hooded jacket, which he'd bought in Harrods, were waiting by the back door.

Sheila came downstairs, wrapping her robe tightly around herself against the cold.

"Should I take some kind of weapon with me?" he asked as he laced up the boots.

"Look, I'm sorry I woke you up. You're like a grumpy bear. You don't have to go out there."

"But I do," he said, putting his coat on and zipping it up. "Anything for you, dear."

She shot him a look that told him she'd had enough of his sarcasm.

Andy retrieved an orange Moncler wool-cashmere hat from the jacket pocket and pulled it tightly over his head. After adding a pair of Bogner gloves to his ensemble, he felt he was stylish enough to brave the winter weather.

He opened the back door and turned to Sheila. "If I don't come back, always know that I loved you."

She sighed. "I wish I'd never said anything now."

Chuckling to himself, he closed the door behind him and trudged through the snow towards the distant building. There was no way Sheila had heard a noise from that far away. A bloody mariachi band could be playing in there and the sound wouldn't reach the house.

He looked back at the house. Sheila's worried face was framed in the kitchen window, watching him. After this fiasco, she'd never wake him up early when he was on holiday again. He'd just say, "Remember the time you thought you heard a hammering noise in the barn?" and roll over and go back to sleep. It might even be worth this short trudge through the snow if it meant he'd get uninterrupted mornings from now on.

The barn—*The Annexe*, he reminded himself—stood alone in the snow, a dark shape against the expanse of the moors behind it. Andy wished he'd brought a torch; it was bloody dark out here. He wasn't sure if the builders had fitted the lights yet. Sheila had probably told him at some point, but he couldn't remember having a conversation about it. He sometimes tuned out when she enthused about her little project. His mind was filled with more important things like stocks, shares, and bonds.

By the time he reached *The Annexe*'s door, he was out of breath. Walking through deep snow was no joke. He leaned against the building's stone wall for a moment and sucked in the cold winter air.

The door to *The Annexe* wasn't locked. The building was empty so there was nothing worth stealing in there. Andy opened it and recoiled when a blast of fetid air hit him in the face.

It smelled like an animal had died somewhere in there. He supposed that was possible if the builders had left the door open while they were working and a fox or a badger or something had sneaked inside, only to get trapped in there when the builders shut the place up for the Christmas holiday.

He stepped inside and felt along the wall, searching for the light switch in the dark. The smell was really bad. Once he hit the lights, he was going to have to find whatever creature had met its end here.

His fingers contacted with the switch and he flicked it on.

The lights sparked into life, flooding the barn with light. Andy's eyes were drawn to something handing on the opposite wall, something that didn't belong. When he realised what it was, he turned and stumbled out of the door, retching sour vomit onto the snow.

He tried to run to the house, but his boots slipped, and he sprawled headlong to the ground. The snow clung to his face, chilling his teeth and caking his eyelids.

Scrambling to his feet, he ran as fast as he could, refusing to think about what he'd just seen.

The lights of the house seemed so distant suddenly. Andy cast a frightened gaze at the darkness around him. If the person who had done...that—he risked a glance back at the barn—was still around...

He couldn't think like that, must not scare himself to death.

He saw Sheila's face in the kitchen window, and he shouted to her. "Call the police!" The wind snatched his voice away and carried his words into the darkness.

His wife was watching him run towards the house with a frown on her face, probably wondering why he was slipping and sliding like a maniac.

"Call the police!" he shouted again.

She shook her head and held a hand to her ear, indicating that she couldn't hear him.

"Open the door," he gasped but there was no way she could hear him. He was too breathless. "Open the door so you can hear me."

She may not have heard his breathless pleading but now that he was getting closer to the house, Sheila went to the back door and opened it.

Andy wanted to shout to her, but he was too out of breath. He could barely breathe.

He reached the door and tumbled inside, lying on the kitchen floor while he tried to catch his breath.

Sheila leaned over him. "Andy, what is it? What's wrong?"

When he finally managed to speak, his words were breathless and frightened.

"Call the police," he gasped. "Call the police."

CHAPTER SIX

Dani got to Brambleberry Farm at 9:45 and found at least half a dozen police cars and a Forensics van parked in front of the farmhouse. She parked next to the Forensics van and climbed out of her car to be greeted by Matt Flowers.

"Why did it take them so long to call us?" she asked by way of a greeting. She'd only received the call an hour ago but had been informed that a body had been discovered here at around 6:30 a.m.

"When the occupants of the farmhouse phoned the police, they just said there was a woman in their barn. According to the operator, they weren't very coherent. So a couple of uniforms were dispatched to see what the problem was. Took them a while to get here because of the snow on the roads. When they found the body in the barn, we were called."

The body in the barn, Dani thought. It sounded like the title of an Agatha Christie story. But from what she'd been told, this was more gruesome than any Poirot or Marple novel.

"Who lives here?" she asked, pointing at the house as she and Matt walked around it, following a path of churned up snow left by the police personnel who'd got here before her.

Matt consulted his notebook. "Andy and Sheila Clifton. They were having the barn converted into a guesthouse."

They rounded the house and now Dani could see the barn in question. It stood alone, some distance from the house. "What were they doing in the barn at 6:30?"

"Sheila thought she heard hammering and Andy went out to investigate. The hammering makes perfect sense when you see the state of the body, guv."

She'd been told it wasn't pretty but hadn't been given any details.

The snow had stopped falling so she supposed she should be grateful for small mercies, but she couldn't help thinking that here she was in the wintertime about to see another dead woman. The snow had brought with it more than bad memories; it had brought tragedy and death, as it always did.

A number stood around the barn, including a number of SOCOs who were coming out and putting their white Tyvek suits into evidence bags. The suits would be checked for trace evidence later, along with everything else that had been removed from the barn.

Some of the SOCOs were already heading back to

the vehicles, including Ray Rickman, the head of Scenes of Crimes.

Dani waved to him. "Ray, anything to tell me?"

He shook his head. "Not until we analyse everything. We've collected what we can from the body and the room. The fact that the building is surrounded by snow means that's about all we can get. And because the snow was still falling, there aren't any footprints." He paused and then added, "Judging by the way the body's been posed, your best bet to catch this one is probably a psychologist."

"Let me know as soon as you have those test results," she said.

He nodded. "I will." He led his team back to the van.

Dani wanted to ask Matt exactly how gruesome the sight about to greet her was going to be but to do so would be a sign of weakness and she had to look no matter what.

Two uniforms flanked the barn door. They nodded to Dani as she walked past them and into the building.

The smell—a mixture of death and the various chemicals used by the SOCOs—was familiar to her. The sight of the naked woman nailed to the wall took her aback for a moment.

The woman looked to be in her late thirties. She had long black hair which partially covered her face. Her body was marked with dozens of wounds that looked like they'd been caused by a knife. The red marks crisscrossed each other on the woman's torso, legs and arms.

She had been nailed by her wrists to a wooden beam that ran through the wall. The builders had probably left it exposed as a quaint feature but now it was the method by which the dead woman was suspended above the floor. Her arms and body formed a "Y" shape.

"She wasn't killed here," Dani said. "There isn't enough blood on the floor beneath her body. She was killed somewhere else and then left here like this."

Why? she asked herself. Why would the killer do this? The woman had been crucified. Was the killer making some statement about her?

Now she knew why Rickman had suggested a psychologist.

"Do we know who she is?" she asked Matt.

He shook his head. "Not yet, guv."

A Jane Doe crucified in a barn in the middle of nowhere. It didn't make any sense at the moment. She had to trust that with time and investigation, answers would be found.

Her phone rang. As soon as she answered, Holloway's voice boomed in her ear. "Summers, where are you?"

"I'm at Brambleberry Farm, sir."

"I want to see you in my office right away."

She resisted letting out a frustrated sigh. "That will be a bit difficult, sir. I'm miles away."

"Well get here as soon as you can." He hung up.

As she put the phone back into her coat pocket, Dani let out the sigh she'd been holding in.

"Problem?" Matt asked.

"Holloway wants to see me."

He nodded sympathetically. No one liked being called to Holloway's office and Matt knew there was bad blood between Dani and the superintendent. "I can hold down the fort here," he offered. "We probably won't have much to go on until Forensics get those test results and the coroner does an autopsy. In the meantime, I'll try and find out who she is and put out an appeal for witnesses."

"Thanks, Matt." She left the barn and walked back towards her car. When she was halfway between the barn and the farmhouse, she turned and let her eyes wander over the moors.

Someone had carried the woman's body over that bleak landscape in the early hours of the morning during a snowstorm. They were determined, she had to give them that. But why go to such lengths to leave the poor woman crucified in a barn? The killer was either trying to recreate a scene or make a statement. Which was it?

She resumed her journey to the car and on the way, fished the phone back out of her pocket. She rang Holloway.

"What is it?" he said when he answered.

"Sir, I'd like to request a forensic psychologist to help us with the Brambleberry Farm case."

"There's no need for that, Summers."

"Sir, I feel there is a need. The way the body has been posed—"

"No, I don't mean that. I mean there's no need for you to request a psychologist."

She didn't know what he meant by that. "Sir, I'm not sure what you—"

"Just get to my office, Summers, and you'll understand soon enough." He ended the call.

His cryptic manner was grating on her nerves. She had half a mind to take the scenic route to HQ and get there in her own time just to piss him off. But his enigmatic comments had piqued her curiosity and she wanted to know exactly what he meant by saying there was no need to request a psychologist. He obviously knew something she didn't.

So instead of taking her time, she drove directly to Headquarters at Northallerton.

When she got up to the floor where Holloway's office was situated, she saw that his door was closed. Had he got tired of waiting for her to get here and started a meeting? How long was she going to have to wait to see him? She didn't want to be loitering around HQ when there was a dead woman's case to investigate.

Holloway's door opened and he stuck his head out. "Summers, get in here."

"Yes, sir." So she wasn't going to have to wait after all.

When she entered the office, she was surprised to see Battle sitting on the side of the desk closest to her and a man she didn't recognise on the other. That man wore a chief superintendent's uniform. He had close-cropped black hair and steel grey eyes, which he used to look Dani over as she entered.

"Sit down," Holloway said, indicating a seat next to Battle. He took his own seat on the opposite side of the desk with the unknown superintendent.

Dani sat and waited. Even though she hadn't done anything wrong as far as she knew, she felt as if she were about to receive some sort of disciplinary warning. With Battle here, though, that didn't make sense. He worked for a completely different force so there was no way he'd be in Holloway's office for a disciplinary hearing.

"This is Chief Superintendent Gallow," Holloway said, indicating the man next to him. "He's come here all the way from the Met."

"Pleased to meet you Detective Inspector," Gallow said, reaching across the desk towards Dani with his right hand.

They shook. His grip was firm, and Dani made sure she matched it. It might seem like a trivial thing but as a woman in the police force, she knew she must not show any sign of weakness.

"I'll let the Chief Superintendent explain why you've both been called in here," Holloway said.

Dani looked at Battle. She'd assumed that because he'd already been in the office when she'd arrived, he must have been told what he was doing there. Battle gave her a look and minuscule shrug that said he was just as clueless as she was.

"As Brian said, I'm here from the Met," Gallow said. "I was in Derbyshire yesterday, speaking to Superintendent Powers. I also wanted to speak to DCI Battle while I was there but there seems to have been some sort of mix up in communication." He looked at Battle with accusation in his steel grey eyes. Dani had no idea what that was about.

"I was coming to Northallerton to speak with you today, DI Summers," Gallow continued, "So it's fortuitous that you two have already met because now I can speak to you both together." He offered them a smile. Dani didn't return it; she still had no idea what this was all about and the details of Gallow's journey around the country didn't interest her.

"I'll get straight to the point," Gallow said. "The Home Office has decided that people don't feel safe anymore due to a decline in the number of police officers and the fact that there are unsolved murders appearing in the media all the time. It's bad press for the police and according to a recent survey, the general public don't think we're doing enough to protect them."

"We're working as hard as we can, sir," Battle said.

"Yes, we are," Gallow said. "But we're not *seen* to be doing anything different. In the eyes of the average man or woman on the street, we're just carrying on as we always have, with no forward thinking. Reactive rather than proactive."

He paused—probably for dramatic effect, Dani

thought to herself—and then said, "So we're going to do something proactive and we're going to make damned sure everyone knows about it."

He got up and walked over to the other end of the office, where a flip chart had been set up on an easel. Gallow flipped to the first page where two words were written in black marker.

Murder Force.

"The high-ups in the Met were tasked by the Home Office to come up with a way to get people on our side again. To show them that we can be proactive. This is what they came up with." He pointed at the chart.

"Murder Force," Dani said. "It sounds a bit dramatic, sir. What is it?"

"I'll come to that," he said. "And yes, it sounds dramatic, but it's meant to. They wanted a name that's down-to-earth, something everyone will understand. When people hear that the Murder Force is investigating, they'll feel safe in the knowledge that the best of the best are on the case."

"So it's a department?" Dani asked.

"It's a team," Gallow said. "An elite team of detectives that will reignite public trust in the police."

"Sounds like a tall order," Battle said. "How will it do that exactly?"

"By solving the high-profile crimes," Gallow said. "The ones everyone reads about in the papers. We sort those out and our reputation goes up. It's all about optics. The general public doesn't know or probably

EYES OF THE WICKED 61

care about our new initiatives to fight crime, but they'll take notice when the cases that the media latches onto are dealt with quickly and efficiently."

To Dani, it sounded like this Murder Force was set up to fail. Not every crime could easily be tackled, and some would never be solved. She didn't like that any more than anyone else, but it was the way things were.

Gallow flipped over the page to reveal an outline of Britain with a line of blue dots drawn through it just north of London. "There are going to be two teams," he said. "One will be part of the Met and serve London, the south of England, Wales, and Northern Ireland. A second team, run by me, will serve the Midlands, the north of England, and Scotland. I've been asked to recruit personnel for that team. You two are the first detectives who came to mind."

Dani groaned inwardly. The only reason she and Battle had "come to mind" was because they'd both been involved in high profile cases and had both been in the papers. What was that word that Gallow had used? Optics. She and Battle were good optics because they were known to the public as detectives who had solved complex murder cases.

"No offence, sir," Battle said, leaning forward in his chair, "but have you chosen us simply because we're good PR?"

"I'll be honest with you," Gallow said. "The answer is yes. You're both known to the public. You've both been involved in high profile cases and you solved them. You're good press. But, you're also damn fine detectives. You didn't solve those cases by chance or good luck. You worked hard. I've read your personnel records and you're the sort of people I want on my team."

Now Dani knew why Holloway had been particularly salty with her today. She was being recruited to a new team that would get a lot of media attention. If he'd been jealous about the media attention she'd been getting after solving just one high profile case, how much more jealous must he be knowing she was being asked to join a team that actively chased them?

She was convinced that this offer had only come because of her—she hated the word but had to use it—celebrity status. What Gallow was proposing—being in the public eye all the time—was everything she hated. And she didn't know the logistics regarding this new team.

"Where will the team be based, sir?" she asked Gallow.

"The headquarters will be in York," he said. "It's a good central point for the areas we'll be serving and far enough north that we won't be stepping on the London team's toes. The building we're going to use as a headquarters is on the eastern outskirts of York, so you won't even have to move, DI Summers. You can drive there in less than an hour." He turned his attention to Battle. "I'm afraid the same isn't true for you, DCI Battle, but we can sort out the details of all that later."

Battle nodded. He looked, to Dani, as if he was

deep in thought. She guessed that his opinions on this new team were probably the same as hers.

"Now, we want to get the full team up and running as soon as possible," Gallow said, "I'm going to have to recruit support staff, uniformed officers, and more detectives by then. But I'd like to get you two on board as soon as possible. I know this isn't a decision to be taken lightly so take some time to think about it."

He handed each of them a business card. "My mobile number is on the back. Give me a call as soon as you make a decision." He looked from Battle to Dani. "Any questions?"

Dani shook her head. She had her misgivings about this new team and doubts about the exact reason it was being formed—it seemed like a PR exercise more than anything else—but she also had to consider how much important work the team would be taking on. High profile cases usually involved serial killings or abductions and solving those cases meant saving lives.

"Dismissed," Holloway said.

Dani left the room, followed by Battle.

As they crossed the floor to the lift, Battle said, "I heard a body was discovered today. Foul play?"

"Definitely," Dani said as they reached the lift. "Unless she nailed *herself* to a barn wall."

Battle's nose wrinkled. "Sounds gruesome."

Dani shrugged. As dead bodies went, she'd seen worse. A lot worse.

The lift arrived and the door opened. They both got on and Dani hit the button for the ground floor.

When the door closed, Battle asked, "What do you think about this new team Gallow's putting together?"

"The Murder Force?" Saying the name out loud made it seem even more ridiculous. "I think he's looking for pretty faces he can parade in front of the press."

"Well that's me out then," Battle said.

"No, you're his grizzled, world-weary detective," she told him. "You fit the bill perfectly."

"Grizzled?" He stroked his stubbly chin. "Maybe I need to level up my grooming routine." He grinned at her.

"The thing is," she said, "a team like that could put some serious criminals away. Despite Gallow's underlying agenda of creating an easily digestible media presence, it's certainly something worth thinking about."

"I'm in," he said.

That surprised her. Battle didn't seem like the type of man who would rush to a decision without giving it long consideration first.

"I just need to ring my wife," he said. "We've been talking about retiring to the coast all of our lives. York is only an hour's commute from the east coast. This way, we can have the house by the sea, and I can still work. Seems like the best of both worlds."

"Sounds ideal," Dani agreed.

The doors opened with a *ding* and Battle said to her, "Come and be a part of it. I know you're a good detective. Gallow might only want something he can show off to the media but he's only going to be the figurehead. The success of the team will depend on people like you and me. Just think how we can shape it and build it into something good. As you said, we could put some very bad people away. And we'll probably save a lot of lives while we're at it."

"It's certainly tempting," she said truthfully as they crossed the foyer to the entrance doors. Outside, the snow had started to fall again. It was nothing more than a few white wisps floating on the breeze at the moment, but Dani knew that could change at any moment.

"Are you going to the hospital?" she asked Battle. "How is Abigail?"

"Still not talking," he said. "And no, I'm not going over there. My boss has taken me off the case. He was so sure I'd take Gallow's offer when he met with him yesterday that he pulled me off duty. He obviously doesn't want me to be in the middle of an investigation when I leave his force. So he's sending another DCI up here to work the Abigail Newton case with DS Morgan."

Dani paused at the doors. "So where does that leave you, guv?"

He looked at the snowy car park and let out a long breath. "In snowy Yorkshire with nothing to do. I suppose I should go home and have a quiet Christmas. I'll call Rowena first and see what she thinks about moving up here. Although this weather isn't much of a selling point."

"All right. I need to go and find out if my body has

been identified. Nice meeting you." She held out her hand.

Battle shook it. "We'll hopefully meet again. Think about what I said."

They left the building. Dani went to her car while Battle, holding his hat on his head and stooping against the wind, made his way to a green Range Rover.

Dani got behind the wheel of her car and watched Battle pull out a mobile and make a call, presumably to his wife.

He had a point; whatever Gallow envisaged regarding the Murder Force, it would be detectives like herself and Battle who shaped the team. And from what she knew of the DCI from Derbyshire, she'd have no problem having him as her guv'nor. He was nothing like Holloway and seemed to be doing the job for all the right reasons.

She called Matt. He was probably still at Brambleberry Farm since he hadn't returned to the office.

"Guv," he said when he answered. "I'm still here. They're taking the body away now."

"Any new leads?"

"Nothing. Although apparently it wasn't the knife wounds that killed the victim. She was struck on the back of the head. Looks like the cause of death is blunt force trauma."

"So why all the cuts?" Dani said under her breath.

Matt didn't answer; he was used to her thinking out loud.

She remembered the conversation she'd had with

Holloway on the phone about a psychologist. He'd said she didn't need to request one and had said everything would become clear when she got to his office. The Murder Force business had distracted her.

"Matt, I've got to see Holloway again."

"I'll be coming to the office now anyway," he said. "There's nothing more to do here at the moment."

"Okay, I'll see you when you get here, and you can fill me in on the details regarding our Jane Doe."

"Will do, guv. See you later."

Dani hung up and got out of the Land Rover. Battle was still sitting in his car, talking on the phone as she stalked back into the building. How could she have forgotten about the psychologist? In a case like this, where the killer was obviously living some sort of internal fantasy life, a psychologist could offer valuable insights.

Instead of waiting for the lift, she took the stairs. When she got to Holloway's office, the door was open but Gallow was still in there and the two officers seemed to be deep in conversation.

Dani knocked on the open door and both men looked up at her.

"Sir," she said to Holloway. "I rang you earlier about requesting a forensic psychologist and you said there would be no need. I wasn't sure what you meant by that."

"The answer's simple," Gallow said. "I'm taking over the Brambleberry Farm case and Murder Force already has a psychologist."

CHAPTER SEVEN

"I don't understand, sir" Dani said to Gallow. "You said the Murder Force isn't up and running yet."

"It isn't," he said. "But I have some personnel, including a forensic psychologist, as I just mentioned. I also have a DCI. Battle just rang me to accept his position on the team."

That was quick, Dani thought. Battle's wife must have jumped at the chance to move up here. If it had been her lifelong dream, then why not?

"But the Brambleberry Farm case isn't high profile, sir," she said.

He looked at her incredulously. "An unknown woman crucified in a barn in the middle of a snowy moor? The papers will be all over it."

"You'll still be working on the case, whether you accept Chief Superintendent Gallow's offer or not," Holloway said. "The only difference is that DCI Battle will now be in charge." He gave her a grin and Dani wondered if he had handed over her case so readily just to piss her off.

"Because my team isn't at full strength yet," Gallow said, "I'll be utilising the resources and personnel here, along with the ones I already have. Perhaps I'll find some more new recruits while I'm at it. I'm sure someone here will impress me."

"We have an impressive team here," Holloway said nervously. "But don't poach all of them, sir."

Gallow chuckled. "Don't worry, Brian, I'll leave you some staff."

Dani wasn't sure if he was joking or if he actually intended to gut the North Yorkshire police department for the sake of his Murder Force.

Gallow turned to Dani. "So it looks like we'll be working together after all, Detective Inspector."

"Yes, sir."

Holloway said, "Dismissed, Summers."

Dani went to her desk and sat down, deep in thought. Did Holloway despise her so much that he had gladly handed over a murder case to a half-formed team? Perhaps she should ask to be seconded to Derbyshire and help the DCI who was on the way here to investigate the Abigail Newton case.

The Brambleberry Farm investigation was leaving a bad taste in her mouth. A woman was dead, horrifically murdered, and the Super and Chief Super were using her case as a piece in some sort of political game.

Battle appeared from the lift and walked across to Holloway's office. He spotted Dani and gave her a little wave on his way. He went into the office and closed the door.

When Matt arrived an hour later, Dani was nursing a cold coffee and looking at a map of the North Yorkshire Moor National Park. She'd marked two locations with red circles: Brambleberry Farm and the place where Melissa and Jeff Wood had picked up Abigail Newton.

She wasn't certain of her accuracy regarding the latter location because she'd gleaned it from the written statement an officer had taken from Melissa and Jeff in Deirdre Murray's house and the couple weren't familiar with the area they'd been driving through when they'd found the girl.

But her mark on the map was in the correct general area, she was sure of it.

"Any news, guv?" Matt asked as he sat down at his desk across from hers.

"Plenty," she said. "But I'll let Holloway explain it. Have a look at this. I've been thinking about our Jane Doe in the barn. Brambleberry Farm is only ten or so miles from the spot where Abigail Newton was found."

He came around the desk and looked at the red circles on the map. "Do you think they're connected in some way?"

"Don't you think it's a bit of a coincidence that a missing girl is found on exactly the same night that a woman is murdered and placed in a barn ten miles away?"

He thought about it for a few moments and then

nodded. "I suppose it does seem like the two things are connected."

"The question is how." She studied the map. "What if the killer of the woman in the barn was also planning to murder Abigail at the same time but she got away somehow?"

Matt nodded and leaned closer to the map. "It sounds logical. That might mean that the place where he murdered Jane Doe is somewhere near where Abigail was found. She couldn't have gone far in bare feet and a nightgown on a night like that so she must have escaped her captor somewhere near here." He pointed at the red circle where Dani had guessed Melissa and Jeff Wood had found Abigail.

"What if she escaped while he was busy with Jane Doe?" Matt continued. "Perhaps he was distracted enough that Abigail was able to run away. The killer looks for Abigail but doesn't find her or realises she's got into a car, so he resumes his grisly task and then later takes his victim to the barn at Brambleberry Farm."

"It makes sense," Dani said. "We know Abigail was abducted three weeks ago in Derbyshire. Perhaps Jane Doe was taken at the same time, maybe even at the same place. It might help us to identify her if the DNA and fingerprints don't give us a name."

"We have a name," a voice said.

Dani looked up to see Battle standing by her desk.

"The fingerprints came back," he said. "Her name is Tanya Ward. She worked as a psychiatric nurse at a mental health facility near York." He consulted his notepad and added, "Her husband reported her missing three days ago when she didn't return home from a late shift."

"So she's from around here," Dani said. That blew her theory of Tanya being taken at the same time and place as Abigail out of the water.

Battle nodded. "We've sent uniforms to her house to inform her husband. We'll need him to make a positive ID as well."

"What about a connection with Abigail?" Dani pointed at the circles she'd drawn on the map. "Brambleberry Farm is quite close to where Abigail was wandering on the moors."

Battle inspected the map and stroked his chin. "It's compelling, I'll admit, but unless we have a solid piece of evidence linking the two of them, we have to treat Abigail and Tanya as victims of separate crimes."

"That took place on the same night, in the same area," Dani said incredulously.

Battle leaned closer to her and Matt and said in a low voice, "If the crimes are regarded as separate, we'll have twice as many people working on them than we would have if it was just one single case."

Dani had to admit that the man was shrewd. He wasn't dismissing a connection between Abigail and Tanya but was using the system to get as many people working on solving the case as he could.

"What's our next move?" she asked.

"We need to get some uniforms out to the moor where Abigail was found while it's still light. It may be snowing but we can't neglect a proper search of the area. I'll rustle up some willing participants. We also need to learn more about Tanya Ward."

He held up a folder. "This is the missing persons file. Everything we know about her last known movements is in there, but it isn't a lot and some of it's a bit vague. Now that it's a murder inquiry, we need to make sure we've got this nailed down tight."

"We can work that angle if you like," Dani told him.

He nodded and handed her the slim file. "Excellent. Let me know what you find. I'll be on the moors, taking part in the search. This new job isn't turning out to be so glamorous after all."

"Will do, guv," she said. She looked at Matt and nodded towards the lift.

He grabbed his coat and followed her. They rode the lift to the ground floor with a number of other people and it wasn't until they were alone in the foyer that Matt asked, "Why is the Derbyshire DCI in charge of our murder case?"

"It isn't our case anymore, Matt," she said as she pushed through the door and they stepped out into the snowy car park. "It belongs to the Murder Force now."

He screwed his face up and said, "The what?"

CHAPTER EIGHT

"The Murder Force," Dani said as she got into the passenger seat of Matt's Kodiaq. She hadn't been told not to say anything to anyone about Gallow's project and everyone would find out soon enough anyway since the formative Murder Force would be working with their department. "It's a new team being put together by Chief Superintendent Gallow, the guy who's been in Holloway's office for most of the day. Apparently, the existence of the Murder Force is supposed to reassure the general public that they're being looked after by the police by tackling high profile cases."

"Strange name," he said, reversing carefully out of the parking space and exiting the car park. "Where are we going, guv?"

She opened the file on her lap and scanned the pages. "Tanya worked at a place called Larkmoor

House near the village of Sutton-on-the-Forest. We might as well start there."

Matt pulled over and typed their destination into the SatNav.

The snow was coming down thick and fast now, melting on the windscreen and forming rivulets of water that the wipers swept away. Dani didn't envy Battle or the others who would be searching the moors later.

When Matt had programmed the SatNav and rejoined the traffic on the road, he said, "So, this new team. Are you joining?"

"I don't know," she said honestly.

"I'd jump at the chance."

"Would you? Why?"

"High profile crimes are usually the interesting ones. And for a crime to be high profile in the first place, there's something about it that grabs the public's attention. That usually means serial killings or the abduction of children. Who wouldn't want to be a member of a team dedicated to finding and catching the type of people who commit those crimes?"

Probably me, Dani thought. She agreed with Matt's opinion regarding a team dedicated to catching the worst criminals, but it was everything else that came with it. The media attention. Details of the case being leaked to the press. Matt hadn't been there when Gallow had described his vision for Murder Force. That vision had mainly been about public perception and public relations more than putting criminals away.

Although she supposed that catching criminals was the only way Murder Force would be perceived positively by the public so perhaps Gallow had assumed that was a given and that was why he hadn't focused much on that aspect of the team's work.

"What about the media spotlight?" she asked Matt. "You'd be willing to endure having reporters following your every move? Writing about the details of your case in the papers and on the Net?"

"It wouldn't be a matter of enduring it," he said. "I'd probably like it."

"Really? So you didn't mind when we were investigating the Snow Killer, and someone leaked to the press about the red ribbons left at the crime scenes and the press started calling him the Red Ribbon Killer?"

He shrugged. "I suppose that was a bit problematic."

"Yes, it was. I was trying to hold that information back in case we got a suspect in the interview room. It was more than a bit problematic, Matt."

He went quiet and then he said, "It wasn't me who leaked it to the press, guv."

"I never thought it was. I'm just pointing out that a case is twice as hard when it becomes a media circus."

"True," he conceded. "But you could give them false or misleading information to make a suspect think he's safe when actually, you're closing in on him. You can use the media to suit your purposes."

She grinned. "You sound like an ideal candidate for Murder Force."

"You think so?" He sounded eager.

"Matt, if you want me to put in a good word with Gallow, I will." She'd have no problem recommending him for anyone's team. Matt was a good DS. His work ethic and reasoning skills would be an asset to any investigation he worked on.

"Thank you. I'd like that."

It must be nice to be as decisive as Matt. She was still struggling with the media aspect of the job. The Snow Killer case had left a bad taste in her mouth. As far as reporters went, she was still weighing up the fact that she'd be in the media spotlight against the fact that she'd be chasing down some really bad people and helping victims of the worst types of crime.

To take her mind off her own indecisiveness, she pored over Tanya Ward's missing persons file. The photograph in the file showed a dark-haired young woman smiling at the camera. She was standing on a beach in a peach-coloured T-shirt and jeans. The day was sunny, and Tanya looked like she didn't have a care in the world.

It was hard for Dani to reconcile the image of the smiling woman in the sun with the body that had been found at Brambleberry Farm. Her mind refused to recognise that the happy woman in the photograph, full of life and seemingly enjoying it, could be the same person Dani had seen hanging from the barn wall, her body marked with hundreds of knife wounds.

She scanned the woman's history—or at least as much of it as had been written down by the officers on the missing persons case. There was scant information other than the fact that Tanya was 37 years old, worked at Larkmoor House as a psychiatric nurse, had been married to her husband Chris for 10 years, and was well-liked by her work colleagues.

It was all standard stuff, and nothing jumped out at Dani that could explain why Tanya had been murdered. There didn't have to be any reason at all, of course; she'd seen enough motiveless killings to know that. Sometimes, having your life snuffed out by someone else was merely a matter of being in the wrong place at the wrong time.

One piece of information that stuck out was the fact that Tanya Ward's car hadn't been found yet. She'd left the Larkmoor House hospital on the night she'd disappeared and then just seemed to have vanished into thin air, along with her orange Volkswagen Beetle.

The killer had left her body at Brambleberry Farm, but the car was still missing.

Finding that car was important; it could hold a wealth of DNA evidence.

She found a page that showed the victim's usual route from the hospital to her home. Tanya lived on the outskirts of York and her eight-mile journey took her mainly through countryside.

If the killer hadn't taken the car and hidden it somewhere, it could still be anywhere along those remote stretches of road. A typed report in the file stated that a cursory search for the Beetle had taken place a couple of days ago but it had been hampered by bad weather and the extensive size of the search area.

In other words, no one knew where to look. The last person to see Tanya alive had been a security guard at Larkmoor named John Morris. He'd seen Tanya get into the now-missing Beetle and drive away from the hospital car park. Another member of staff, a nurse named Sheila Hopkins, had also seen the Beetle leave the car park. Tanya had driven into the night and that was the last anyone had seen of her until she'd turned up at Brambleberry Farm.

Hopefully, Forensics would get some piece of evidence from the barn or Tanya's body that pointed to a suspect. Because as things stood, there were no leads at all. Nothing.

The husband had an airtight alibi; he'd been working a late shift himself, at York Hospital. Like his wife, Chris Ward was a nurse. His shift had finished at 2 a.m. the same time as his Tanya's. He'd had to navigate the streets of York to get home, she the eight miles of country roads. They should have arrived at their house at virtually the same time, but Tanya had never made it.

"Who did you meet on your way home?" Dani whispered to the photograph of the smiling woman on the beach.

The woman in the image offered no answers.

The interviews that had been carried out when Tanya was thought to be simply missing didn't offer any answers either. Sometimes when reading the transcripts of interviews, a remark made in the interview might stick out, seem odd, or be worded so carefully that it indicated a lie. There were no such remarks in these interviews. Everyone whose life intersected with Tanya Ward's seemed completely baffled by her disappearance.

The police, unable to tease out even a weak lead from the statements they'd taken, were also baffled.

That made Dani think that Tanya's killer had been someone unknown to her. But had she met with her death purely by random chance—by simply being in the wrong place at the wrong time—or had her killer chosen her beforehand, perhaps stalked her and waited for an opportune moment to strike? Just because he was unknown to Tanya didn't mean she was unknown to him. He might have followed her, fantasised about her, perhaps even taken something of hers without her knowledge.

If that was the case, more in-depth interviews might reveal a clue. One of Tanya's friends or work colleagues might have seen someone suspicious hanging around or perhaps spotted a car that seemed familiar because they'd seen it a number of times before.

Tanya might even have confided in someone that she thought she was being followed. Dani knew sometimes these things might never come to light. It might seem a no-brainer to mention to the police that your missing friend had told you that she thought she was being followed but such things were often not revealed in interviews simply because the right question hadn't been asked.

Beyond the car windows, the falling snow had become less intense. The wind blew flurries of tiny flakes over the road but for the most part, the heavy fall seemed to be done. At least that would be better for Battle and his search of the moors.

Dani was sure the snow would have covered any useful evidence by now but as Battle had said, a search couldn't be neglected. It was the least they could do for Abigail.

She finished reading the slim stack of sheets that made up the missing persons case file and closed the folder.

Following the SatNav's instruction, Matt turned onto a long driveway that led to a large Victorian building set among the trees and surrounded by large, snow-covered lawns.

"This place looks classy for a mental hospital, guv," he said as he pulled into the car park.

Dani nodded in agreement. This didn't look like an NHS facility; it was probably private.

"Must cost a pretty penny to stay here," Matt said, parking the Kodiaq next to a dark green Jaguar.

"Even rich people can have mental issues," Dani said. "Probably more than the rest of us."

"You think?" he asked, raising his eyebrows incredulously.

"Having all that money," she said, getting out of the car. "It brings with it a lot of stress."

"In that case, I wouldn't mind a bit more stress," he said, getting out and locking the doors. "I can think of worse places to end up than here."

Dani was only half listening. Her eyes scanned the woods surrounding Larkmoor House. If someone *had* been stalking Tanya Ward, they would have had plenty of places to hide around here. Especially at night.

Her phone rang. She retrieved it from her coat pocket and answered. "DI Summers."

It was Battle. "I thought you should know that your theory was correct," he said.

"Theory?"

"About the two cases being linked. Abigail and Tanya, I mean."

"Did you find something on the moors?"

"No, we've not gone out there yet. I'm still getting everyone together. However, I've had a call from Forensics."

Dani felt her fingers tighten on the phone. Sometimes, you could do months of leg work and come up with nothing, yet a single strand of hair or flake of skin found by Forensics could blow the case wide open.

"The bloodstains on the nightgown Abigail Newton was wearing," Battle said. He paused and then added, "They're Tanya Ward's blood."

CHAPTER NINE

"Samuel, where are you?"

His mother's voice came floating on the wind, reaching him even out here in the barn. She never came this far from the house and he regarded it as his domain, so the fact that her words could penetrate his sanctum annoyed him. He should take the knife from its hiding place in the barn's stone wall, march through the snow to the house and...

Eventually, he told himself, *she will pay for what she's done. But not yet. Not yet.*

"Samuel!" she shouted, her voice harsher now. Harsher even than the cold wind that blew over the farm, whirling the snow into devilish shapes that arose from the ground momentarily and then scattered on the breeze. Maybe they were old ghosts come to haunt him.

He wanted to go to the open barn door and shout at her, "My name isn't Samuel!" but there was no point.

She'd given them new names years ago and ignored any talk of their old ones. Like demons evading conjuration, they kept their true names secret.

He did go to the barn door but instead of shouting at her, he waved. She was standing on the porch, dressed as always in one of her white ankle-length robes. Today, the robe seemed to reflect the whiteness of the snow covering the farm, almost shimmering in harmony with it. Her uniform, she called it. Her uniform as a servant of God.

Funnily enough, Samuel couldn't recall anyone in the Bible wearing a uniform. His mother's brand of faith was definitely unique.

And hypocritical.

He knew where her religious fervour came from and it was nothing to do with a faith in God and more to do with a desire to bury her past sins. That was why he was now called Samuel and she had named herself Mary.

That was a joke in itself, unless her name referred to Mary Magdalene.

She beckoned to him to come back to the house. He sighed and left the barn, making his way towards her through the snow, surrounded by the whirling snow devils. He imagined they were whispering to him.

"Do it."

"Don't wait. Get the knife now."

"Make her pay for what she did."

"We're watching you."

"Ruth is watching you."

"Avenge her death."

As tempting as it might be to follow their instructions, he ignored the voices in his head He couldn't do what they wanted—what *he* wanted— just yet.

As he got closer to the porch, he could see her belly protruding beneath the robe. One of the many men she met from the Internet had planted his seed inside her and now it was growing to fruition.

Samuel could not kill her while she had the innocent baby inside her.

He turned to look back at the barn. Behind the building, buried beneath the snow, was Ruth's grave. Marked with only a simple rock, upon which he had painted his sister's name in red paint, it was a place where he often stood and reflected on what he must do.

It was while standing there, looking down at the red-painted rock, that he had finally understood his calling. It had been the day his mother had told him she was pregnant. Blessed with a child was how she'd put it.

After his mother had told him her news, he'd gone out to Ruth's grave and for the first time since her death, he'd felt how disappointed she was in him. A profound sense of failure had washed over him. He'd told Ruth he would protect her, and he had been neglectful in that duty.

And now she was dead.

He had to put things right.

The idea of taking a woman and a girl had come to him.

He turned away from the barn and hurried to the house where his mother waited on the porch. He wondered how she could bear to be out here in the cold with only the robe protecting her from the elements. Despite the fact that he was wearing a thick, padded jacket and gloves, he felt the chill of the wind deep in his bones.

"What are you doing up there in the barn?" she asked him. There was no malice or suspicion in her voice. She had no idea what he was planning to do to her. It was just a simple question.

"Just checking the hens," he said. That wasn't a lie; he'd gone to the barn to make sure the hens were fed. He'd thrown food pellets and grain onto the ground and watched the birds pick at it with their beaks.

He liked animals. Unlike people, they were simple. The people he had to deal with at the delivery depot where he worked were mind-bogglingly complex and he didn't know how to interact with them at all. So he avoided them as much as possible. That made them think he was weird, and they avoided him as well.

His job as a courier meant he spent most of his workday on the road in his van anyway, which suited him perfectly. The van was his sanctum, shutting out the outside world when he was behind the wheel. And he didn't have to interact with the customers other than handing them their parcels and asking them to sign for them if required. He could handle that no problem.

"Come inside," his mother said. "It's freezing out here."

So she did feel the cold after all.

He went into the house and took off his jacket, gloves, and boots. His mother took the jacket from him and hung it on a hook behind the door before placing the boots neatly beneath it. "I don't know why you spend so much time in that barn," she said. "Those birds can take care of themselves."

Samuel knew that what she actually didn't like was him spending time *behind* the barn where the little red-painted rock marked his sister's final resting place. But she'd never say that because she never mentioned Ruth or the grave. He wasn't allowed to either. Even the mention of his sister's name was taboo and would bring about a harsh punishment.

His mother might believe her sins were forgiven but she obviously didn't want to be reminded of them.

"Look at you," she said, flicking her hands through his hair. "You're covered with snow."

"I'm fine," he said, trying to bat her hand away. "Leave me alone."

She ignored his protestations and continued fussing over him until she was satisfied. "There," she said, stepping back and looking him over. "That's much better."

He went into the living room and looked at the telly, which was on with the sound turned down. The News was on and Samuel could see a photograph of a girl's face and the words *Abigail Newton Found* on the screen.

She wasn't just any girl, of course; she was the girl he'd looked after for three weeks.

Three weeks ago, he'd seen her from his van. She'd been strolling along a country lane like she didn't have a care in the world. At that moment, he'd been struck by how much like Ruth she looked. The same long, dark hair. The same slight figure. And most of all, there'd been a lightness about her movements, almost as if she wasn't completely a part of this world at all, that had reminded him of his sister.

He'd pulled over and stopped the van a few yards in front of her. He could remember that moment vividly. Every detail. Although it was Winter, the day had been warm, the sun beating down from an azure blue cloudless sky.

The birds had been singing in the trees and their song had sounded like a joyous celebration of his chance meeting with this girl on a lonely road.

She wore a red padded jacket and jeans. Ruth had worn a red jacket. As he waited for the girl to reach his van, he had to blink at her a couple of times to assure himself that this wasn't actually his sister strolling along a Derbyshire road with not a care in the world.

It wasn't Ruth, of course. But she looked so much like her that he couldn't just leave her here. Everyone knew that pretty girls shouldn't wander on their own. It was dangerous. To simply drive past and leave her on this country road would be wrong. What if he saw her face on the News in a few days' time and heard that she'd been murdered? He'd never forgive himself for not protecting her when he had a chance.

He was looking at her face on the News right now, but she hadn't been murdered. She hadn't been hurt at all. He'd looked after her.

But now, he wasn't so sure that Abigail looked like his sister at all. She had the same hair and build but that was all. When he'd seen her from his van on that country road in Derbyshire, he'd been fooled. The Devil had placed scales over his eyes and made him think that Abigail Newton was similar to his sister.

Now, watching the silent television, the scales had been lifted. She was nothing like Ruth.

That was why he didn't feel a sense of satisfaction from what he'd done last night. He'd believed his actions would quiet the voices in his head, show them that he was seeking repentance for failing his sister.

It hadn't worked as he'd hoped. It hadn't worked at all.

The news report about Abigail ended and her photo was replaced with a video that showed men in white overalls stepping carefully into the barn where he'd left the whore.

The video was replaced with a photograph of a woman's face and a caption that read, *Missing Woman Tanya Ward Found Dead.*

He leaned forward and frowned at the photograph on the screen and then looked over at his mother, who was standing in the doorway, watching him.

He returned his gaze to the television and felt a sinking feeling. The Devil had fooled him a second time; the woman on the screen looked nothing like his mother.

He was going to have to find another one.

CHAPTER TEN

"I don't know what else to say." The nurse sitting across the table shrugged. "Tanya worked her shift and went home as normal. Well, we thought she'd gone home."

Dani nodded and resisted letting out a sigh of frustration. She and Matt had interviewed everyone currently on duty in the small mental hospital. No one knew anything and no one seemed to be lying about that fact. They'd all spoken to the police already and had nothing else they could add to their previous statements.

No strange vehicles had been seen in the vicinity of Larkmoor House. No one had been loitering outside the building or hanging around in the woods, as far as anyone knew.

Dani looked at Matt, who was sitting next to her, and saw the same look of disappointment on his face that she knew was on her own. They'd been here for three hours now, interviewing the staff in a tiny meeting room that smelled of sweat and cheese. The cup of tea she'd been given, in a brown plastic cup, had tasted stale and after one sip, she'd left the rest to go cold.

"Okay, thanks," Matt said to the nurse.

She got up out of her chair and nodded solemnly before leaving the room.

Matt looked up at the ceiling and threw his pen onto the table. "Well that was a waste of time."

"It had to be done," she said, getting up and stretching her back and shoulders. "Now let's get the hell out of here."

Matt gathered his things, which included photo-copied pages from the hospital's Visitor's Log, and strode to the door before Dani had a chance to put her coat on.

"Hang on," she said.

"Sorry, guv, it's just that this place gives me the creeps."

"The hospital? Why?"

"When I was a kid, my grandmother ended up in a place like this. My parents took me to see her every weekend and the place terrified me. When people lose their minds, it isn't a pretty sight."

"It isn't," she agreed, gathering her things and following him out of the door.

When they got to the reception area, they were buzzed out of the front door and stepped out into the chilly night. It was dark and quiet outside. The snow had stopped falling but thick, grey clouds loomed overhead.

Looking out over the surrounding countryside, Dani had a sudden sense of just how isolated Larkmoor House was.

Matt, who was loading his things into the boot of the car, saw Dani contemplating their surroundings and did the same, looking at the vast space around them as if trying to figure out what his boss was seeing that he was not.

"He probably has a connection to this place," Dani said finally, her eyes on the far horizon.

"Guv?"

"You wouldn't know Larkmoor House existed unless you worked here, visited a patient here, or were a patient yourself. There's nothing else for miles around."

"There's nothing to suggest he came into contact with Tanya here, though," he said, taking her things from her and placing them in the boot with his own. "He might have seen her anywhere."

"The file suggests she lived a quiet life in a small village," Dani said. "She hardly ever went anywhere except to work and the occasional night out with her husband and friends at a local pub."

"Not much of a life," Matt observed, getting into the Kodiaq and starting the engine.

"No," Dani said, putting her seatbelt on. "But it makes our job easier."

Matt pursed his lips and seemed to be lost in thought as they drove away from Larkmoor House. "He could be a random killer," he said when they reached the main road. "He's driving along this road and he sees Tanya's car. He gets her to pull over and grabs her. After he's dragged her into his own vehicle, he hides her car and continues on his way."

"I don't know," she said. "If you were hunting for someone to abduct, would you be driving along this road at two in the morning? There's nothing here."

"Nice and isolated," Matt said. "The perfect place to grab someone. The chance of anyone seeing you is almost non-existent."

"So is the chance of finding a victim. You could probably drive along this road all night and not see another car. He must have known that Tanya would be here, on this road, at that exact time."

Matt considered this. "So you think he met her at the hospital at some point and, I don't know, fixated on her or something? Then, three nights ago, he followed her along this road from the hospital and abducted her?" He sighed. "I don't know, guv, are you sure he couldn't just be some random guy?"

"I don't think so," she said. "I think she knew him. If he was a stranger, why would she stop her car, in the early hours of the morning, on an empty stretch of road? No woman would do that."

"Perhaps he forced her off the road," he said. "He could have come up alongside her and bullied her into the ditch. Maybe he had a larger vehicle, like a lorry or a van."

" So where's Tanya's car?"

"He moved it into the trees."

"If he wanted to hide her car, he couldn't risk crashing it. It might have ended up disabled by the side of the road. Tanya might have been killed. Then his efforts would have been for nothing."

"So you think he got her to pull over?"

Dani nodded. The more she thought about it, the more it made sense. She wasn't going to rule out any other possibility, especially at this early stage of the investigation, but she was sure the killer had followed Tanya from Larkmoor House along this road and had somehow persuaded his victim to pull over.

Assuming he was someone Tanya knew, and assuming he wasn't someone from her close-knit group of friends, the most logical place for him to have met her was at her place of work. Members of the public must come and go all the time at the hospital.

But for Tanya to have trusted this person enough to stop her car on a lonely road, he had to have been more than just a member of the public who'd been visiting a patient at the hospital. He had to be someone the victim knew.

That suggested a staff member. But everyone who worked at Larkmoor House, whether on duty during the night of Tanya's abduction or not, had been accounted for by the police officers who had conducted the initial inquiry into Tanya's disappearance.

She rubbed her eyes. Her theory seemed to make sense at the moment, but her sleep-deprived mind might be ignoring holes in the logic that would be obvious in the cold light of day.

"I don't know," she said to Matt. "I think I just need some sleep."

"We both do, guv," he said sympathetically.

Until she was able to think more clearly, she wasn't even going to consider how Tanya Ward's blood had ended up on the nightgown that Abigail Newton had been wearing.

Hopefully, that was something Abigail could explain. The girl was the key to solving this case.

Matt dropped her at HQ and Dani drove her Land Rover home with eighties pop hits blaring from the radio. She sang along with the ones she knew the words to, trying to distract her mind from the case. She couldn't allow herself to overthink it, especially when she was tired.

At the cottage, the dogs greeted her and she went out into the back garden with them for a while before turning in.

When she slept, she dreamt of a girl in a white nightgown watching with terrified eyes as a man with no face slashed a dark-haired woman over and over with a knife. A rain of blood splattered onto the girl's nightgown, turning the white fabric a dark, bloody crimson.

CHAPTER ELEVEN

December 23rd

BATTLE STOOD in the newly created incident room at the Northallerton HQ building. At the moment, he was the only person in there; everyone else was getting ready for the painstaking search of the moors they were about to carry out.

The search should have been conducted yesterday but the news from Forensics that linked Abigail to Tanya widened the area that Battle wanted the search team to examine. A corridor leading over the moors between the place Abigail had been picked up and Brambleberry Farm had been marked on a map. It was a huge area and searching it would be no easy task. He'd decided to hold off until this morning so that they could devote every hour of daylight to it.

Thankfully, the snowstorm had moved on and

today, the sky was cloudless and bright blue. Now if the sun could just melt the snow off the moors, conditions would be ideal.

The room in which he now stood contained a number of desks, telephone lines, and whiteboards fixed to the walls. One of these boards was devoted to Tanya Ward and photographs of her—both alive and dead—were affixed to it. Another board focused on Abigail and photos of her—all alive, thankfully—were arranged neatly down the left-hand side.

The scant information they had on the girl and the woman was detailed on each board in blue marker.

Between the two boards was a third that held no photos, and had only three words written on it, in red ink.

Link Between Victims

A silhouette of a man's head with a question mark where the face should be had been drawn in the centre of the board. As far as anyone knew, this man—Tanya Ward's killer and Abigail Newton's abductor—was the only link between the two.

They would look for other possible connections, of course, but Battle couldn't see how a 15-year-old girl in Derbyshire was connected to a 37-year-old woman in York who kept herself to herself, by all accounts.

It had probably been pure chance—or bad luck—that had caused Abigail and Tanya to end up here, on the same incident room wall.

Both of them had encountered the unknown

subject of the investigation, the man with the question mark face. And both had paid a price for that meeting.

Abigail still wasn't talking to anyone, not even her parents. The last Battle had heard, the girl was still under heavy sedation.

Battle scowled at the question mark face. When a real face finally replaced that question mark— when they knew who had done this—there'd be a price to pay all right...

The door opened and a slight man in a dark blue shirt and black trousers entered the room. He was in his forties, with collar-length hair and stubble that Battle couldn't decide was there because the man hadn't had time to shave or was an affectation.

"DCI Battle?" the man asked.

His voice was friendly enough, if perhaps a little nervous. Battle decided the stubble was the result of the man forgetting to shave this morning.

"That's me," he said.

"Ah, great." The man held out his hand. "Tony Sheridan. I'm with the Murder Force. As are you, of course. I mean, I'm the psychologist."

Battle shook the man's hand. "Glad to have you on board. You'll have your work cut out for you with this one, though. I assume you've seen the crime scene photos."

Sheridan nodded. "The posing of the body is interesting indeed. The killer is either mocking or revering his victim. Or at least mocking or revering the person she was playing in his twisted little one act play."

"The person she was playing?"

"Well, not willingly, of course. Tanya wasn't playing a part. She was probably fighting for her life. But in his mind, she had some role or other. That's why he chose her; she reminded him of someone else."

"Chose her? You don't think this could be random?" Battle had worked with forensic psychologists before and he wasn't sure how much store he put in their theories.

He was willing to give Sheridan the benefit of the doubt, though. At this stage, he needed all the help he could get, and the crime certainly seemed to have some sort of psychological element to it. If Sheridan could untangle it, then more power to him.

"Oh, I'm sure of it," the psychologist said. He gestured to the pictures of Tanya Ward on the whiteboard. "He went to a lot of trouble and risk to stage that scene. He wouldn't do that with just any old victim. This wasn't your average killer dumping a body in a river to erase forensic evidence or burying a victim in the woods to keep the body hidden for as long as possible. This is a statement. A message. He would have chosen his victim carefully."

"Can you write me a report on what you've gleaned from the information we have so far?"

Sheridan nodded and grinned. "It's already written."

"Excellent," Battle said, clapping the man on the back. "In that case, come with me." He headed for the door.

Sheridan looked confused. "Where are we going?"

"Well, since your report's already done, you can help with the search of the moors. We need every available pair of hands."

Sheridan hesitated.

"Come on," Battle urged. "We'll get you a decent pair of boots. Those shoes won't last five minutes out there."

Sheridan looked down at his expensive-looking shoes and then back at Battle. Then he shrugged and said, "All right. I'll help any way I can."

"That's the spirit," Battle said, leading the man to the locker room.

———

AN HOUR LATER, hundreds of police officers and volunteers, all wearing Hi-Vis jackets over their clothing, stood at the edge of the moors . The sun hadn't melted the snow as Battle had hoped. The white expanse stretched out before the search team, sparkling beneath the clear sky.

The searchers had been split into groups, each group having a warden in charge. Any findings were to be reported to the warden, who would bag and document the items.

"Everyone's ready to go, guv," said a uniformed officer who was acting as warden to the team closest to Battle.

"All right, let's do it," Battle said. "Slowly and methodically."

The officer blew a whistle. In answer, the wardens down the line did the same. Hundreds of people stepped forward onto the snowy moors.

Sheridan was somewhere among them. Battle had allocated him to a team upon their arrival. At least the psychologist was mucking in.

Battle joined the line and inspected the ground in front of him. Nothing but snow. He kicked at it and examined the grass underneath. Moving forward a step, he repeated the action. More snow, more grass.

This was going to be a very long day.

CHAPTER TWELVE

Dani parked and got out of her Land Rover in the car park of Whitby Hospital and found Matt waiting by the hospital doors.

She'd woken up to a text from Battle that said, *Searching moors today. Check on Abigail,* so here she was.

"Morning, guv," Matt said, stamping his feet against the cold. The day was sunny and crisp.

"Been waiting long?" she asked him.

"About half an hour," he said.

She checked her watch. This was the exact time she'd told Matt to meet her here. She wasn't late; he was early. "Couldn't sleep?"

"It's Charlene," he said. "She was up at the crack of dawn. Thought she'd heard a noise in the garden. So I had to check, of course."

"Anything there?"

He shook his head. "Just next door's bloody cat."

"And then you couldn't go back to sleep," she said, entering the hospital through the automatic doors.

"Not only that but even after I told Charlene it was the cat, she was lying there fretting. She wasn't making a sound, but I could feel the anxiety coming off her in waves."

"Have you told her about Murder Force?" Dani asked as they reached the lifts.

"Yeah, I told her last night before we went to bed. Told her I'd hopefully have a chance to be on the team."

"Well there you are, then," Dani said, getting into the lift. "That's why she's worrying."

He frowned. "What do you mean, guv?"

"She's worried about you, Matt. Working the Snow Killer case was one thing but if there's a chance you might be on a team that constantly deals with high profile serial killers, that's something else entirely. It's dangerous."

He looked worried for a moment. "Dangerous?"

"Haven't you seen *Silence of the Lambs*?"

"We're not going after Hannibal Lecter, guv."

"Not exactly," she admitted, "but there are people out there who are just as deadly. Real people, not characters in a book or a movie. Charlene is probably worried that you might put yourself in danger."

"But I won't."

"I'm sure that's what Clarice Starling thought... until she ended up in Buffalo Bill's basement."

Matt's eyes widened.

The lift doors opened, and they stepped out onto the floor where Abigail's room was located. A uniformed officer stood outside. He knew both Dani and Matt but perfunctorily checked their warrant cards anyway before allowing them into the room.

Abigail was sitting on the bed, dressed in jeans and a dark blue jumper. She looked a hundred times better than she had the last time Dani saw her. The fear was still in her eyes but now it was dulled—probably by drugs, Dani thought—and the girl had obviously had a shower and washed her hair, which was currently tied back in a ponytail.

A vase of yellow roses sat on the windowsill, lending their sweet fragrance to the air in the room. A dark-haired woman who looked like she was in her forties but had been aged by worry sat in a high-backed chair by the bed.

When Abigail saw Dani, her lips curled into a slight smile.

Dani smiled back and said, "Hey, how are you, Abigail?"

"She's doing all right, considering what she's been through," said the woman in the chair.

"I'm Detective Inspector Danica Summers and this is my colleague, Detective Sergeant Matt Flowers."

"I'm Sarah Newton, Abigail's mother. Nice to meet you. I believe you're the person I have to thank for getting my daughter back alive."

"Not me. Some kind-hearted members of the public."

"But you're the person we'll be thanking when you catch whoever did this," said a bespectacled man—obviously Mr Newton—standing in the doorway. He was holding two plastic cups of tea in his hands. He came into the room and handed one to his wife.

"I hope that's the case, Mr Newton," Dani said.

"Do you have any leads?"

"The moors are being searched at the moment and we're following a number of lines of inquiry," Dani said, giving him the stock police answer that elicited neither despair nor hope.

"Does that actually mean anything or are you lot clutching at straws?"

"Eric!" his wife chided.

"I'm only saying that someone has hurt our daughter," he said. "And he should be locked up."

"They're doing everything they can," Sarah Newton said, shooting him a look.

"I've seen enough true crime documentaries to know what that means," he said, carrying on regardless of his wife's unspoken warning. "Things get missed. The bad guys get away. Even if they're caught, they slip through the legal system and they're out on the streets again in no time."

"I can assure you, Mr Newton, that we're doing everything we can," Dani said.

A sudden scream from the bed made everyone turn to Abigail. The girl's eyes were wide, transfixed to a silent TV that was bolted to the wall. Abigail was backing up on the bed, as if trying to get away from the television set and sink into the wall behind her.

"Abigail, what is it? What's wrong?" her mother asked, her face anguished.

Dani turned her attention to the TV. The News was on and a photograph of Tanya Ward's face filled the screen. A caption beneath the photo said, *Missing Woman Tanya Ward Found Dead.*

Turning to Abigail, who was being comforted by her mother, Dani said, "Abigail, do you know this woman?"

Abigail didn't answer. Her eyes were still fixed to the screen, her body rigid in her mother's embrace.

Eric Newton marched over to the TV and turned it off. "Am I the only person in this room with any sense? The News upsets her so don't let her see it. It isn't rocket science, for God's sake!"

"Mr Newton," Dani said, facing him, "Abigail is going to need to talk about her experience at some point. Ignoring the fact that something bad has happened to her is going to do more harm than good. And it won't help us catch whoever did this."

"That wasn't even about her," he said, gesturing angrily at the black screen. "It was about that other woman. The one they found dead."

Abigail whimpered and buried her face against her mother's chest.

"Mr Newton, we believe there is a link between Tanya Ward and Abigail," said Dani. "The same person may be responsible for both crimes."

The anger fell from his face and was replaced by a look of confusion. He stared at the dead TV. "But...that woman they found. He..." The rest of the sentence was left hanging.

"He murdered her," Dani said.

Eric Newton's gaze crept across the room to his daughter. "Then how is Abigail here? How did she..?"

"We think she escaped," Dani told him.

He leaned heavily against the wall and tears sprang into his eyes. "Oh my God."

"You might want to sit down, sir," Matt said, taking the man by the arm and leading him to a plastic chair in the corner of the room.

Eric Newton sat down heavily, his eyes fixed on the floor. Until this moment, he hadn't been aware that the person who'd taken his daughter was a murderer. He hadn't known how close to death Abigail had come.

He placed his face in his hands and his chest hitched as he released emotions that had probably been pent up for weeks.

Dani turned her attention to Abigail. She wasn't going to get anything out of the girl at the moment; Abigail's emotions were too raw.

The door opened and a tall woman with blonde hair cut into a shoulder length bob entered the room, followed by DS Morgan.

The blonde woman wore a dark suit jacket and trousers and had an officious air to her. She took in the scene before her and looked at Dani. "What's going on here?"

"DI Summers and DS Flowers," Dani said. "North Yorkshire Police. We're investigating the murder of Tanya Ward." She could tell the woman was in law enforcement herself.

"DCI Cormoran," the woman said in clipped tones. "Derbyshire Police. I'm investigating Abigail Newton's abduction."

"Then our cases are linked, ma'am."

"Yes," Cormoran said. "It would seem so." She didn't seem too pleased about the idea.

"Well, we were just leaving," Dani said, eager to get away before she became embroiled in inter-force politics. She headed for the door, followed closely by Matt.

DS Morgan gave them a smile as they passed her. Cormoran, without turning, said, "Make sure DCI Battle keeps me informed of all progress being made regarding the Tanya Ward case. As you say, it's linked to our investigation. We don't want to be left in the dark."

"I'll be sure to tell him, ma'am." Dani said, pushing through the door.

As she and Matt made their way through the hospital and back to the car park, he said, "Is it me or did the temperature in the room plummet when the DCI walked in?"

"She doesn't seem very friendly," Dani admitted. "At least we got something useful out of our visit before she arrived."

"Something useful, guv?"

She nodded. "Abigail's reaction to the News report."

"We already knew there was a link, guv. The blood on Abigail's nightgown."

"Yes, we knew there was an evidentiary link but now we know more than that. Abigail recognised Tanya's face. That means she wasn't blindfolded or kept in a pitch-black room. What else did she see? Did she and Tanya talk to each other? If Tanya knew who the man was, she might have told Abigail his name."

"You think it could be that easy?" Matt asked. "So all we have to do is get her to tell us who he is, and we'll get the bastard."

"She's been through a traumatic experience, Matt. Any information she may know is locked inside her for now. It might come out eventually, but we can't rely on that happening. We have to throw everything we've got into the investigation and find the man who did this."

"Of course, guv. So what's our next move?"

They were standing in the hospital foyer now, just inside the main doors. Outside, the sun was beating down and glaring off the cars in the car park.

"I want to have another look at Brambleberry Farm. Holloway pulled me away from the scene yesterday before I had a chance to really look around."

They left the hospital and got into their cars. As Dani started the Land Rover, her phone rang. The name that appeared on the hands-free dashboard display said *SOCO*, which probably meant that Ray Rickman was calling her.

She answered as she followed Matt's Kodiaq out of the car park and joined the traffic on the road. "DI Summers."

Ray Rickman's voice came from the speakers. "I've got some of the test results back from Tanya Ward's body. Luckily, our man either isn't forensically aware or he's just not bothered about leaving DNA everywhere."

"Sounds good. What have you got?"

"Well, first of all, we found hairs belonging to both Abigail Newton and a person unknown on Tanya's body. We also found traces of cereal grains mixed with animal fat and canola oil."

"Something she ate?" Dani asked.

"Not unless she was fed pellets that are meant for chickens. The substances were compacted. It's animal feed, so I'd venture a guess that she was at a farm at some point. We only found minute amounts of it, so it probably fell from her killer's clothing or hair."

"Okay. It's something to go on, at least."

"He most likely wore gloves when he nailed her up. There aren't any fingerprints on that section of the wall. However, the rest of the barn is full of them and we need prints from the builders that were working there for elimination purposes. So our man might have left a print somewhere but going by the absence of them in the immediate vicinity of the body, I doubt it."

"So he doesn't care about his DNA being discovered but he doesn't want us finding his fingerprints,"

Dani mused. "Maybe his prints are in the system somewhere."

"Perhaps," Rickman said. "He's been sloppy with the hairs and chicken feed, so his DNA probably isn't on record anywhere. He probably knows we can only use that if we find out who he is and get a sample from him to connect him to the crime. He seems cocksure of himself."

"Or maybe just forensically unaware, like you said." Dani hoped that was the case. Despite the amount of coverage DNA got these days, she was constantly amazed to discover that many criminals were unaware of the fact that they were leaving forensic signposts at every crime scene. It was good for the police, of course, but the lack of awareness still surprised her.

"Anything else?" she asked Rickman.

"Nothing else so far but we're still waiting for some of the results."

"Okay, thanks, Ray." She hung up.

The fact that Abigail's hair was found on Tanya's body meant that not only had the girl seen Tanya, she'd been in physical contact with her. Had they been held in the same room? What had they spoken about?

As she left Whitby and then followed Matt along the roads that cut through the moors, she dialled Battle's number.

"DCI Battle," he said when he answered, his voice gruff.

"It's Dani," she said. "Gallow promised us a

psychologist. I was wondering when he was going to get here."

"He's here," Battle said. "In fact, I can see him right now. Tony Sheridan. He's helping us search the moors. Do you need him?"

"I'm on my to Brambleberry Farm. I could probably use his insight."

"No problem. I'll send him over there."

"Thanks, guv. Find anything yet?"

"Just bits and pieces of rubbish. It's slow going."

"I'll see you later. Oh, I have a message for you. I met the DCI from Derbyshire at the hospital. She asked me to tell you that she wants to be informed of our progress with the Tanya Ward case."

"What? Of course we'll keep her informed; our cases are linked. Who is it?"

"DCI Cormoran, guv."

She heard him sigh on the other end of the line. "Julia Cormoran," he said. "That's all we need."

CHAPTER THIRTEEN

When Dani arrived at Brambleberry Farm, the road in front of the property was lined with News vans from various television companies. Some of the journalists were talking to camera, with the farmhouse behind them.

A couple of uniformed officers had been posted on the driveway that led to the farm, to keep out unwanted journalists and the inevitable ghouls who wanted to see where a dead body had been found.

Dani rolled down her window and showed her warrant card. The officer who checked it said, "There's a member of your team here already ma'am." He waved her on.

The psychologist had made good time if he was already here. Dani had expected that they'd have to wait for him to get off the moors and drive here.

She followed Matt's car onto the property and noticed a dark green Aston Martin parked outside the farmhouse. If that was his car, it looked like the psychologist wasn't short of a bob or two and he liked to show off his wealth.

Parking next to the prestige car, she climbed out of her Land Rover.

Matt was already standing by the Aston Martin and casting admiring looks in its direction. "That's a nice motor," he said, nodding.

"I think it might belong to the Murder Force psychologist," she told him. "He's supposed to meet us here."

"Looks like I'm in the wrong job." Matt gently touched the Aston Martin's roof as if placing his hand on a holy relic. "Maybe I should become a shrink."

Dani laughed. "You'd be bored to death within a week. Stuck in an office, listening to other people's problems, just isn't you, Matt."

"What do you mean? I'm a good listener, guv."

"You're better at hunting and catching killers than you'd be at analysing them."

"Like the car?" said a voice from the side of the house.

Dani turned to see a short, muscular man with close-cropped black hair approaching. He wore jeans and a black bomber jacket. As he got closer, he held it hand out to Dani. "DC Tom Ryan, ma'am. You must be DI Summers."

"DC Ryan? So you're not the psychologist?"

He grinned widely. "No, not me, ma'am. I'm one of the Murder Force detective constables. Chief Superintendent Gallow told me to come up here to Yorkshire and report to DCI Battle. He was busy on the moors, so he told me to come to this address and report to you."

"Guv is fine," she told him. "How much do you know about our case?"

"Just the basics, guv. I know that Tanya Ward's body was discovered in a barn at the rear of this property."

"That's right. We're going to walk the scene with the psychologist when he gets here," she said. "Hopefully, he can shed some light on why the body was posed in the way it was, what the killer's motive was, and if it's likely that he'll do it again."

Ryan nodded.

"I also want to know how the killer got to the barn and how he got away," she said. "He couldn't have walked for miles over the moors carrying a body. That means he must have had a vehicle nearby. If we can work out where it was been parked, perhaps we can figure out which route he took in and out of this area."

"And then we can check traffic cameras?" Ryan asked.

"Possibly, although they're few and far between out here. Where did you work before Gallow recruited you for Murder Force?"

"This is my first policing role," he said.

That didn't surprise her. She'd already thought to herself that Ryan looked mature for a constable. She'd put him in his forties. Most DCs had moved up to DS by that age. So it made sense that he'd only just joined the force. Must have had a well-paying job before that, judging by the car. But why had Gallow recruited a brand-new DC into his flagship team? She'd have thought the Chief Super would have only wanted seasoned personnel.

"What did you do before?" she asked.

"I was in the military, guv."

She nodded. That explained his erect posture, neat appearance, and obvious level of fitness. But there seemed to be something more about him than the outward signs of a military career; he had an air of self-assurance. An inner confidence. She took a stab and said, "Special forces?"

"That's right," he said. "The Regiment."

The Regiment. The SAS. So Ryan had been much more than just a common-or-garden soldier. He'd belonged to the elite regiment of the British Army that recruited rugged individualists. The SAS carried out clandestine missions all over the world. So what was Ryan doing here, at a crime scene in Yorkshire?

The sound of a car behind her caught her attention and she turned to see an old blue Mini trundling towards the house. It stopped and a slight man got out. He was bundled up in an oversized orange padded winter jacket that was so large, it made Dani wonder how he'd managed to fit into such a small car while wearing it. A pale blue beanie sat on his head and he wore boots that also looked too big.

"That must be the psychologist," Matt said.

The man approached them and asked, "DI Summers?"

"That's me," Dani said. "I assume you're Tony Sheridan?"

"Yes. Tony Sheridan. Psychologist. Murder Force. DCI Battle sent me to have a look at a barn with you."

"It's this way," she said, leading the three men around the side of the house.

This area had been trampled by so many feet that a clear path had been formed from the house to the barn. Dani followed it and stopped at the barn door. Although the scene had been processed, crime scene tape still surrounded the building. She broke it and stepped inside, expecting the same foul stench she'd experienced yesterday. But the interior of the barn smelled of chemicals more than anything else.

"That's where we found her," she said, pointing at the wall that still had marks where the nails had been. The entire area was smudged with aluminium powder where Forensics had dusted for prints.

Sheridan regarded the wall and nodded. "The door we just came through is the only way in here, correct?"

"Yes," Matt said.

Stepping forward, the psychologist said, half under his breath, "Look what I've done."

"Sorry?" Dani asked. She wasn't sure if Sheridan was talking to himself or to her.

"That's what he's saying," the psychologist said, turning to face them, the wall behind him. He raised his arms into a "Y" shape, mimicking the pose in which they'd discovered Tanya Ward. "The moment you come through that door, you see her there in front of you. You can't miss her. But is he mocking the viewer? Is he telling us that he's done this and got away with it? Laughing at us? Or is he showing us his sins and asking for repentance?"

He turned to face the wall again, his gaze travelling up to the place where Tanya had been crucified. "His sins laid bare."

Dani looked at Matt. He raised an eyebrow.

"Had she been sexually assaulted?" Sheridan asked, turning to face Dani again.

"We don't know. We haven't had the pathologist's report yet."

"That will tell us what he thinks about the person he hung here for everyone to see. I don't mean Tanya Ward herself; he has no feelings for her, probably doesn't even know her in any real way. He chose her because she represents someone else, someone he does know and has a relationship with."

"So he chose Tanya," Dani ventured. "He didn't meet her by chance?"

"Their paths might have *initially* crossed *entirely* by chance. But she didn't end up here by chance. This isn't opportunistic. He didn't meet her one minute and then do this the next. He's playing out a complex fantasy and people like him are very particular regarding the participants in their fantasies. Tanya was chosen because she reminds him of the person he really wants to nail to that wall but can't."

"Why can't he?" Ryan asked. "If he can do that to Tanya, why can't he do it to the person he actually hates?"

"His psychology isn't that simple. Something is holding him back." He looked back at the wall. "I don't think he sexually assaulted Tanya. He slashed her with a knife instead. There's a rage inside him; a rage that is focused on one person."

"Shouldn't that be two people?" Matt asked. "He took Abigail Newton as well."

Sheridan considered that for a moment, narrowing his eyes and pursing his lips. "She got away before he could make her part of his fantasy, so we don't know where she fits into all of this. If she hadn't escaped, her body would probably have ended up here as well, as part of a tableau. It's positioning in relation to the cruci-fied body might have given us more insight into what drives this guy."

The psychologist seemed almost disappointed that he hadn't been able to see both bodies arranged in the barn.

Dani wasn't sure how any of this was going to help. Sheridan could theorise on tableaux and victims repre-senting other people all day, but it wouldn't help them catch the killer.

"Do you have anything we can use?" she asked out of frustration. "Something concrete that will tell us where to look for him?"

"I can't give you a name and address," Sheridan said. "It doesn't work like that. What I can do is sketch a psychological picture of who our man is, how he functions. That way, we can narrow down the suspect pool. As more killings occur, and he leaves us more clues—or messages, if you will—I'll be able to paint a much clearer picture."

"More killings? You think he's going to kill again?" Dani felt a sinking feeling in her gut. She'd tried to convince herself that this crime was a one-off, that there wouldn't be any more bodies. Deep down, she'd known she was lying to herself.

"Oh, yes," Sheridan said. "That's one thing I can tell you for certain."

He gestured to the nail holes in the wall. "He won't stop here."

CHAPTER FOURTEEN

Dani led the men outside. She needed to find something concrete that would lead them to an arrest before
the body count increased. SOCO had combed the barn
and the immediate area so she knew there was no point
looking anywhere within the cordon of police tape. But
if she could figure out how the killer had travelled to
this area, how he'd transported his victim, it would be
something.

It would be more helpful than Tony Sheridan's
theorising.

"Right," she said, surveying the expanse of pristine
white moorland behind the barn. "How did he get
here? Which direction did he come from? He was
carrying a body, remember, so he couldn't have come
far on foot."

"Are we sure he didn't just park up by the house
and come that way?" Ryan asked.

"No, he didn't. The wife heard hammering coming

from the barn but neither she nor her husband heard a vehicle. When they got downstairs, there were no foot-prints in the snow near the house." She pointed at the moors. "He came and went this way."

"That suggests a knowledge of the area," Sheridan said. "He could be a local."

"He could be," Dani agreed. "But unless he's Superman, he didn't hike over the moors with Tanya Ward's body on his back."

"Perhaps he killed her nearby," Ryan said. "That way, he wouldn't have to carry the corpse very far."

"I'm no pathologist but Tanya had been dead a while before being put in the barn," she told him. "We know he didn't park at the farmhouse so where's the closest place he could have parked without someone hearing his vehicle?"

"Depends on the vehicle, guv," Ryan said. "If he's got a four-wheel drive, he could have left the road and driven over the moor with the body in the boot."

It was a possibility. Due to the mix-up in calling the police, it had been some time before the proper people had arrived here and by then, the snow could have covered any vehicle tracks.

"All right," she said. "Let's work on that theory." She made her way onto the moors, the three men close behind. She stopped and positioned her gloved hand over her eyes, shielding them from the sun's glare. In the distance, she could see the road she'd driven along to get to Brambleberry Farm.

A low stone wall separated the road from the moorland. "If someone exited the road and proceeded cross country," she said, "they'd have had to break through the wall. From here, it looks intact."

She could get a couple of officers to check the state of the wall later and look for possible access points.

"Let's say he came here in a vehicle," she said. "He had to stop somewhere in this area and unload the body before carrying it to the barn. The snow has covered over the tracks but they're still there somewhere, underneath the snow. The ground is frozen but a vehicle as heavy as a 4X4 would have left its mark on the terrain."

"Do you want me to get a shovel, guv?" Ryan asked.

"Have you got one in the boot of that fancy car of yours?"

He shook his head, grinning. "No, but I'm sure the people in the farmhouse will have one."

"All right. If you want to do some digging, I won't stop you."

He nodded once and set off back to the house.

"Come on," she said to Matt and Sheridan. "Let's have a look a bit further on." Leading them away from the barn, she checked the ground at her feet with each step, even though there was nothing there but snow. She didn't envy Battle and his search team; meticulously searching the ground in these conditions must be mind-numbing.

"What's that, guv?" Matt asked, pointing into the distance.

Dani followed his gaze but all she could see was an endless stretch of whiteness, like a blank piece of paper, punctuated here and there by the odd rock or tuft of grass.

"What are you looking at?" she asked.

"Just there. The land seems to dip."

She saw it as well now; an uneven line on the landscape the length of a football pitch away from where they stood. "Let's have a look."

They made their way through the snow towards the dip and as they got closer, Dani heard running water. A stream.

It was no more than five feet wide. The water had been frozen at some point, or if not frozen, then covered with a layer of ice.

But the ice was broken.

It hadn't melted. It had been shattered. Shards of it lay in the water and on the frozen muddy banks.

"He came this way," Dani said. She knew that was a leap of reason. *Someone* had come this way but not necessarily the person they were hunting. It could have been a reporter trying to get a picture of the barn. It could have been hikers on a day trip. Hell, it could even have been an animal if it was something heavy enough, like a deer.

But something in her gut told her it was their man.

He'd been here.

She followed the stream towards the road. In that direction, the water was still frozen over, gurgling beneath a sheet of ice.

She moved in the opposite direction, away from the road. More shattered ice.

"He followed the stream to this point and then he left it, probably on foot, and made his way to the barn," she said. She tried to keep her voice calm. Here was a real clue, something she could work with.

"So his vehicle was parked here," Matt said, crouching next to the broken ice. "A Land Rover maybe?"

Dani shook her head. "A Land Rover Defender is over six and a half feet wide. An average car is around six. Neither of them would fit into this depression, it's too narrow. He didn't use a car; he used something else."

"If we follow the stream, we might find some tracks," he said.

"My thoughts exactly." She turned to Sheridan. "You wait here for DC Ryan. Tell him to clear the snow in a line from this point to the barn. Carrying a body would have weighed the killer down so we might get some boot prints, even in the frozen soil."

Sheridan nodded.

"Come on," Dani said to Matt. "Let's see how far he came downstream."

They moved along the edge of the stream. It took them northwards and deeper into the moorland.

"This points to a local," Matt said. "He must have known the stream was here and where it would take him."

Dani nodded. It was unlikely the killer stumbled upon the stream and it just happened to lead him to the barn. "We need to canvass for witness, see if anyone has been hanging around in this area. Or driving some sort of vehicle over the moors around here."

"Could be a motorbike, guv," Matt suggested.

"It could be. Although I'd think that riding a motorbike over an icy stream wouldn't be the best idea in the world. And how would he carry the body?"

Matt thought for a moment and then said, "He could have tied it behind him, like a pillion passenger."

That conjured a gruesome image up in Dani's mind. Would anyone really ride a motorbike with a dead person strapped to them? It was possible, but not likely. And if Tanya had been tied to the killer, there'd have been a lot more DNA and particulate evidence.

"Guv, there's a track!" Matt said, pointing at the muddy stream bank. In the frozen soil, the edge of a tyre tread was clearly visible.

"Looks like he tried to stay in the water but veered off course a little here," she said. Taking her phone from her pocket, she took a photo of the tread mark and then called Ray Rickman.

When he answered, she said, "We need a SOCO team at Brambleberry Farm. On the moors behind the barn. We've got a tyre track."

"All right," Rickman said. "Give me an hour to get some people together and I'll meet you down there."

Dani hung up. She and Matt needed to explore further upstream in case there were any more tracks, but she didn't want to lose the location of this one. She moved a few feet away from the stream and kicked a large "X" in the snow with her boots.

Then they moved on, following the stream for at least another quarter of a mile without seeing any other sign—other than the broken ice—that a vehicle had come this way.

Moving through the frozen, snowy landscape was tough. There was absolutely no way Tanya's body had been carried very far in these conditions. The vehicle that had left the track in the frozen mud had to belong to the killer.

The difficult conditions on the moors also meant that Abigail couldn't have gone far on foot either, especially considering the fact that she'd been barefoot when the Woods had found her. There was no way she'd escaped from captivity and then run for miles over the moors to arrive at the road. She'd travelled to that location by some other means.

She rang Battle.

"Got anything for me?" he asked gruffly when he answered.

"We've found a tyre track in a stream behind Brambleberry Farm. SOCO are on their way. But that's not why I'm calling. There's no way Abigail got to your location by walking over the moors. I think she might have jumped from a vehicle."

"All right," he said. "I'm listening."

"Melissa and Jeff Wood assumed that Abigail came from the moors and ran into the road. We assumed the same thing. But what if she'd been on the road a few moments before, in a vehicle? She jumps from it and runs onto the moors. Assuming the killer is driving, he pulls over and tries to find her. He can't. And he can't draw a lot of attention to himself or his vehicle, so he gets back in and drives away. Abigail waits until she sees a car coming, maybe one that has a couple in it because that seems safer, and then she runs out in front of it and gets in."

There was a silence on the line for a moment, then Battle said, "It makes more sense than her running for miles over the moors in the dead of winter, I'll give you that. So this search we're conducting is pointless. Our man was never here, other than in a car on the road."

"It seems to be the most likely explanation," she said.

Battle sighed. "We haven't found anything out here anyway. I'm going to call it a day and send everyone home. See you back at headquarters."

"Okay, guv." She hung up and slid the phone into her coat pocket.

"I think you're right," Matt said. "There's no way Abigail travelled far on foot."

In her head, Dani created a mental timeline of the night of December 21st and the morning of the 22nd. Assuming Abigail hadn't spent too long on the moors before running in front of the Woods' Volvo, the killer had been driving in that area at around ten o' clock at night. Where was he going to or coming from? Why did he have Abigail in the vehicle with him?

Sheila Clifton heard the hammering in her barn at around 6:30 the following morning. So between 10 p.m. on the night of the 21st and 6:30 a.m. on the morning of the 22nd, the killer had driven some sort of vehicle along this frozen stream, transporting Tanya Ward's body to the barn. That was a large window of time and did nothing to narrow down his likely location.

Tanya must have already been dead by 10 p.m. on the 21st, when the killer was on the road with Abigail, because her blood was all over the nightgown Abigail was wearing when the Woods picked her up.

"Why was she in the car with him?" she asked Matt. "Any ideas? He'd already killed Tanya, so where was he taking Abigail?"

Matt shrugged. "Your guess is as good as mine, guv."

"He took a big risk, transporting her like that. A risk that didn't pay off in the end because she escaped. Whatever he was up to, it must have been something important."

"Who knows how his mind works?" Matt asked. Then he grinned and added, "Probably not that psychologist."

"You don't rate forensic psychology as a useful field in understanding criminals?" she asked. Personally, she still wasn't sure what to make of Tony Sheridan, but she'd worked with a helpful psychologist on the snow killer case and knew that behavioural investigation could be useful.

Matt shrugged. "Well, I don't know, guv. I prefer something solid, like that tyre track. I'm not sure how helpful understanding the criminal's brain is, if it's not going to lead us to his address."

Dani sighed and looked over the windswept moors. A killer was out there somewhere. He'd killed at least one woman that they knew of and, if Sheridan was correct, would strike again.

The evidence they had was scant and didn't point the finger at anyone. Never mind a list of likely suspects; they didn't even have a single name.

"At this point, Matt," she said. "I'll take all the help I can get."

CHAPTER FIFTEEN

"Samuel, I'm going out," his mother said. "You get to bed at your normal time. Don't wait up for me."

He turned from the kitchen sink, where he'd been washing the supper dishes. The meal had consisted of bread and some sort of stew his mother had made. She was a terrible cook.

He couldn't wait until tomorrow when he'd be at work and would get his meals from service stations, garages, and fast food restaurants. Even food that was made mostly by machines and mass-produced tasted better than his mother's home cooking.

She stood by the front door with her going-out clothes on: a long dark blue skirt, high heels, and a colourful low-cut jumper. Her hair was freshly washed, and she wore it down. It reached to well below her shoulders. Her face was heavily made up.

It was almost as if she were a totally different

person to the white-robed woman who wore no makeup and tied her hair back when she was at home.

This get up was a lure to attract men, in the same way a flower's colourful petals entice bees to pollen.

"How do I look?" she asked, grinning inanely.

"Great," he lied. He hated her even more when she dressed like this because he knew what she was going to be doing while she was out. Those colourful petals would be falling to the floor of some seedy hotel room somewhere while the latest man she'd picked up watched and waited.

Samuel was surprised she was going out with the bump in her belly so obvious. Maybe some men were into that kind of thing.

She took her coat from the hook near the door and leaned forward, offering her cheek to him. "Come and give me a kiss goodbye, then."

He sighed, went over to her and leaned toward the offered cheek.

"Don't smudge my makeup," she said.

He kissed her perfunctorily, the chemical taste of her foundation repulsive on his lips.

"Bye," she said, opening the door and going out to her car, a cherry red Nissan. He waited at the door and watched her drive away before closing it and going back into the house.

He finished the dishes and dried his hands on the tea towel before going to the back door and putting on his coat, boots, and gloves. He left the house and crossed the cold yard to the outbuilding where his ATV quad bike waited.

He unhooked the trailer and got onto the bike, starting the engine. It thrummed beneath him, the vibrations rising through his legs and into his body. Samuel put on the black safety helmet he always wore when riding the bike and pushed the visor down. He gunned the engine and rode out of the building, turning the handlebars towards the back of the yard.

He approached the barn where the hens were kept and rode past it. He glanced at the rock behind the barn that marked Ruth's grave, but he didn't stop. Tonight, he was going further than that.

The ATV bumped over the frozen ground, churning through the snow with no problem. Samuel surveyed the landscape around him. He was alone. Other than the distant lights of faraway villages, there were no signs of life out here. He could be the last person alive on the planet. He wouldn't mind that. He wouldn't mind that at all.

In the distance, he saw his destination, a small, insignificant looking dark shape against the snow. Some time ago, he'd considered throwing a camouflage net over it to hide it even better—he'd seen such nets on an army surplus site on the Internet—but the truth was that it was hidden well enough already. And this land belonged to the farm and was fenced off, so members of the red sock brigade weren't going to stumble across it during their rambles over the countryside.

He didn't like ramblers. In the Summer, they

seemed to be everywhere, like an army of ants marching nowhere in particular with their ridiculous ski poles, wearing rucksacks that looked like they were made for a polar expedition rather than a stroll over the moors.

He arrived at this destination and cut the ATV's engine.

Removing his helmet and checking the landscape around him again, he went over to the waist high, green-painted, metallic structure and removed his gloves to open the combination padlock that secured the hatch.

When the padlock was unlocked, he removed it and carefully opened the metal hatch to reveal a ladder that descended into darkness.

Samuel called this place The Bunker. The land upon which it had been built had been leased to the government in the 50s by his grandfather and they'd built this installation, along with hundreds of others, in case of a nuclear attack by the Russians. It had been a waste of government money. Eventually, the lease had run out and the land on which the Bunker had been built had been returned to the farm.

The installation may have been useless as far as the government was concerned but Samuel had found a use for it.

A torch hung from a nail just inside the hatch. He unhooked it and switched it on, casting the beam down the shaft to the room below. The air smelled stale, despite a vent that was built into the metal structure and another, smaller vent that projected through the ground some distance away.

Samuel supposed that having the girl live here for three weeks was bound to make the place smell. Tanya had been here for a short while as well. He was glad he'd decided to kill her somewhere else and not in the bunker because if he'd done it here, the smell would have been unbearable.

He climbed part way down the ladder and closed the hatch before descending the rest of the way to the subterranean room.

He assumed that in the 50s, when the bunker had been built, there must have been furnishing down here and maybe even electricity provided by a generator. The government had stripped the bunker of those things when the lease had run out and now there was nothing more down here than a large space and an archway that led to a chemical toilet. The lighting was provided by battery powered LED lights fixed to the walls

Samuel clicked one on and turned the torch off. The light cast by the wall light was weak, barely illuminating the sleeping bags on the floor at the far end of the room.

He remembered how Abigail had begged to be let out of here. He supposed he couldn't blame her for that; three weeks in an underground room would make anyone desperate to see the sun again. He'd underestimated her, though. Three weeks down here hadn't made her quite as pliable as he'd thought it would and when he was taking her on her final journey, believing that her spirit had been broken and therefore not taking the precautions he should have taken if he was being sensible, she'd escaped.

That had hurt his feelings. He'd looked after her every day for those three weeks and spent time with her, sitting in the darkness with her, telling her about Ruth. At times, he'd believed she *was* Ruth.

He should have realised his mistake when she reacted the way she did to the woman's death. That wasn't how Ruth would have reacted.

And then, when he was so close to putting right the wrongs of the past, she'd jumped from the van. He still found that hard to believe. One minute, he'd been driving along the road, humming along with the radio, happy that everything was going to be okay, and the next, she was gone.

He pulled over and searched frantically for her, calling into the night for her to come back, but she vanished so completely that he wondered if she'd existed at all. Maybe he wasn't here on the moors calling for her in the dead of night but was actually still sitting in his van on that country road in Derbyshire and the past three weeks had been nothing more than a dream. He'd had episodes like this before.

If the girl hadn't existed, then neither had the woman.

That had proved to be untrue when he got back home and found Tanya Ward's body exactly where he'd left it.

Realising that the last three weeks *had* happened, and he had to deal with it, he bundled the body onto the ATV's trailer and drove it away. He'd been clever and had ridden along an icy stream as he got closer to the barn where he'd already decided he was going to leave Tanya. He'd seen enough cop shows to know that water washed evidence away.

He grinned as he remembered the pose he'd left the woman in. How fitting. His mother thought she was a saint so what could be more appropriate than a crucifixion?

He hit the LED light, plunging the bunker into darkness, and contemplated his next move. It was obvious to him now that everything had gone wrong because Abigail was no Ruth. The Devil had deceived him into believing she was.

He would not be deceived again. Instead of waiting until he chanced upon a suitable girl, he was going to go looking for one. He wasn't going to let the Devil put the wrong girl in his path again. He would search for the *right* girl to take, the right girl who would be just like Ruth.

Finding a woman like his mother would be more difficult. Tanya had been chosen specifically. He'd chosen her a long time ago. He wasn't going to wait that long again.

No, he wasn't going to wait that long at all.

He turned the torch on and ascended the ladder. When he opened the hatch at the top, the crisp night air greeted him. He climbed out of the bunker, locked it with the combination padlock, and got back on the ATV.

Leaving his helmet hanging on the handlebars, he rode back to the house with the cold wind blowing on his face and through his hair. He felt so alive.

His mother often spoke about being born again and that was how he felt right now. As the bike thrummed beneath him and ploughed through the snow, spraying cold wet flakes onto his face, he formulated a plan.

Tomorrow was Christmas Eve. He would be out in the van delivering people's last-minute purchases and presents. And he would use the time to hunt for two presents for himself.

A woman and a girl.

CHAPTER SIXTEEN

December 24th

WHEN THE ALARM on her bedside table chirped, Dani reached out from under the covers and turned it off before trying to drift off to sleep again. Today and tomorrow were her days off. She'd booked them months ago, when she'd thought Charlie would be home from Uni and they'd go shopping together in Newcastle.

Now that Charlie was spending the holiday with her boyfriend's family, a shopping trip was off the table, so Dani just wanted to sleep. She should have turned her alarm off last night before going to bed, but it had slipped her mind. She'd gone to bed thinking about the tyre track in the stream and a partial boot print that Ryan's digging had revealed.

She heard the dogs' claws on the bedroom floor and then two sets of paws pressing against the duvet.

Barney and Jack knew her routine and as far as they were concerned, the alarm meant it was time to get up. They didn't understand annual leave.

Dani sat up in bed and smiled at her two companions. "You two think it's time for breakfast, huh? Yes, I suppose you're right." She sat on the edge of the bed and slid her feet into her fur-lined slippers while the dogs roamed about the room agitatedly.

"We'll go for a long walk today" Dani promised as she made her way to the kitchen. She unlocked the dog door, but the German Shepherds remained in the kitchen; they wouldn't go outside until they'd eaten. She filled their bowls with food and replenished their water dishes.

While the dogs ate, she put the kettle on and spooned coffee into a mug Charlie had bought her that bore the slogan, *You Have the Right to Remain Caffeinated.*

After pouring hot water into the mug and splashing some milk into it, she put a few spoons of porridge oats into a saucepan with some water, added a pinch of salt, and ignited the gas ring beneath it.

While the porridge was simmering on the hob, she placed a bowl, a spoon, and a plastic container of honey on the counter.

Barney and Jack, finished with their breakfast, pushed through the dog door and chased each other up the garden, frolicking in the snow.

Dani took her breakfast to the living room, kicked off the slippers, and sat on the settee with her feet tucked under her while she watched TV. A morning chat show called *Live With Jo and Martin* was on and the titular presenters—a blonde-haired, buxom woman named Joanna Rose and Martin Parish, a grey-haired man in his late fifties who wore too much fake tan— were discussing the newspaper headlines, all of which involved the discoveries of Abigail Newton and Tanya Ward.

Jo and Martin couldn't decide if the two discoveries were linked and if the police should be looking for two perpetrators of two very different crimes or one perpe- trator of a single crime that involved both Abigail and Tanya. The media hadn't been given any information regarding the link Dani and her colleagues knew existed.

After their debate in the subject, Jo looked into the camera and said, "Well, Martin, we might get the answers to our questions after the break when we talk to Chief Superintendent Ian Gallow, the man who is heading the police's new crime-busting initiative called Murder Force. Stay tuned for that, coming up next."

She smiled and the show's title appeared on the screen, along with a catchy piece of music . Then the adverts came on.

Dani sat forward on the settee. She didn't know Gallow was going to be on breakfast TV. She supposed it made sense since he wanted to elevate public aware- ness of Murder Force but his name being mentioned on the telly while she was eating breakfast had taken her by surprise.

After the adverts, the title appeared again along with the catchy music. The shot of the studio that opened this segment was a wide-angle one, and Dani saw Gallow sitting on the *Live with Jo and Martin* pink settee in full uniform, his hat next to him on the arm of the sofa.

The shot switched to a closer angle that showed Jo and Martin sitting on a sofa across from Gallow, ready to ask their questions.

Jo looked into the camera with an earnest expression on her face. "We're all aware of the tragic murder of Yorkshire nurse Tanya Ward. Her untimely death was reported just one day after 15-year-old Derbyshire schoolgirl Abigail Newton was found wandering over the Yorkshire moors. Here to talk about the two crimes, and a new police team tasked with finding the perpetrators, is Chief Superintendent Ian Gallow."

She turned to Gallow. "Chief Superintendent, thanks for joining us. What can you tell us about the abduction of Abigail Newton? We've been told that she isn't talking about her ordeal. Is that correct?"

Gallow nodded. "That's right. At the present time, Abigail is with her family, safe and well. She hasn't spoken of her ordeal yet but we're confident she'll be giving us some information in the near future."

"Information that could help you apprehend the person who kidnapped her?" Martin asked.

"That's the hope, yes," Gallow said.

"So are you saying you need Abigail's statement before you can solve this case?" Jo asked.

"Well, it would be helpful, but we don't need it, no. We're already working on a number of leads and our officers are uncovering new evidence every day."

"And are these officers all members of Murder Force, the new police team?" Martin said. "What can you tell us about that?"

"Murder Force isn't fully operational just yet," Gallow said. "So we're working alongside the North Yorkshire and Derbyshire police forces at the moment. However, Murder Force detectives are taking the lead in this investigation and that of Tanya Ward's murder."

"So the two crimes are linked?" Martin asked.

"I can't comment on that aspect of the investigation at the moment." Gallow gave Martin Parish a thin-lipped smile that clearly told the TV presenter that he wasn't going to be making any big reveals this morning. "I will simply say that Murder Force is working tire-lessly on these cases and no stone is being left unturned."

Dani supposed that this TV appearance was Gallow's way of getting Murder Force's name out there in the public consciousness. This was the beginning of the high-profile PR the Chief Superintendent had mentioned in Holloway's office. As far as daytime TV went, it didn't get much more high profile than *Live With Jo and Martin*.

"And why does this country need a new team of detectives?" Jo asked. She was either playing devil's advocate or she was feeding Gallow the right questions to lead him to his next statement.

Dani suspected the latter; Gallow would have made sure that the first TV appearance in which he was going to introduce Murder Force to millions of viewers would be carefully scripted.

"I'm glad you asked that question," he said with a smile, affirming Dani's suspicions. "Let me be clear; we have wonderful policemen and women in this country. They do a fine job. However, mistakes have been made in the past; mistakes that have come about because of a lack of communication between various police forces. Names have slipped through the system unnoticed. Evidence has been missed. Murder Force's priority is to make sure that these kinds of mistakes aren't repeated in the future and the worst criminals in our society are brought to swift justice."

"And how do you intend to do that?" Jo asked.

"By eliminating inter-force politics and broken lines of communication. The investigations of certain crimes will be handled by the highly experienced Murder Force officers. We will also be collating information regarding crimes around the country that may be linked. These links are sometimes missed because different forces are sometimes working on different aspects of the same case without realising it."

"What exactly do you mean by that?" Martin asked, leaning forward on the sofa and putting his hand on his chin.

"Simply that two or three different police forces might be working on separate murder cases, unaware that they are all looking for the same perpetrator. It's happened in the past."

Martin nodded. "So you're talking about serial killers?"

"I am. Murder Force will be examining the details of various cases around the country and searching for links that the investigating officers are unaware of. A murder in Newcastle, for example, might have been committed by the same perpetrator as a murder in Nottingham and the two forces investigating each crime might not know that their cases are linked."

Jo raised an eyebrow and nodded. "So Murder Force will be hunting serial killers."

"We'll be looking for linked crimes," Gallow said. But his knowing smile and almost imperceptible nod said, *Yes, we'll be hunting serial killers.*

"And I believe you have some well-known detectives on the team," Martin said. "Detectives who have appeared in the media before because of their work catching serial killers."

"That's right. I'm sure your viewers will be familiar with DCI Stewart Battle, the man in charge of our team. He solved a forty-year-old murder case in Derbyshire recently and caught a serial killer while he was at it."

A photograph of the front page of *The Sun* from a couple of years ago appeared on the screen, showing Battle walking away from a crime scene beneath the headline *Hero Detective Solves Forty-Year-Old Murder*.

"And do you remember the Snow Killer in North Yorkshire?" Gallow asked.

Jo and Martin both nodded. Martin looked toward the camera. "Also called the Red Ribbon Killer because he left a red ribbon at the crime scenes."

Dani froze, a spoon of porridge halfway between the bowl and her mouth. Gallow wasn't going to say she was part of Murder Force, was he? She hadn't decided if she was joining or not. If Gallow said she was part of the team, he'd be lying to the media, which would make her decision a lot easier; she couldn't work for a boss who wasn't truthful.

"Yes," Gallow said. "Well, we've got Detective Inspector Danica Summers working with us. She's the detective who was in charge of the investigation that brought the Snow Killer to justice. You may remember seeing her in the papers a year ago."

The *Sun* front page was replaced by one from the *Mirror*, this one bearing the headline *DI Summers Gets Her Man* and a photo of Dani walking across the moors, unaware that her picture was being taken.

"Yes, we all remember her," Jo said, making Dani cringe. "So she's part of Murder Force as well?"

"Not yet," Gallow said, raising a finger. "But I'm hoping she soon will be."

Dani put the spoonful of porridge into her mouth and chewed it thoughtfully. At least Gallow had been honest about her involvement with the team.

"We also have Tony Sheridan on the team," Gallow said. "He's the psychologist who was instrumental in the arrest of the Lake Erie Ripper in Canada a couple of years ago."

That gave Dani pause. So Sheridan had worked on a high-profile investigation as well. She'd heard of the Lake Erie Ripper case but only vaguely. From what she could remember of the case, a forensic psychologist working with the Ontario Police Department had personally rescued two girls from the Ripper's house and had faced the serial killer alone until help had arrived.

She seemed to remember that the psychologist had required mental as well as physical care after the encounter. Was that Sheridan?

Martin held a finger to his ear and said, "That's all we have time for Chief Superintendent. We wish you luck in finding the person or persons responsible for the abduction of Abigail Newton and the murder of Tanya Ward."

"Thank you," Gallow said. "And please be assured that the members of Murder Force will do the best job they can to serve the people of this country."

The camera cut to a close up of Martin's face. "After the break, we'll be discussing reality TV shows. Are they damaging our children?"

The title screen appeared, along with the music, and Dani turned off the TV.

She showered and got dressed in an old jumper and jeans and put her coat and boots on while the dogs, who had sensed that a walk was on the cards, whirled excitedly around her legs, almost knocking her over.

Putting collars and leads on two excited Shepherds was no easy task but Dani managed it and led Barney and Jack out through the front door. She walked them through the small village and then onto the moors, where she took the leads off and watched the dogs skitter about in the snow.

Twenty minutes later, while she was watching the dogs and wondering if she should have lunch at a local pub, her phone rang. It was Battle.

"Where are you?" he asked.

"I'm walking my dogs. It's my day off."

"Oh, sorry, I didn't know. Does that mean you won't be coming in today?"

"That's what a day off usually means," she said.

"Ah, all right. I'll see you tomorrow."

"I'm off tomorrow as well." She paused and then asked, "Has something happened, guv?"

"You could say that. Some hikers have stumbled across Tanya Ward's car in a ditch."

"Send me the location, I'll be there as soon as I can."

She called the dogs and ran with them back to the cottage.

CHAPTER SEVENTEEN

The orange Volkswagen Beetle wasn't exactly in a ditch as the uniformed officer who'd attended the scene had told dispatch. It was actually hidden in a small copse of trees near the road. Battle got out of his Range Rover and trudged through the snow to the car.

SOCO were crawling over the car, taking samples, dusting for prints, and shining various lights into the Beetle's interior. The area in which they worked had been cordoned off by crime scene tape. A second, smaller area a few yards away had also been taped off. One Scenes of Crimes Officer was working in that area.

"What's over there?" Battle asked the nearest uniformed officer, pointing to the smaller section of tape.

"I'm not sure, sir," the officer said.

Ray Rickman, who Battle knew as the head of SOCO, came to the edge of the tape and removed his face mask. "It's one of the wheels," he said to Battle.

"The car was probably sabotaged. It came off the road here and then someone pushed it into the trees so it wouldn't be seen."

Battle nodded. So the killer hadn't been opportunistic; he'd arranged for Tanya's car to crash.

He went back to the Range Rover and fished a map of the area out of the glove box. Unfolding it on the bonnet, he located the area in which he now stood and used his finger to follow the road back to Larkmoor House, Tanya's place of work. It wasn't far at all. No more than a couple of miles.

The Beetle had probably been sabotaged while Tanya was working her shift. She'd only managed to get a couple of miles down the road before the killer had struck.

DI Summers' Land Rover pulled up behind Battle's car and she got out. When she saw Battle consulting the map, she came over to him. "What have we got, guv?"

"Tanya's car was sabotaged," he told her. "Probably at Larkmoor House. She got this far before one of the wheels fell off. He hid the car in the trees over there."

She surveyed the scene and Battle knew her brain was working overtime, coming up with questions, hoping for an insight that would narrow the search for the killer. He hoped she was going to join Murder Force because from what he'd seen of her, she was a very capable detective with a sharp, inquiring mind.

"And no one at Larkmoor saw anything," Battle mused out loud. He'd read through the interviews Dani and her DS had conducted and even reading between the lines of the statements given by the hospital staff, he couldn't see anything that indicated someone was covering something up.

Each member of staff could account for the others on shift that night. Nobody had left the building that night until Tanya went home at 2 a.m.

"Nothing," Dani said. "Tanya arrived at six and went home eight hours later. There were no suspicious vehicles in the car park, no one hanging around."

"We need to check the CCTV," he said. "That car didn't sabotage itself." Footage from a camera in the Larkmoor House car park had been reviewed by the missing persons officers when Tanya had first disappeared. According to their report, the footage showed nothing out of the ordinary, but Battle wanted to see it for himself.

He gestured to the car and the SOCOs swarming all over it. "There's not much more we can do here. You might as well go back to your day off. I need to get to Whitby. My wife's coming up on the train and I've got to meet her at the station."

"What about the CCTV, guv? Don't you want me to check that?"

"That can wait until tomorrow. Oh, you're off tomorrow as well, aren't you?"

She shook her head. "I'm going to come in. I booked the day off when I had...other arrangements."

A sadness crossed her face. Battle was surprised that a young, attractive woman like Dani didn't have plans for Christmas Day. He didn't know much about her personal life other than the fact that her husband had died some years ago. And she had a daughter. He seemed to think he'd heard that somewhere.

"Listen," he said. "Why don't we review that footage in the morning and then you can come and have Christmas dinner with me and Rowena." The thought of DI Summers being alone on Christmas Day didn't sit well with him.

She looked taken aback by the suggestion. "I really couldn't impose, guv."

"Nonsense. We're only going to a restaurant anyway."

"Won't your wife mind?"

"Of course not. She'll be glad to have someone else to talk to. I warn you, though; she'll probably bend your ear about the best shops and places to eat in Whitby and she'll want to know all the details."

"All right," she said. "I'll come. Thank you."

"Right, I've got to get to Whitby," he said. "Enjoy the rest of your day off and I'll see you in the morning."

He folded the map and stuffed it back into the glove box as he got behind the wheel of the Range Rover.

Forty minutes later, after a short drive across the moors, he was looking for a space in the Co-op car park next to the train station in Whitby. Christmas Eve had brought the last-minute shoppers out in droves and it took Battle ten minutes to find a place to park the Range Rover.

When he got out and hurried towards the station, he saw Rowena lugging her suitcase down the stone steps that led from the station to the car park.

"I've got it, love," he said, taking the suitcase from her. "How was your journey?"

She gave him a peck on the cheek. "It was fine but I'm glad to finally be here. Are you rushing back to work after taking me to the hotel or are we spending the day together?"

"Things are a bit quiet today," he told her. "Some new evidence has turned up but it's going to take a while for Forensics to process it. So I thought we might get a bite to eat and have a look round the shops."

Like DI Summers, he'd already booked today and tomorrow off as well. Also like her, he'd decided to have a look at the car despite being on holiday. There were plenty of personnel—some members of Murder Force and other members of the North Yorkshire Police—who were working on the case during his absence. If anything else important like the car turned up, they had instructions to contact him.

He'd pop in tomorrow to look at the CCTV footage but until then, he had to wait for the cogs in the investigative machine to turn slowly and deliberately. Such was the curse of police work.

They went back to the car and he put the case in the boot. As he got behind the wheel, he said to Rowena, "I've invited DI Summers...Dani...to lunch with us tomorrow. She didn't seem to have anywhere else to go and I didn't like to think of her being on her own on Christmas Day."

His wife gave him a warm smile. "Always thinking of others. That's one of the reasons I love you, you know."

"I know." He smiled at her, but the smile faded when he saw half a dozen journalists standing at the car park exit. A couple of them held small cameras, the others digital recorders and microphones. "Shit," Battle said.

"What's wrong?" Rowena followed his gaze and her face dropped when she saw the reporters. "You don't have to say anything to them, Stewart. They'll get out of the way if you don't stop."

"I know that," he said, "but Gallow told us we've got to be media-friendly."

"They can't just follow you around everywhere expecting an interview, though. There are limits."

Unfortunately, Gallow hadn't mentioned what those limits were. He said he wanted the Murder Force personnel to be "good optics" as far as the media was concerned. If Battle drove through the reporters with his head down or shouted, "No comment!" at them through the window and it appeared in the papers or on the News, that wasn't good optics.

Battle sighed and unfastened his seat belt. "I'll have a quick word with them. Maybe then they'll leave me alone."

Rowena looked from him to the journalists but said nothing.

He got out and walked across the car park to the exit, fixing a smile on his face. The cameras turned in his direction as he approached.

One of the journalists, a woman with a hand-held recorder that she shoved in Battle's face, said, "Chief Inspector Battle, what can you tell us about Tanya Ward's body being nailed to a cross. Is there a madman loose on the streets?"

"Mrs Ward's body was not fixed to a cross," he said firmly.

"Is her husband a suspect?" Someone else asked.

"He's not a suspect, no."

Dozens of questions were thrown at him. Battle held up his hands to calm everyone down, remembering to keep the smile fixed on his face even though he felt like shouting at the lot of them to bugger off. Didn't they have better things to do on Christmas Eve than harass him and his wife?

"I'll take one question," he said, "but then I have to get on with my day."

Again, a jumble of words spilled from the journalists' mouths.

Battle pointed at a woman he recognised from the BBC. She held a microphone and was accompanied by a burly cameraman.

"You," Battle said. "What's your question?"

"What will happen now that Abigail Newton is going back to Derbyshire later today? Shouldn't she be kept here, in the area where she was found, in case she has vital evidence that might lead to an arrest?"

That took Battle aback slightly. He had no idea Abigail was going home today. It made sense, of course; her parents would want to take her home and try to get on with their lives.

He gave an answer of which he was sure Gallow would approve. "If this were being handled by two separate police forces, it might present some logistical problems. But Murder Force operates across the country so there won't be an issue."

More questions were asked but he held up his hand. "I'm afraid that's all I have time for right now. If you need any more information, go through the proper channels instead of following police officers around. Have a good Christmas." He turned and walked back to his car, still keeping the smile on his face. He was determined to keep it there until he was out of the car park and away from the cameras.

When he got back in the car, Rowena asked, "How did it go?"

"Not too bad," he said, getting his phone out of his pocket. He found the number for Tony Sheridan, the Murder Force psychologist, and rang it.

Sheridan answered immediately. "Hi, boss."

"Tony, I need you to get to the hospital and visit Abigail. She's going home today."

"Going home?" the psychologist said. "I haven't even spoken to her yet."

"I know. That's why you need to get over there right now."

"I'm on my way. If she's leaving, this will be our last

chance to talk to her while everything is still fresh in her mind. Once she gets home, details will be repressed. That's good for her but bad for us."

"Let me know if she says anything," Battle said.

"No problem, boss. Leave it with me."

Battle hung up and put the phone back into his pocket before starting the engine. The reporters were still milling around at the car park exit so he gave them a cheery wave as he drove past them. No one could say he wasn't being media friendly.

"Do you think Abigail Newton will talk to your man?" Rowena asked as they left the car park behind.

"I'm not holding out much hope," Battle said truthfully. "But we have to try. The key to this entire investigation is probably locked away inside her head."

CHAPTER EIGHTEEN

When Dani got back to the cottage, she let the dogs out and made herself a quick lunch of beans on toast. While she ate, she mentally reconstructed the events of the night Tanya disappeared. The nurse had arrived at Larkmoor House at 6 p.m. and left her car in the car park.

Dani had seen that car park with her own eyes and knew it wasn't exactly large. If someone had been messing around with the Volkswagen Beetle's wheel, surely they'd have been seen. If not by the staff in the building, then at least by the CCTV camera that pointed into the car park its position just above the entrance door.

She closed her eyes and tried to recall if she'd seen any lights in the car park. At this time of year, sunset was around 4 p.m. so Tanya would have arrived in the dark. If the car park wasn't adequately lit, maybe someone could have crept around, unseen by the security guard or even the camera.

The footage would reveal more when she reviewed it with Battle tomorrow. If the images were grainy or showed shadowy areas near Tanya's Beetle, it was likely that someone had used the cover of darkness to sabotage the car.

Every member of staff had agreed that there were no strange vehicles at the hospital that night so the perpetrator must have entered the car park on foot. The woods were the most logical access point.

The killer had a vehicle, though, because he'd used it to follow Tanya from Larkmoor House along the road where her car would inevitably break down. Had he followed at a safe distance, waiting for the wheel to fall off?

Perhaps he hadn't sabotaged the car at the hospital. In America in 1970, the Zodiac had flashed his headlights at a woman on a highway and, after she'd pulled over, had told her that she had a loose rear wheel and he could fix it. While she waited in the car, he went through the charade of tightening the wheel but actually loosened it. After the woman drove away, the wheel fell off and the Zodiac was waiting to pick her up.

Dani was sure that hadn't happened to Tanya Ward. She found it hard to believe that Tanya—a woman driving alone across the moors on a winter's night—would pull over if a man in the car behind her flashed his headlights.

What if it was a woman in the car behind her? Would she have pulled over then? There was no concrete evidence to categorically conclude that the perpetrator was a man. Statistically, it was unlikely, but Dani wasn't willing to discount anything at this stage.

She finished eating and loaded the plates and cutlery into the dishwasher. Her phone rang. Wondering if Battle was calling her to relay the news of another break in the case, she rushed to the table, where she'd left the phone, and picked it up.

The name on the screen wasn't Battle's at all, or any of her work colleagues' for that matter.

Liz Summers, Shaun's mother, was video calling her.

Dani missed her husband all year round, but this time of year was particularly difficult. She had fond memories of past Christmas times, memories that would never be added to. And each Christmas marked the passing of time since Shaun's death, pushing the memories back yet another year. It was for that reason that Dani didn't care for the holidays.

She guessed that Liz felt exactly the same way. They'd had a good relationship in happier times and Dani, Shaun and Charlie had sometimes spent this time of year in Edinburgh, where Liz and Rob—Shaun's dad—lived. Now, they barely spoke, and Dani was sure the reason for that was that Liz cherished those past Christmas times and seeing Dani and Charlie without Shaun reminded her that those times were gone and were never coming back.

Dani answered the call and Liz's face appeared on the screen. She looked older than Dani remembered but, of course, she was older. Dani had spoken to the woman on Charlie's birthday a few months but hadn't actually seen her for a couple of years.

"Dani," Liz said, smiling gently, "How are you?"

"Keeping busy," Dan said. "How are you and Rob?"

Liz's faces fell slightly. "Well, you know we don't like this time of year. We put a brave face on, I suppose, but it isn't like it used to be. Oh, here's Rob."

Rob leaned into shot and waved. "Hello, Dani. How are you and Charlie?"

"We're fine, Rob."

"Is she there?"

"No, she's spending Christmas with her boyfriend's family."

"Boyfriend?" He looked surprised.

Dani nodded.

"So you'll be on your own?" Liz said. "You could have come up here. We're not doing anything special but you're very welcome."

"Thank you," Dani said, "but I'm working tomorrow."

"Aye, we saw you on the telly," Rob said. "You're part of that new police team. The Murder Squad."

Dani didn't correct him.

"Terrible business with that woman," Liz said, shaking her head in disgust. "How could anyone do that to another human being? I don't know what the world is coming to."

"Yes, it is terrible," Dani agreed.

"Well he'd better watch out now that you're on the case," Rob said. "He won't know what's hit him once you get your hands on him."

Dani smiled. "I've got to find him first."

"Oh, you'll find him," he said. "You got that bastard who was killing all those women in the snow and you'll get this one as well." A sadness crossed his face and he added, "It's just a shame Shaun isn't here to see how well you're doing." He wiped his eye and said, "Anyway, you have a good Christmas." With that, he moved out of shot. Dani heard a door close and Liz's gaze moved away from the camera.

"He's gone out to the garden," she told Dani. "He often goes out there when he wants to be on his own. But I'm going to have to take his coat out to him. It's freezing out there and there's more snow on the way."

"All right, I'll let you go," Dani said. "Thanks for calling."

"Just remember you're always welcome if you want to come up here," Liz said. "Anytime you want, just let us know and we'll make up the spare bed for you in Shaun's old room."

"Thank you, I appreciate it."

The screen went blank as Liz disconnected from the call.

Dani pondered the open invitation to stay in Edinburgh. Perhaps her theory about Liz avoiding her because she didn't want to be reminded of the happy times was wrong. Or Liz had changed her outlook and now wanted to remember those times.

She got up from the table and wandered over to the sofa, checking the weather report on her phone. The forecast said there was a 100% chance of snow today and probably tomorrow as well.

Dani sat on the sofa and closed her eyes, the phone in her lap. Her premonition a couple of days ago that the snow was a harbinger of death had been correct.

She wondered if this new, approaching snowstorm was also bringing something terrible with it.

CHAPTER NINETEEN

Tony Sheridan sat inside his Mini in the hospital car park, staring at the building and feeling the tight grip of terror in his gut. It felt as if a huge hand had reached inside him and was squeezing his vital organs.

A light flurry of snow had begun to fall over the car park, but he barely noticed it; his focus was on the hospital. The rest of the world seemed blurry in his peripheral vision. Only that building dominated his sight and his thoughts.

"Get a hold of yourself, Tony," he chastised himself.

He tried to control his breathing—a technique he often taught to his patients—but it did nothing to calm his racing heart and mind. Since his rehabilitation—both mental and physical—in various medical facilities in Canada, he'd managed to avoid such places, fearing that they'd bring back the memories he tried every day to lock away behind a door in his mind.

The fact that he was sitting here in his car like a scared mouse in its hole proved that he'd been right to have such a fear.

His hand instinctively went to his side and his fingers traced over the raised scar he could feel under his shirt. That scar was the only visible souvenir of his encounter with the Lake Erie Ripper, but he had many mental mementos to go along with it.

Sometimes, when he closed his eyes at night, memories of the house where he'd found the girls flashed into his head. His remembrances weren't limited to images, either. Smells, sounds, and even emotions accompanied the visions.

He knew, from a clinical perspective, that he was suffering from PTSD but knowing that didn't help to alleviate it.

He also knew that the aversion therapy he'd prescribed himself—avoiding all hospitals—wasn't practical, especially in his line of work. Battle had sent him here to talk to Abigail Newton because there was one last chance to do so before she returned home to Derbyshire. The DCI had put his trust in him, and Tony wasn't going to let his boss down now.

Attempting to focus purely on the task at hand and ignore all of the emotional baggage that came with it, he got out of the Mini and walked around to the boot, where he'd stowed his padded jacket and hat.

He put them on and immediately felt swamped by the jacket. He'd bought it in Canada, to stay warm while he worked on the Lake Erie case, but he'd lost a lot of weight since then and now it looked ridiculous on him. At least the beanie still fit his head.

His briefcase was also in the boot, but he left it there; he didn't want to appear as a figure of authority or "part of the system" to Abigail when he met her. He wanted her to identify with him and something as innocuous as a briefcase could be a barrier to that process.

Locking the car, he took a few tentative steps towards the hospital entrance, his hands shoved in his pockets.

A constant stream of people entered and exited through the automatic doors and Tony knew that if he was going to speak to Abigail, he had to do the same. It seemed so simple and easy.

But it wasn't. Not for him.

"Get a grip," he told himself through gritted teeth.

He took another few steps towards the building but then found himself turning away with beads of sweat breaking out on his forehead.

He leaned against the hospital wall and closed his eyes, breathing icy, wintry air deep into his lungs.

"Sheridan!"

He opened his eyes again when he heard the voice calling his name. Looking back at the car park, he saw DC Tom Ryan walking towards him, waving to get his attention.

What did he want? When Tony had left the incident room, Ryan had been sitting at one of desks, staring at a computer screen. What was he doing here at the hospital?

For one mortifying instant, he wondered if Battle—knowing about Tony's PTSD—had sent Ryan to make sure he made it into the hospital. No, that was impossible; Battle didn't know about Tony's PTSD. No one did other than Tony's therapist and there was no way he'd talk to the police about his patient's condition thanks to the confidentiality rules surrounding private therapy sessions.

So why the hell was Ryan here?

As the ex-soldier got within earshot, Tony voiced his question. "What are you doing here?"

"I was getting bored in the office," Ryan said with a grin. "When I saw you take that phone call and leave, I thought you might be going somewhere interesting."

"So you followed me?"

Ryan shrugged. "I suppose so."

"What? You can't just follow me. You do your work and I do mine."

"Yeah, but my work was getting boring. I wasn't doing anyone any good sitting there like a zombie behind a desk. I'm better at field work." He gestured to the hospital. "What are we doing?"

"*We're* not doing anything. *I'm* going to see if I can get Abigail Newton to talk to me."

"You see," Ryan said. "That's much more useful than staring at computerised reports. Let's go." He started towards the automatic doors.

"Wait a minute. I have to do this, not you. I'm

trained to talk to patients suffering from stress. This is my speciality."

"All right, I'll stand in the corner and watch." He moved towards the doors again.

"No," Tony said, following him. "No, you won't. You might scare the poor girl even further."

"I don't think I'm scary." He gave Tony a big grin.

They were in the foyer now, walking to the lifts.

"You're not listening to me," Tony said. "This is a very sensitive situation. It needs a professional touch."

"I was a professional soldier for ten years. What floor?" They'd entered the lift now and Ryan's finger hovered over the control panel.

"Floor two. And you know that's not what I mean when I say professional. I'm talking about a being a professional in a profession that deals with this sort of thing."

"I'm sure I'll learn simply by watching you," Ryan said.

"No, you won't because you won't be watching me. You can stay outside the room. I don't want you in there, do you hear me?" He raised his finger to emphasise his point, but he was sure the ex-SAS soldier in front of him wasn't intimidated in the slightest.

As the lift door opened with a *ding* and they stepped out, Ryan said, "All right, doc, I'll wait outside."

"Good," Tony said. He suddenly realised where he was. Ryan had distracted him so much with his bullish attitude that Tony's fear of entering the building had been overridden by his need to reign in the DC.

A tremor of fear passed through his body. The last time he'd been in a hospital had been during the lowest point in his life. His mind had been so messed up and the doctors had pumped him with so many meds that he hadn't been sure where he was, or even who he was. Being here, inside a hospital again, made him feel unstable both on his feet and in his mind.

"Come on, doc," Ryan said, taking Tony by the shoulders and leading him along the corridor to a room at the far end where a uniformed police officer stood guard. He flashed his warrant card at the officer and knocked on the door.

A man's voice within said, "Come in."

Ryan led Tony inside and said, "I'll wait outside." He went back out into the corridor and closed the door behind him.

If Tony didn't know better, he'd swear that Ryan somehow knew about his problem getting to this room and had just helped him every step of the way.

He fixed a smile on his face when he saw Mr and Mrs Newton standing by the window with their daughter Abigail.

"Hi," he said. "I'm Tony, a psychologist. I was wondering if I could speak to Abigail."

Mr Newton shrugged. "She hasn't spoken a word to us, so I don't see why she'd tell you anything, but you're welcome to try."

"If it's all right with Abigail, of course," Tony said,

turning to the dark-haired girl who regarded him with inquisitive eyes. At least he saw was no fear there, which was positive.

She looked him up and down and gave him a barely imperceptible nod.

"Would you like to sit down?" he asked her, indicating a chair by the bed.

Abigail shook her head.

"Okay, that's fine. Do you mind if I sit down? I hate hospitals."

She smiled.

Tony dropped into the chair, feeling much more secure now that he was sitting than he had done when he was on his feet. "Okay," he said, taking off his beanie and unzipping his coat. He puffed out his cheeks. "It's very warm in here."

"They never turn the heating off and the windows don't open," Mrs Newton said.

"A wonderful breeding ground for bugs and germs," he said. Turning his attention to Abigail, he said, "Do you know that I had to force myself to come inside this building? In fact, if my colleague outside the door there hadn't distracted me, I probably wouldn't be here at all."

He wondered again if Ryan's distraction tactics had been deliberate.

"Well, that may not be strictly true," Tony admitted. "I wanted to speak to you so badly that I probably would have overcome my fear on my own. But talking to my friend made it much easier. It helped me do something I was afraid of."

He pulled his jacket off awkwardly and wiped his forehead with the back of his hand. "I suppose you're wondering why I'm afraid of hospitals."

Abigail said nothing but watched him intently.

"A couple of years ago," he said, "the Canadian Government contacted me. They wanted me to help them find a very bad man. So I went all the way to Canada. Have you ever been to Canada?"

She shook her head.

"Well, it's a long way from here. It takes eight hours to get there on a plane. And it's very cold. At least it was when I was there. Anyway, I worked with the police there to track this man who had been doing terrible things to people in places that were all situated around a lake called Lake Erie. Lake Erie is huge. It's one of the Great Lakes and its surface area is almost ten thousand square miles."

He caught himself going off on a tangent and said, "Anyway, it's big. So as well as physically searching for this guy, the police were also trying to find him by using psychology, which is my field of expertise. I tried to put myself in his shoes so I could predict what he was going to do next. We didn't have much luck. I was certain I knew a lot about the person we were looking for but there were no leads so there was no one for me to match against my profile."

He took a deep breath before continuing. "One day I hired a Jeep Wrangler and went for a long drive. I had a few days off and I needed some time to think. Two girls were missing, and I was trying to work out how I could help the police get them back to their families. So I drove around for a while and stayed in some cheap motels and tried to get inside the head of this bad guy we were chasing."

The scar in his side felt suddenly itchy but Tony resisted the urge to scratch it. He realised his hands were gripping the arms of the chair so tightly that his knuckles had gone white. "I came to a small town called Lakeshore," he said. "Lakeshore, as the name implies, is on the shore of a lake. Lake St Clair, which is much smaller than Lake Erie. Anyway, I stopped for petrol—or gas, as they call it over there—and as I was paying for it, a sudden chill came over me. It was like my brain was sounding an alarm in my head, telling me to get out of there. I looked at the guy who was serving me and he looked at me and as our eyes met, I knew. It was him. The man we were looking for was right here in front of me, handing me my change."

As he remembered those eyes looking at him across the gas station counter—and the feeling that they were reaching into his soul—he gripped the chair even tighter. "I should have called my police colleagues but what could I tell them? I met a guy at a gas station who I thought was the Lake Erie Ripper? No, that wouldn't bring them to Lakeshore. They'd already told me that I was overworked and getting too close to the case; that was why they'd given me those days off in the first place. So if I called them and said I'd bumped into the

Ripper, they'd just think I was being paranoid or delusional."

That was an understatement. The Canadian police had thought him a bit eccentric from the moment they'd met him. He didn't blame them; he *was* a bit eccentric. But that didn't mean he couldn't do his job. As time passed, though, and he became embroiled in the Lake Erie Ripper's thought processes, some of the officers he worked with amended their assessment of him from eccentric to downright weird.

He forced himself to release his grip on the chair. "So I got back in the Jeep and drove it a few yards down the street. Then I sat there and waited. I needed to know where this man lived, and the only way I could do that was by following him home. If I was right, you see, and he had those two missing girls hidden away somewhere, the only way I was going to find them was by finding out where his house was."

"Is this relevant?" Mr Newton asked.

Tony nodded. "Yes, it is."

"I don't see how—"

"When he came out of the gas station, it was getting dark," Tony said, cutting Newton off. He focused all of his attention on Abigail, who was listening with interest.

"He got into a beat-up old car and drove home," Tony told her. "I followed. I waited outside his house for half an hour after he went inside, wondering if the missing girls were in there. Finally, I couldn't stand waiting there and not doing anything any longer. I got out of the car and crept up to the house. As I got closer, I noticed that the front door had been left open. So I went inside."

He took a deep breath as he felt an anxious tightness in his chest. The next part of the story—what happened after he entered the house—was the stuff of nightmares. He wasn't going to recount that now, to Abigail. What was important was that she realised that, like her, he was a survivor.

"He was the Lake Erie Ripper after all," he said, his voice breaking as he tried to keep his emotions in check. "When I'd recognised him in the gas station, he'd recognised me as well. He knew I'd followed him home. And he'd left the door open to lure me inside."

Abigail's eyes widened.

"What happened next is something I can never forget, no matter how much I'd like to. But I won't go into that now," he added when he saw Mr Newton's alarmed face. Despite what Abigail's father feared, Tony wasn't about to add to his daughter's mental anguish by telling her what happened in that house.

"Suffice to say, I ended up in hospital," he said. "That's why I hate the places; they remind me of that time. A time in my life when I was utterly broken."

He leaned towards her and said, "The doctors and nurses wanted me to tell them what had happened but for a long time, I wouldn't speak of it. I just wanted to lock it all away. I thought that if I pushed it deep down inside myself, it would be as if it had never happened."

He paused, remembering his refusal to speak about

what had happened in the Ripper's house. He'd frustrated all of the medical professionals who were trying to help him come to terms with the traumatic event but at the time, it had seemed more important for him to refuse to acknowledge that the event had happened at all.

"The thing is, I was wrong. Keeping it all inside of me just meant it had a place to fester and grow. My mental state got worse. I couldn't sleep. The memories, unspoken, were becoming more and more overwhelming. It wasn't until I finally spoke aloud what had happened in that house that the memories lost their power over me."

He shrugged. "Abigail, I'm not telling you that you have to speak to me right now. Or ever. You might feel that you can only tell your mum about what happened. Or your dad. And that could be some time from now. But I just want to say that when you're a survivor, like we both are, then it seems easier to try and forget everything that happened to you. But it's acknowledging that it happened and getting on with your life that makes you a true survivor."

He got to his feet and smiled at her. "I'm not going to try and force you to say anything." He fished in his inside pocket and found one of his business cards. "But if you ever feel that you want to talk to a fellow survivor, this is my number."

He handed her the card and she stared down at it in her hand.

"Right," Tony said. "I'd better get back. I hope you all have a safe journey home."

Nodding to Abigail's parents, he turned to the door.

"He told me about his sister," Abigail said.

Tony turned back to her, relief making him smile.

Mrs Newton's hand flew to her mouth and tears sprang into her eyes. "Abigail!"

"He told me about his sister," Abigail repeated, looking up at Tony. "He told me lots of stories."

Tony knelt in front of her and said, "Tell me all about them."

CHAPTER TWENTY

"He called me Ruth," Abigail said. She was sitting on the bed now and Tony was back in the chair. Mr and Mrs Newton stood by the window, watching their daughter with relief on their faces. Tony wondered if they'd believed Abigail might never speak again.

He wished he had a paper and a pen to take notes, but he wasn't going to interrupt the girl sitting in front of him. He wasn't even going to get his phone out of his pocket and find the voice recorder app on it. His full attention was directed at Abigail. She was in a flow state and he didn't want to break it by distracting her.

"Ruth was his sister's name," she said.

Tony let Abigail tell her story her own way. Another interviewer might interrupt at this point and ask questions like, "Where did he keep you? What did he look like?" or "Describe the room you were in." Tony did none of that. Instead, he nodded slightly, encouraging Abigail to continue.

"It was pitch black. Somewhere underground. There were lights on the walls, but they were dim, and they kept going off. I was there on my own for a long time. Sometimes, he'd visit me in the dark and when he did, he kept saying things had gone wrong, but he was going to make them right again. I didn't know what he meant by that, so I stayed quiet."

"That's good," Mr Newton said. "You did the right thing."

Tony held a hand up and shot him a look that told him to keep quiet.

"Sometimes, he seemed to know I wasn't Ruth," Abigail continued. "That was when he told me that Ruth was his sister and his mother's name was Mary. He said Mary hated Ruth and she was the reason his sister was dead. He was going to get revenge."

She paused and looked down at the ground. "He... killed someone. Right in front of me." She didn't lift her head. Tears dropped from her face onto the tiled floor.

Mrs Newton made a move towards her daughter but Tony lifted a finger, signalling for her to wait. He reached out and gently placed a hand on Abigail's shoulder.

"He said there was something he wanted me to see but he had to tie me up to make sure I didn't run away. He tied my hands and climbed up a ladder that led to a hatch where I could see the night sky. He told me to climb up as well. He said he had a shotgun and if I tried to run away, he'd use it. I climbed up and then I was in a big open area with a few trees. There was a quad bike with a trailer. I couldn't see his face because he had a baseball cap on, and a scarf pulled up over his mouth and nose. He told me to get in the trailer, and when I did, he tied the bindings on my hand to a metal bracket on the side of the trailer. Then he took me to a house."

Tony wanted to stop her and make her describe more details. She couldn't see his face but what colour were his eyes? Did the baseball cap have any kind of logo on it? What did the house look like? He knew he couldn't ask any of these things yet. Abigail had to get the story out in broad terms; the details could come later.

"There was a basement in the house," she said. "And in the basement, there was a lady tied to a chair. The lady whose face was on the News. He made me kneel on the floor in front of her. There was a gag in her mouth so she couldn't speak. Her eyes were wild, terrified. The man walked behind her and picked up something from a shelf. I think it was a hammer. Then he said, "Look, Ruth, I'm going to do what you wanted me to do. I can do it. I can." And then he...he..." She put her hands to her face and wept. "He killed her," she managed between sobs.

The flow state was broken. Abigail had purged herself of some of the emotions tied up with seeing another human being killed.

Tony looked at Mrs Newton and nodded. She went to her daughter and held her in her arms.

"Abigail," Tony said as gently as he could. "Did he

only use the hammer? Did he use anything else as well?"

Abigail shook her head.

"Not a knife?"

"No," she said.

"What happened after that?"

"He took me back to the underground place and untied me. He was talking under his breath the whole time, but I couldn't tell what he was saying."

"Do you want to tell me how you escaped?"

"A long time passed. He didn't come to the underground room except to bring me food and water. Then, one night, he opened the hatch and said, "Come on, Ruth, we're going to our special place." I had no idea what he was talking about, so I stayed in the dark, frightened to go up.

He shouted at me until I climbed up the ladder. This time, he didn't tie my hands. I got into the trailer and he drove us back to the house. I thought it was my turn to be tied to the chair in the basement, but we didn't go into the house. Instead, he put me in a van. I think it was the same van I'd been in the back of when he first took me. But this time, I was in the passenger seat."

"Was he wearing the scarf over his face?" Tony asked.

She shook her head slowly. "That scared me the most. Something about him had changed. Before, when he wore the scarf, I felt like he wasn't letting me see his face because he was planning to let me go. But when we were in the van, I knew he was going to kill me."

Tony wasn't going to ask for a description at this moment; that could come later. "Did he say anything to you?"

"He was rambling again. He kept repeating, "This is how it should have been," over and over. He said other things as well, but I couldn't hear them. He was talking to himself, not to me. I knew I had to get out of the van, that this was my last chance. We seemed to be in the middle of nowhere, but I thought that if I could run into the dark, I could hide, and he might not find me. But we were going too fast for me to jump out of the van."

She let out a long sigh. "Then, in the headlights, I saw a rabbit on the road. It was just sitting there. I thought he'd speed up and try to kill it, but he hit the brakes and the van slowed down to an almost stop. The rabbit leapt into the darkness at the side of the road and at the same time, I pushed the door open and jumped. He tried to grab me, but he was too late. I landed in the grass and ran as fast as I could.

I heard him calling me...or calling Ruth, anyway... but I kept going. After a few minutes, he drove away. I was cold and I knew I couldn't stay out on the moors for long or I'd freeze to death. So I crept back to the road but stayed out of sight in case he came back. Then I saw a car coming and I ran out in front of it. There were two nice people inside and they helped me." She began to cry again, burying her face against her mother's chest.

Tony knew he'd got as much information as he was going to get out of Abigail today. She'd taken the first step and told her story. She'd find it easier to tell it again later, hopefully with more details.

"Abigail, you've been amazing," he said. "Thank you for talking to me."

He stood up and went over to Mr Newton, who was still standing by the window. "Mr Newton, Abigail is making great progress but taking her home today might not be the best idea."

Mr Newton sighed. "Well, we're not staying in this hospital a moment longer, but I suppose we can find a hotel. It's not like we can drive home in this, anyway." He waved his hand at the window.

Tony looked outside. The snow was coming down so thick and fast, he could barely see the car park.

He gave Newton the same business card he'd given Abigail. "If any of you need to talk to me, my number is on there."

He turned to Abigail and her mother. "I'll see you soon, Abigail. You've done brilliantly today. Thank you."

Tony left the room and found Ryan leaning against the wall in the corridor, waiting for him.

"You were in there a while, Doc," the DC said.

"She told me what happened to her," Tony said.

Ryan's eyes widened. "Wow, you must be as good as they say you are."

"As good as *who* says I am?" Tony asked as they made their way along the corridor to the lifts.

"I don't know," Ryan said, shrugging. "Just a figure of speech."

Tony wasn't convinced by that explanation. As they got into the lift, he said, "What was all that about earlier? When we arrived you wouldn't stop talking. What were you up to?"

"I don't know what you mean. I wasn't up to anything. I'm a friendly guy. I talk a lot."

"It seemed like more than that to me."

"Just banter, doc."

Still unconvinced, Tony remained silent during the short lift ride to the ground floor. There was more to DC Tom Ryan than met the eye, that much was certain.

"So what's our next move?" Ryan asked as the lift doors opened and they stepped out into the foyer. "Did the girl tell you anything useful?"

"Plenty," Tony said, "but nothing that's going to have us banging on anyone's door today. She's going to need time to get all the details out. At least they're not going home today. They've decided to stay."

"I'm not surprised," Ryan said, looking out at the snowstorm beyond the automatic doors. "Who'd want to drive in this?"

"Well, we've got to get back to headquarters." Tony zipped up his oversize coat and pulled the beanie over his head. "I've got to write up my report and tell Battle that Abigail is speaking."

"Right," Ryan said. "And what about me?"

Tony grinned at him. "You can get back to those computerised reports."

CHAPTER TWENTY-ONE

The snow beat against the van's windscreen and the wipers thrummed with a steady, heartbeat rhythm. Samuel had been on the road since early morning, his eyes hunting for Ruth among the faces of the people he passed as he drove to his various delivery destinations.

When he'd started his rounds this morning, there had been a few people out and about but now, the snow had driven everyone indoors. He felt like he was the only person in the world, driving through a pure white landscape. Was this what the world would look like when it was finally cleansed of sin? Everything white and pristine?

His mother often said that a day would come when the evildoers were punished and the righteous rewarded. When all wrongs would be avenged by God. Until that day came, Samuel was just going to have to right the wrongs himself.

But unless he found a woman and a girl to help him, evil would go unpunished.

His phone—which was clipped into a holder on the van's dashboard as it showed him the route to his next delivery—rang and the number displayed was that of Simon Beale, the depot manager at the branch of Anytime Deliveries where Samuel worked. What the hell did he want?

Samuel considered ignoring it, but Simon rarely rang him, so it must be something important. He jabbed the screen. "Yeah?"

"It's Simon," a tinny voice said from the phone's speaker as if Samuel hadn't seen the manager's name on the screen. "You're going to have to finish your round and go home. The Met Office has issued a weather alert. I'm recalling all drivers. It isn't safe."

"But I'm almost at my next destination." Before he'd been interrupted, the phone's navigation system had told him he was only 2 minutes away from the next delivery.

"Well just do that one and then take your vehicle home. Don't come back to the depot; I can't have drivers stranded here. We can finish these deliveries after Christmas. There'll probably be a few disappointed kids tomorrow morning but no one can blame us for that. I can't let my drivers work in unsafe conditions and I'll get in trouble from Head Office if our vehicles get stuck and have to use the emergency call out service. So after your next delivery, get yourself home."

"Understood," Samuel said. He ended the call and the map reappeared on the phone's screen. He was just one minute away. Once he'd delivered the parcel for this address, he was free. But he wasn't going home as Simon had suggested; he was going hunting.

According to the map, he was in a village called Tarnby. As well as older, stone cottages, the village had an estate of newly built houses and it was to this estate that the navigation system was leading him.

The houses here were all uniform, with yellow bricks and bay windows. Samuel found No. 24 Lime Avenue—his destination—and stopped the van at the end of the house's short drive. Pulling his baseball cap low over his eyes and pulling up his parka hood, he felt ready to brave the weather.

He got out and opened the back of the van, searching among the few remaining packages for the one destined for this address. When he found it—a large thin cardboard box that contained a flatscreen TV according to the writing and picture on the packaging— he scanned the bar code on the label with his phone. The label said that the person who lived in the house was a T. Matthews.

Leaving the phone in the back of the van while he manhandled the unwieldy parcel up the drive, he ducked his head against the swirling snow and wind that bit at his face.

The door of No. 24 was painted black, like all the other doors on the street. The only thing that differenti- ated this house from those around it was a ceramic tile on the wall next to the door that had the house number painted on it, along with flowers, vines, and bees.

Samuel pressed the doorbell. It wouldn't take long to get a signature for the TV and then he'd be on his way, free to spend the rest of the day looking for the perfect presents for himself.

An attractive woman in her late thirties opened the door. She had short dark hair and she was in the process of fastening an earring in her ear. She was dressed in a dark skirt and tight-fitting jumper that did nothing to hide her curves. Her face was made up and she looked like she was getting ready to go out.

"Oh, hi," she said when she saw Samuel. "Does that need to be signed for?"

He nodded.

"Gemma," the woman shouted as she walked away from the door and back into the house. "Come and sign for the TV."

Samuel watched her as she went into the kitchen and used a compact mirror to check her makeup. She reminded him of his mother getting ready for a night with one of her many men, painting on a mask to lure them in like unwary animals.

A girl with long dark hair came down the stairs, her face lighting up when she saw the large box Samuel had leaned against the door frame. "At last! It's here!" She looked at Samuel and said, "Our old one broke. Where do I sign?"

"I'll just get my phone from the van," he said, giving her a cheery smile. As he walked back down the drive, head bowed against the elements, his mind began to race. He didn't need to go hunting. This woman and her daughter were perfect.

When he got to the van's open rear door, he climbed inside and picked his way among the boxes to the canvas bag he carried with him at all times. He opened it and checked the contents, even though he examined them a thousand times a day, dreaming about what he would do with them and what he'd already done with them.

Everything was there. The hammer, a roll of duct tape, a length of rope, and a wicked-looking kitchen knife. He slung it over his shoulder and emerged from the van. A quick check of the street as he walked back up the drive to the house confirmed that there was no one else about.

The girl had pulled the TV inside and it was now leaning against the wall just inside the door. She was waiting for him expectantly.

He held the phone out to her, as if for her to sign, but as she reached for it, he pushed her backwards into the hall and entered the house.

CHAPTER TWENTY-TWO

December 25th

DANI WAS PULLED out of sleep by the sound of her phone's ringtone. She reached over to the bedside table and grabbed it, checking the screen with bleary eyes to see who was calling her at this hour. She had no idea what the time actually was, but it was dark outside, and she was sure she hadn't got enough sleep.

It was Charlie, video calling her.

Dani pressed the green icon on the screen and rested her head against the headboard as the call connected. According to the phone's clock, it was 7 a.m. Dani had never known her daughter to emerge from her bed early in the morning, so she must be making an extra special effort while she was staying with her boyfriend's family.

Charlie's face appeared on the screen. "Merry

Christmas, Mum. I wanted to catch you before you go to work."

"Merry Christmas," Dani said, although she felt anything but merry. She wished she'd taken the day off after all and could just crawl back under the covers for a few more hours. "How are things?"

"Great! Elliott's parents and sisters are really nice. We were up late last night playing board games and drinking mulled wine."

Then how can you look so fresh-faced at this hour? Dani thought. It must be the resilience of youth. Charlie could stay up all night playing games and look wide awake at 7 a.m. whereas she'd gone to bed at ten and felt like death warmed up.

"I saw that murder on the News," Charlie said. "Is that the case you're working on?"

"Yes," Dani said.

"Are you part of that new team? Murder Force?"

"No. Not yet, anyway."

Charlie frowned. "What do you mean?"

"I've been offered a job but I'm not sure I'm taking it."

"You should do it, Mum. What have you got to lose?"

She sighed and rubbed her eyes. "It's all very much in the media spotlight. You know I try to avoid that kind of thing."

"But you can't avoid it. You'll always be the detective who caught the Snow Killer. The media is going to be interested in you anyway, so that isn't really a factor.

And you like working on murder cases. You should totally take the job. Then I can point you out on the telly and tell my friends that you're my mum."

Dani grinned. It made her feel warm inside to know that her daughter was proud of her. Maybe she *should* join Murder Force. It wasn't like the press was going to leave her alone if she didn't. There'd always be some reporter or other chasing after her for an interview or a comment. It wouldn't be any different if she joined Murder Force.

Changing the subject, she asked, "Did you get any nice presents?"

Charlie shrugged and grinned. "We haven't opened any yet. Elliot's parents have a tradition of opening them at lunchtime when the rest of the family gets here."

"Oh, there are more people coming?"

"Yeah. Some uncles, aunts, cousins, and Elliot's granny."

"Sounds like it's going to be a full house." It certainly sounded different from last year, when Dani and Charlie spent the day together.

"Well, there's plenty of room. This house is huge." Charlie swept the camera around the room and Dani saw how spacious it was. Fitted with dark wood panelling and bookshelves, it looked like a library. Elliot's parents were obviously well off.

"Anyway, Mum, I've got to go," Charlie said. "Have a great day, even though you're at work. And think about that new job. You'd be amazing!"

"I will. You have a great day as well."

"Oh, and look in the top drawer of my bedside table," Charlie said. "Your present is in there." She waved at the camera. "See you, Mum."

The screen went black.

Dani looked at the blank screen for a moment. Things were changing. Her girl was growing up. She'd felt that way ever since Charlie had gone to Birmingham Uni but something about her daughter not being here on Christmas Day brought home the fact that she was now living her own life.

Which was fine. Dani was just going to have to get used to it. Nothing lasted forever.

She got out of bed and went into the kitchen, followed closely by the dogs. After fussing each of them in turn, she put down their food and unlocked the dog door.

The back garden had been covered by another couple of inches of snow overnight and although it wasn't snowing at the moment, the clouds overhead were dark and grey.

Dani made a cup of coffee and a bowl of porridge. Sitting at the kitchen table while the dogs went out into the garden, she let her mind wander over the details of the case. Hopefully, the CCTV footage which she was going to review with Battle today, would reveal something useful. Larkmoor House—and what had happened to Tanya's car while it had been parked there —seemed to be the key to finding the killer.

He had been in the car park that evening and he

had tampered with the Volkswagen. Even if none of the hospital staff had seen him, the camera must have captured something. The fact that the missing persons team had already seen the footage and dismissed it didn't fill Dani with hope, but she had to believe that a fresh set of eyes—hers and Battle's— would see something the others had missed.

Her phone rang. It was Battle.

Dani swallowed a mouthful of porridge and answered. "Morning, guv."

"Morning," he said. "Merry Christmas and all that. We didn't arrange a time to meet at the station. How does nine-thirty sound?"

"Great," she said.

"Also, I've got some news," he said. "Sheridan got the girl to talk."

Dani pushed up from the table. "Did he? What did she say?"

"Not much yet. Some clues, maybe, but it's all a bit vague. Sheridan didn't want to push Abigail when she'd just opened up."

"That's understandable."

"Yes, it is. You can read his report when you come in."

"Are you already there? In the station, I mean."

"Yeah, I'm here."

"I'll come in now, then. I'll just get ready and then I'll be on my way."

"All right, see you soon." He hung up.

Dani quickly showered and dressed. As she was

about to leave the house, she remembered what Charlie had said to her about a present. She went into her daughter's room and opened the top drawer of the bedside table, where she found a small square object wrapped in silver paper. Dani took it into the kitchen and opened it.

Inside the silver paper, which she ripped open and placed on the worktop, there was a dark blue jewellery box. Dani opened it to reveal a pendant on a delicate gold chain. The pendant was also gold, and shaped like a sun.

There was a note in the box. Dani unfolded it.

The note was written in Charlie's neat handwriting. She'd always had neat handwriting, even when she was a child, which was more than Dani could say for herself; her own handwriting was an untidy scrawl.

———

MUM,

———

I KNOW you don't like winter so here's a sun that will be with you all year round.

———

LOTS OF LOVE
  Charlie

XXX

———

DANI FELT a tear spring into her eye. She wiped it away and texted Charlie. *It's beautiful! Thank you! xxx*

She put the necklace on and inspected herself in the mirror by the front door. Since she was meeting Battle's wife today and wanted to make a good impression, she'd put on her nicest dark blue blouse and black trousers. She opened a button on the blouse to show off the sun pendant. She supposed she'd pass muster.

She wasn't feeling very glamorous five minutes later when—swaddled in her winter jacket with her woolly hat on her head—she was wiping snow off the Land Rover's windows. It had started snowing again. The cold morning air bit at her face and the wind blew snow off the Land Rover's bonnet into her eyes.

When the car was finally snow-free, she got inside and put the heater on full-blast. Throwing her hat onto the passenger seat, she reversed onto the road and drove carefully to Northallerton.

There was very little traffic about. On any other day, that might mean that she'd make good time to headquarters but the horrendous driving conditions prevented her from taking advantage of the quiet roads. She had the wipers on to combat the snow that whipped against the windscreen and she had to be careful where she drove because the edge of the road was lost beneath a thick white blanket. If she wasn't careful, she'd end up in a ditch.

When she finally got to the headquarters building at Northallerton, she had a low-grade headache from concentrating on the glaring, white roads.

The building was more quiet than usual. Dani took the lift up to the floor where the incident room had been set up. A few officers, uniformed and plain clothes, sat at their computers. Battle stood in front of the whiteboards, gazing at them as if the name of Tanya Ward's killer would suddenly appear there by magic.

"Summers," he said, when he saw her. "They've set the CCTV footage up in the AV Room, wherever that is."

"One floor down, guv," she told him.

He scooped up a file from his desk and gestured to the door. "Lead the way."

She led him to the lift and while they were waiting for the door to open, he handed her the file. "Tony Sheridan's report. She didn't tell him much, but we now know our man had a sister named Ruth. And he kept Abigail in some sort of underground room."

"A basement?" she asked.

"I don't know. It sounded a bit different to that. It wasn't beneath a house. He had to transport her *to* the house from this place. It sounds like it's in the middle of nowhere."

She frowned, thinking. Had the killer constructed a custom-built dungeon somewhere? If so, why not have it close to the house, where he could keep an eye on his victims? Perhaps he was afraid of visitors or other family members hearing what was going on down there.

But building an underground room somewhere in the countryside was risky. It would attract attention. Heavy machinery would have been involved. A sudden thought struck her.

"The cold war bunkers," she said.

Battle raised an eyebrow. "The what?"

"In the '50s and '60s, the government built a number of bunkers in preparation for a nuclear strike. I don't know how many there are in this area but there are probably a few still remaining. I saw one once, years ago, when I was out walking. From above ground, they don't look like much more than a small stone cube with a hatch on the top."

"And you think he could have kept Abigail in one of these bunkers?"

The lift door opened with a *ding*. They got in and took it down to the next floor. Battle fished his phone out of his pocket and dialled someone. "Morgan," he said when his call was answered. "What are you up to? Yes, yes, Merry Christmas. Listen, I want you to look into cold war bunkers in this area. How many are there and, more importantly, *where* are they? That's right, cold war bunkers. Get that information to me as soon as you can. Thanks." He hung up and put the phone back into his pocket.

"Was that the DS you arrived at the hospital with?" Dani asked.

He nodded. "DS Lorna Morgan."

"Is she working the Tanya Ward case now?" The last Dani had known, DS Morgan had been working the Abigail Newton case under DCI Cormoran.

"She's joined Murder Force," he said. "Gallow recruited her on my suggestion. She's a good copper."

The lift opened and they got off.

"Do you think I could suggest DS Matt Flowers?" she asked.

"Yes, I don't see why not. You'd best get in there quick, though. Since Gallow's appearance on breakfast telly, he's had applications coming in from all over the country." He raised an eyebrow again. "That goes for you too. If you want to be a part of this team, you'd better make a move soon. I don't want to lose you because of numbers."

She nodded, making a decision. "When I recommend Matt, I'm also going to tell Gallow that I'm in."

His face broke into a grin. "Excellent!"

They made their way to the Audio-Visual Room. The room was lined with computers and machines that analysed old-fashioned tapes and other media. Sitting at one of the computers was a young fair-haired technician Dani had seen around the building a few times but didn't know.

When he saw Battle and Dani, he looked up from the screen and said with a grin, "Hi, I'm Chris Toombs. I'll be your technician today."

"DCI Battle and DI Summers," Battle said. "Have you got that footage ready for us?"

"It's all cued up," Toombs said. He gestured to the wheeled office chairs that were dotted around the room. "Grab a seat for the special Christmas Day showing."

"Are you the technician who showed this to the Missing Persons team recently?" Battle asked, wheeling a chair over to Dani and finding one for himself. They sat behind the tech and the screen that currently showed a grainy black and white image of a car park with a time stamp in the top right corner.

"No, that was my colleague," Toombs said. "Unlike me, he had the good sense to take today off. If this snowfall continues, we'll all be stuck here until the new year."

Battle gestured to the screen. "All right, let's have a look."

Toombs pointed at the time stamp on the screen. "You're interested in seeing the car park after the Volkswagen Beetle arrives, right?"

"That's right," Battle said.

"Okay, we've got the vehicle arriving at 5:52 p.m." He hit the keyboard and the image on the screen came to life, showing Tanya Ward's Beetle driving into view. The car stopped at the far end of the car park and Tanya got out. She locked the vehicle and walked out of the shot.

"What speed do you want me to play this at?" Toombs asked. "If we watch it in real-time, we'll be here for hours."

"I just want to know if anyone goes near that car," Battle said.

"Okay," Toombs said. "Let's just do this." He pressed a key and the footage sped up considerably.

Dani kept her eyes glued to the Beetle. A couple of other vehicles came and went but none of the vehicles parked near Tanya's car.

Until 6:32 showed on the rapidly changing time stamp.

A white van entered the car park and came to a stop near Tanya's car, obscuring the camera's view of the Beetle.

"Stop!" Battle shouted.

Toombs jumped as if he'd been woken up from a daydream. He hit the keyboard and the image froze.

"What the hell is that?" Battle said.

"A van," Toombs offered.

"I know it's a van. It's parked between the camera and Tanya's car. Rewind the tape. I want to see that van come in again."

The technician rewound the footage to the moment the van entered the car park. Battle leaned forward towards the screen and Dani found herself doing the same thing. She wanted to see who was in that van.

"I can't see any details of the person driving it," Battle said gruffly. "How about you, Summers?"

"Nothing, guv."

Battle sighed. "All right, wind it on. Perhaps we'll see him when he gets out."

Toombs let the tape play at normal speed. The van

parked next to Tanya Ward's Volkswagen Beetle, blocking it from the camera's view.

The driver's door opened, and someone got out. He walked out of shot, head down, face hidden beneath the brim of a baseball cap. He was holding a box in his hands.

"He's aware of the camera," she said. "That means he's probably been there before."

"And he knows just where to park his van to hide the Beetle," Battle said. "Right, let's see what he does when he comes back out."

By the time the mysterious figure reappeared into view of the camera, the time stamp read 6:39. His head was still lowered, and he no longer had the box. He disappeared again, this time around the opposite side of the van, the side where Tanya Ward's Beetle was parked.

"This is it," Battle said. "He could be doing anything behind there. How the hell did Missing Persons miss this?"

It wasn't until the time stamp read 6:53 that the driver got back into the van and drove away.

"Can you get the van's plate?" Battle asked Toombs. "Enhance it or something?"

Toombs raised his hands from the keyboard and shrugged. "I'll try but the original video is so bad, there's nothing to enhance. Besides, I don't think the number plate is in shot." He rewound and fast-forwarded the images. When the van entered and left the car park, the number plate was below the lower edge of the image.

"Who the hell positioned that camera?" Battle asked no one in particular. "Summers, I didn't see any markings on the van. No company name or logo. Did you?"

"No, Guv."

"What about you?" the DCI asked Toombs.

"No, sir. But most delivery drivers these days don't have company logos on their vans. They use their own vehicles as part of a logistics network. You know, like the people who bring Amazon parcels."

Battle spun his chair to face Dani. "There must be a record of that delivery at Larkmoor House. We need to find it."

"Don't you want to see the rest of this?" Toombs asked, gesturing to the screen. "There might be something else the other team missed."

"If there is, they all need the sack." Battle turned back to the screen. "Right, play the rest on high speed."

Toombs played through the rest of the tape. As evening became night, the Larkmoor House car park became quiet. After a while, no other vehicles entered or left. Tanya's Volkswagen Beetle sat undisturbed at the far end of the car park until Tanya appeared at 2:03 a.m. and got behind the wheel.

She drove out of the gate and into the night.

Never to be seen again, Dani thought, *until she turned up crucified in a barn three days later*.

"Thanks for your help." Battle said. He got out of

his seat and gestured to the door. "Come on, we're going to Larkmoor House."

Dani followed him out, nodding her thanks to Toombs on the way out of the room. He gave her an acknowledging wave.

Battle marched to the lift and jabbed the call button. His face was dark as he looked at Dani and said. "If Tanya died because Missing Persons missed that van, I'll bloody throttle them."

CHAPTER TWENTY-THREE

Battle had suggested they each take their own cars to Larkmoor House instead of leaving one at the station and with his mood being what it currently was, Dani saw no need to argue. So she followed his Range Rover along the snowy roads to the mental hospital in the middle of nowhere.

It was still snowing, and the constant *whirr* of the windscreen wipers did little to help her headache.

The more she thought about the man in the CCTV footage, the more certain she was that he was familiar with Larkmoor House and Tanya Ward. He knew where the camera was and how to use his van to hide Tanya's car from it and he also knew which car Tanya drove.

Unless he had sabotaged a random car and then waited on the road outside to abduct a random victim—which seemed highly unlikely—Tanya had been targeted. The killer had some connection with her.

That had turned out tragically for Tanya but was good from a police point of view. A connection could be discovered and unravelled.

Dani knew that was why Battle hadn't simply called Larkmoor House and asked them about the delivery on the evening of Tanya's disappearance; the place was important, and he wanted to be there in person to ask the question.

If only the weather had been better. The snow reminded her of the sun pendant around her neck and she smiled. She wondered what Charlie was doing now and decided she was probably meeting all of Elliot's relatives.

When they got to Larkmoor House, Battle parked his Range Rover in the same spot the white van had occupied on the CCTV footage. Dani parked her Land Rover next to it and got out.

The wind came whistling off the moors, icy and harsh. She and Battle bowed their heads against it and trudged through the snow to the hospital's entrance door.

"Maybe this is why his head was lowered, guv" she suggested. "It could have been windy that night."

He guffawed. "Yeah, that's what he wants us to think."

As they passed beneath the camera positioned over the door, Dani looked back at the place where Battle's Range Rover was parked. The killer had walked this same short distance from his van to this door. Unfortunately, he'd been wearing gloves—even the grainy

CCTV footage had made that clear—so there was no point dusting the door handle and examining the hundreds of prints that were sure to be lifted from it.

Battle's phone rang. He answered it as he pushed through the door into Reception. "Battle." His face fell as he listened to whatever he was being told. Then he said, "Are there any witnesses? Did anyone see anything?" He listened, nodded, and said, "Thanks, we'll be there soon."

He hung up and looked at Dani. "A woman and her daughter have gone missing from a village near here."

Dani's heart dropped.

"A white van was seen in the area," Battle said.

She nodded. The killer had struck again.

A middle-aged woman in a nurse's uniform sat behind the reception desk. She smiled when she saw Battle and Dani. "Good morning and merry Christmas!"

Battle flashed his warrant card at her. "DCI Battle and DI Summers. We're investigating the murder of Tanya Ward. I'd like to ask you some questions about a delivery that was made here on the night she disappeared."

The nurse frowned. "A delivery? I'm afraid I don't normally work on Reception. I'm only covering for Maureen because she's off today. I don't know anything about a delivery."

Battle pursed his lips. "There must be some kind of record somewhere. Do visitors log in when they arrive?"

She nodded. "Visitors, yes, but not deliveries. There'd be no need for a delivery driver to sign in because they wouldn't be going into the hospital. We take the deliveries here and then they're on their way again. It's all very quick."

Except it hadn't been quick, Dani thought. According to the time stamp on the CCTV, the van driver had been in here for about five minutes.

"Are there any delivery drivers that know the staff?" Battle asked. "Chat with them? That kind of thing?" Obviously, he'd picked up on the time stamp thing as well.

The nurse shrugged. "As I said, I wouldn't know. I usually work in the hospital with the patients, not out here. You'd have to ask Maureen or Deirdre. They're our receptionists."

"And they're both off today?" Battle asked.

She nodded. "It's Christmas."

"Do you know who was working on this desk the night Tanya Ward disappeared?"

"The receptionists don't work at night," she said. "They go home at eight."

"Fine," Battle said. "I'm interested in who was sitting in that seat you're sitting in now at 6:32 on the *evening* Tanya Ward went missing."

"Maureen," she said. "Maureen Williams."

The DCI sighed. "Do you have a home address for Maureen?"

"A home address? No, I wouldn't have that."

"A phone number, then."

She hesitated and then said, "Yes, I have her number."

"Then I'd like you to ring Maureen and tell her that we need her address. We need to speak to her."

"Today?" she asked, a surprised look on her face.

"Yes, today," Battle said evenly. Dani could tell he was trying to suppress his frustration.

"But it's Christmas," the nurse said.

"Listen to me," Battle said, leaning over the counter. "A woman and a girl are missing. Their lives are at stake. Call Maureen now or give me the number and I'll do it myself."

"I'll call her," she said, picking up the phone. She pulled a sheet of paper across the desk towards her and consulted it as she dialled. "She left her number in case of emergencies," she told Battle while she waited for her call to be picked up. "You know, in case I didn't know where the paperclips were or something."

"Maureen, "the nurse said cheerily into the phone. "Merry Christmas! How are Don and the kids? Good. Yes, it's always best when they're younger. They appreciate it so much more. And they still believe in Santa Claus, of course."

Battle turned away from the counter, casting his eyes to the heavens as if asking for the patience he needed to stop himself jumping over the counter and snatching the phone from the nurse's hand.

"Listen, the police are here," she said, her voice becoming more serious. "They want to talk to you. I know, that's what I told them, but they're quite insistent. So if you could let me know your address, I'll pass it on to them. I don't know, I'll ask." She covered the mouthpiece and whispered to Battle, "What time are you going around there?"

"Immediately," Battle said.

"Straight away, apparently," she said into the phone. "Ok, love, I've got a pen." She ripped a yellow Post-It note from a pad and wrote on it. Got it. Thanks, Maureen. Yes, everything's going fine. It's been quite busy, plenty of visitors—"

Battle reached over the counter and plucked the Post-It from where the nurse had stuck it to her desk. He read it and said to Dani, "She lives in Haxby."

"Not too far from here," she said. "We should be there in a couple of minutes."

He nodded. "Good. I'll follow you. Then we need to get over to Tarnby and find out what the situation is with the missing woman and girl."

They went back outside, leaving the nurse chatting on the phone.

As Dani climbed into her Land Rover, the immensity of what she'd just learned struck her. Somewhere, a mother and daughter were in the clutches of a killer and it was up to her and her colleagues to save them.

Battle would be pulling everyone back to work from their day off. It would be all hands on deck until the case was closed.

Christmas was over.

CHAPTER TWENTY-FOUR

"Samuel, wake up." His mother was banging on his bedroom door with her fists.

He sat up in bed and looked around the room with bleary eyes. "I'm awake!"

"Well come down for breakfast. You can't sleep the day away. It's Christmas."

He heard her go back downstairs and he closed his eyes again. His body ached all over and sleep hadn't swept away the exhaustion he felt. Getting the woman and the girl into the bunker last night hadn't been easy, even with the shotgun to control them. He'd worked hard. He deserved a lie in.

But he knew that his mother wouldn't stop bothering him, so he slid out of bed, pulled a black T-shirt over his head and pulled his jeans on. Then he went down to the kitchen, where she was cooking breakfast.

Deciding not to risk the bacon, some of which she'd somehow managed to burn to a crisp while other pieces looked almost raw, he opened the cupboard and took out a packet of cornflakes.

When she saw him pouring them into a bowl, she pouted. "I'm making a special Christmas Day breakfast for us."

"I'm not very hungry," he said, adding milk and sugar to the cornflakes while eyeing the sausages sizzling in the frying pan. He wondered if they were raw inside. Maybe she'd get food poisoning and die, saving him a job.

He sat at the table and chewed on the cornflakes while his mother plated up the sausages and bacon, along with some pale poached eggs.

She sat at the table and began to eat. Samuel finished his cereal quickly and got out of his chair . He had to check on the bunker and its two new occupants.

He wondered if he should take them some food but decided there was no point. The last time, he'd wasted time with the girl, keeping her for weeks before he'd captured Tanya. He'd hesitated, trying to put off what he had to do. This time, he was going to act quickly. No need to feed anyone when it would all be over soon for them. Besides, they had water; he'd left a gallon container down there for them.

"I'm going out to feed the hens," he said.

His mother sighed. "They can wait. Come and have breakfast with me. It's Christmas. God will know if you don't treat your mother well on Christmas Day."

Her words set his anger alight. He remembered Christmas time ten years ago. How could she be so

214 ADAM J. WRIGHT

hypocritical to say that? He wanted to scream at her, "What about treating your daughter well? You killed her! You killed Ruth!" He imagined picking up the cereal bowl he'd just placed in the sink and smashing it into her face. Then, while she was still reeling from the shock, he'd grab the kitchen knife and slash and slash...

"The hens are God's creatures too," he said without a trace of emotion betrayed in his voice. "They need to be fed or they'll die."

He slipped his feet into his boots and took his jacket off the hook, leaving the house before she could protest.

The cold wind bit at him as he walked to the barn, but he liked the sensation on his skin. It made him feel numb.

When he got to the barn, he tossed some feed onto the ground for the hens. They pecked at it and squabbled among themselves as he watched them for a few minutes.

Then he left the barn and walked the short distance to the place which was the real reason he'd come out here.

Ruth's grave.

The rock that marked the place his sister was buried had been covered by snow in the night. Samuel knew the exact spot anyway and cleared the cold, wet snow away with his bare hands. By the time he uncovered the simple rock upon which he'd painted his sister's name in red paint ten years ago, he couldn't feel his fingers anymore.

With numb fingers, he cleared an area next to the rock and sat on the ground next to the grave.

Ten years ago, Ruth had still been here. Alive. If not for him, she'd *still* be alive and that bitch in the kitchen would be dead. If only he'd listened to Ruth. She knew what was coming. He had been her only hope and he'd let her down.

And now she was buried here, in the frozen earth.

He stroked the rock tenderly, even though he couldn't feel it beneath his cold fingertips, and let his mind wander back to a time when Ruth was still here.

It had all ended on Christmas Day, but it had begun three weeks before that, back in the days when he was Michael, not Samuel.

The spiral of tragedy had begun when he'd received a phone call from Ruth.

———

DECEMBER 6TH, ten years ago

"MICHAEL, I NEED YOU." Her voice sounded desperate.

He sat up on his bed quickly. He'd been lying there reading a magazine about American muscle cars and daydreaming about driving along Route 66 in a souped-up Mustang. He'd only just passed his driving test and had to drive his mum's Fiesta, but he dreamed of getting onto the American highway, putting the pedal to the metal, and leaving everything behind in a cloud of dust and exhaust fumes.

The magazine fluttered to the bedroom floor. "Ruth, what the hell? Where are you? You didn't come home last night. Mum is furious."

"Of course she is. I can't do anything right. Listen, I need you to come and meet me, okay? Right now."

"All right. Where are you?"

"Our favourite spot."

He knew exactly where she meant. They often sat on the East Cliff at Whitby, in the shadow of the Abbey, gazing out to sea and talking about nothing in particular. Sometimes they sat there, in the long grass, in silence.

Michael always felt a sense of freedom when he sat there on the cliff, high above the sea, seagulls wheeling and crying overhead.

"I'll be there soon," he said.

"Don't be too long." She hung up.

He went downstairs quickly, hoping to avoid his mother. She'd been in some sort of depression lately and had been spending a lot of time in her bedroom. With any luck, she'd be there now, and Michael could escape the house unseen.

He got to the kitchen without seeing her but that was when his luck ran out. She called to him from the living room.

"Michael, come here."

Sighing, he went to her. He found her lying on the settee in front of the TV. The sound had been muted but he could see some sort of daytime chat show on the screen.

His mother looked like she hadn't slept in a week. Dark rings surrounded her eyes and her hair was a tangled mess.

She was still wearing the same black jumper he'd seen her in yesterday and the day before that. In fact, he was sure she'd been wearing the same clothes for a week and judging by the sour, sweaty smell coming off her, she hadn't bothered to take a shower in all that time either.

An empty bottle of gin lay on the floor next to the settee.

"Michael, you won't leave me, will you?"

"I'm only going out for a little bit," he offered.

"No, I don't mean that. I mean you won't abandon me like your sister has."

"She hasn't abandoned you, Mum."

She nodded emphatically. "Yes, she has. She didn't come home last night."

"I'm sure she'll be back later," he said. Ruth hadn't mentioned leaving home, at least not to him, and they told each other everything. If she planned to leave, she'd have told him.

"She won't," his mother said. "It's that thing growing inside her. It's pulling her away from me."

He frowned at that, not sure how to respond. A week ago, Ruth had told them that she was pregnant. Michael had thought that was great; he'd be Uncle Michael, a title that he felt lent him an air of authority.

Their mother hadn't taken the news so well; it was after Ruth's announcement that she'd taken to her bedroom and started drinking. Michael had no idea what her problem was. Okay, so Ruth was only sixteen, which was a bit young to have a baby, but he was sure she'd make a great mother. Better than his own, anyway. Not that there was a high bar to conquer in that respect.

"You're being silly," he said.

"No, I'm not. You'll understand when you're older."

"Mum, I'm eighteen. I understand stuff."

"You don't know about the world out there. I've protected you from it all your life. I tried to protect your sister as well, but she fell prey to its evil."

He sighed and turned away. "You're talking rubbish. You've been drinking too much."

He went back into the kitchen and put his boots on.

"Michael, don't go," she called pathetically. "I don't want to be on my own."

"I'll be back soon," he said, picking up the car keys from the kitchen counter and stepping out of the back door. "See you later," he said as he closed it behind him.

Once he was outside, he breathed a sigh of relief. The atmosphere in the house was cloying but he felt the cold winter wind blow its sticky tendrils off him.

The day was perfect; cold and crisp with a pale sun looking down from a clear blue sky. Michael got into the Fiesta and turned the key in the ignition. The car was old and didn't like the cold. It often refused to start on days like this. But today, the engine roared to life with just one turn of the key.

He put the radio on and sang along with Taylor Swift's *You Belong with Me* as he drove along the quiet country roads to Whitby. He imagined what it would be like to be behind the wheel of a Mustang, putting his foot down as he raced along Route 66 from Chicago to Los Angeles.

Unfortunately, the speed had to remain firmly in his imagination; the Fiesta started shaking if it got over 60 and these roads were too narrow, with too many blind bends, to go fast anyway.

Still, that didn't dampen his mood. He was free of the house and his mother and he would soon be sitting in his favourite spot with Ruth. Nothing else really mattered.

When he arrived at Whitby, he parked in the Abbey car park but didn't go into the old ruins that stood on the cliff. Instead, he walked across the grass to the cliff, where Ruth was waiting for him.

She sat in the grass at the cliff edge, looking out to sea. The winter breeze snatched her long, dark hair, making it dance in unison with the long grass around her that also stirred in the wind.

Despite the low temperature, Ruth was wearing her denim jacket and jeans. Michael couldn't remember ever seeing her in a winter coat; she seemed to be immune to cold.

"Hey," he said as he sat next to her. "What's up?"

She shrugged, her eyes still fixed on the sea. "I don't know if I should tell you."

He rolled his eyes. "You called me and dragged me all the way out here and now you're not going to tell me why?"

She looked at him and her expression, which was usually carefree, was dark and serious. "When I called you, I thought you'd be able to handle what I have to tell you. Now, I'm not so sure."

He frowned at her. "Why? What's changed since then?"

"I've been sitting here listening to the seagulls."

"And they told you not to trust me?"

"It isn't a matter of trust. It's a matter of how much you can handle."

He sighed, frustrated with her. She sometimes withdrew into these cryptic moods and when she did, nothing would break her out of them. He just had to wait until she gradually became her carefree self again.

"Don't tell me, then," he said, lying back in the grass and looking up at the immensity of the sky. "I don't care."

She lay on her side, facing him. "Don't be like that. I'll tell you part of what I was going to say, okay?"

He shrugged nonchalantly. "Whatever."

Ruth pouted at him. "Come on, Michael, please listen to me. This is important."

He let out a dramatic sigh. "All right. Tell me."

She hesitated for a moment and then said, "I need you to protect me."

"I've always protected you. I'm your big brother."

"Yes, I know that, but I'm talking about a real threat to me and the baby." She put a hand on her slightly swollen stomach.

Michael leaned up onto his elbows. "What threat?"

"Mum," she said.

He laughed, thinking she was joking. Their mother might be a little crazy, but she wasn't a threat to anyone.

"I'm being serious," she said.

"Well, if you're being serious, then you're seriously mistaken. Mum wouldn't hurt you. She might not have come to terms with the fact that you're going to have a baby, but she wouldn't hurt you or it. She's not that mad."

Ruth shook her head. "You don't understand. The reason I didn't come home last night is because I was scared. I've seen the way she looks at me, like she's planning something. Something bad."

"What? I think your hormones are playing tricks on you. Where *did* you spend last night, anyway?"

"In a shop doorway."

"Are you crazy? It's freezing cold. Think about the baby!"

"I am thinking about the baby. That's why I couldn't come home."

He'd thought she'd been exaggerating her fear but if she'd been scared enough to sleep rough, she had to be afraid for her life. But why? Was she just imagining malevolent glances from their mother? That was the most likely explanation; Ruth knew their mum didn't want her to have the baby, so she was imagining crazy things, probably fuelled by her wild hormones.

"Well, you're not sleeping outside tonight," he told her. "You're coming home and sleeping in your own bed where it's nice and warm."

She nodded reluctantly. "I know. I can't spend another night like last night. That's why I called you, to make you aware of the situation. So you can protect me from her when I'm at home. Promise me that you'll protect me, Michael."

"I really think you're imagining this."

"Promise. Or I won't come home."

He let out a long sigh to let her know that he thought she was crazy. "All right, I promise."

She grinned at him. "I knew you would."

He sat up and looked at the sea. The sunlight glinted on the water like a constellation of stars. A gull, circling overhead, called to its mate hovering beyond the cliff edge. When its call was ignored, it repeated the sound and flew closer to the other bird. They both wheeled away out of sight.

"I think that gull was speaking to me," Michael said, trying to look serious.

Ruth shook her head. "No, it was talking to that other one. The one it flew away with."

"No, it was definitely telling me something," he said.

She looked at him and raised a questioning eyebrow. "All right, what was it saying, then?"

"It was telling me that I have to get something to eat. I'm starving."

She punched his shoulder playfully. "Have you got any money?"

He nodded. "I got paid yesterday." He had a job at a garage near their farm. He didn't work behind the till or anything like that; he just had to make sure the shelves were stocked and clean up petrol spills on the forecourt. It only paid minimum wage, but he didn't need much money, anyway. He lived at home rent free and had his meals provided for him, when he could stomach them.

So payday usually meant he could forego his mother's terrible culinary creations and get proper food from cafés and the fast food places down by the harbour.

"What do you fancy?" he asked Ruth.

She smiled. "Fish and chips."

"Okay, you wait here, and I'll be back in a minute." He got up out of the grass and stretched.

"Are you sure?" she said. "You've got go all the way down the steps and back up again."

"If you want fish and chips, then you shall have fish and chips."

She clutched her hands in front of her breasts and pretended to swoon. "My hero."

He made his way back across the car park to the top of the 199 steps that led down to the town. As he descended, he mulled over what Ruth had told him. Could she be right in thinking that she needed to be protected from her own mother?

Michael just couldn't see how that could be so. Their mother wasn't exactly a danger to anyone; she was more pathetic than dangerous.

———

HE LIFTED his numb fingers from the stone that marked his sister's grave. At some point during his remembrance, he must have cried because he could feel the tears drying coldly on his cheeks. The backs of his legs were getting wet from sitting on the ground, melted snow soaking through his jeans to his skin. He didn't care. At least he could feel the cold. Ruth couldn't feel anything anymore.

He should have listened to her.

CHAPTER TWENTY-FIVE

The front door of 37 Carlin Way, Haxby, was opened by a gruff-looking bearded man in his forties. When he saw Dani and Battle on the doorstep, he shook his head as if in disgust. "I just have to say that this is an invasion of our privacy. The police shouldn't be calling round people's houses on Christmas Day. It just isn't on."

"We wouldn't be here if it wasn't important, sir," Battle said, stepping past the man and into the house.

Dani followed, wondering if Maureen's husband would be so stand-offish if he knew that two people's lives were at stake.

"Maureen Williams?" Battle asked, entering the living room, where a woman with dyed black hair sat on the sofa.

She was sitting with a cup of tea while two boys, who looked to be five or six, played with toys among a pile of boxes and discarded pieces of wrapping paper.

"Yes, I'm Maureen," the woman said, looking from

Battle to Dani. "What is this about? I've already talked to the police about Tanya. I don't see why you have to barge in here on my day off."

"Mrs Williams, a delivery was made to the hospital on the evening that Tanya went missing. The driver spent at least five minutes inside before returning to his van. Is he someone you know?"

She frowned at the cup of tea in her hands as if thinking, then said, "Oh, you mean Samuel."

"Samuel?" Battle asked.

Dani took her notebook from her inside pocket and wrote the name down.

"Do you know his surname?" Battle asked.

Maureen shook her head. "No, it's just Samuel. He makes deliveries to the hospital quite often, so we have a chat sometimes. You know, just pleasantries, that kind of thing."

"Do you know the delivery company he works for?"

"No, sorry. He hasn't done something wrong has he? Because he's a very nice young man. I'd hate to think he was in some kind of trouble."

Keeping his cards close to his chest, Battle simply said, "I'm going to need a description of Samuel."

"All right. Well, he's probably in his late twenties. He's got dark hair, kind of collar length."

"Kind of?" Battle asked.

Maureen shrugged. "Well, you know, it's hair. People have different haircuts at different times."

"What was his hair like when you last saw him? On the evening Tanya disappeared?"

"Collar length. And he's tall and thin. Well, perhaps wiry would be a better word."

"When you say tall," Dani said, "could you approximate his height?"

Maureen pursed her lips. "No, not really."

"Over six feet? Under six feet?"

"Over. He's very tall."

Dani wrote that in her notebook, along with everything else Maureen had said.

"He was wearing a baseball cap," she said to Maureen. "Did it have any kind of logo on it?" She hoped that the cap might bear the logo of the delivery company.

"It did have a logo," Maureen said, nodding.

"Can you remember it?"

"Yes, it said NY. You know, for New York. I think it's the logo of a baseball team or something."

The New York Yankees, Dani thought. That wasn't going to help much; there must be thousands of those caps sold every year.

"What else do you know about him?" Battle asked Maureen.

"Nothing, really."

"You must know something; you chatted with him every time he came into the hospital. What did you talk about?"

"Like I said, we just exchanged pleasantries, the way you would with anyone. We talked about the weather, that kind of thing."

"Mrs Williams, he was in your Reception for five

minutes. You didn't spend all that time talking about the weather."

Her husband, who had come into the room and was leaning against the wall behind Dani with his arms folded, spoke up. "I think that's enough, don't you? She's told you what he looks like and that she doesn't know anything else. It's time you left."

Battle wheeled on him. "We'll leave when I say it's time to leave. A woman and her daughter have gone missing and their lives are in danger. Until I've exhausted every avenue of investigation, I'll say when it's enough."

The bearded man shrank back against the wall and Dani was sure he was wishing it would swallow him up.

Turning back to Maureen, Battle said, "You didn't spend five minutes talking about the weather. During any of your conversations, did he tell you anything about himself? Anything at all?"

She looked into her cup of tea for inspiration and then looked up at Battle. "Well, you know, he might have mentioned things about himself sometimes. He talked about his sister quite a lot."

"His sister," Battle said. "Did he mention her name?"

Maureen nodded. "He said her name was Ruth."

Dani wrote the name in her notebook.

"Is there anything else?" Battle promoted. "Did he tell you where he lived? Were there any other names he mentioned apart from Ruth?"

"He's definitely from around here," she said. "York-shire, I mean."

That was something, Dani thought, but Yorkshire just happened to be the largest county in England, so their search had only been narrowed down to an area of almost five thousand square miles.

"Did he mention any other family members apart from his sister?" Battle urged. "How about a holiday he'd been on? Places he'd visited?"

She shook her head. "No, he didn't talk about any of that."

"What about his sister? What did he tell you about her?"

"Just that he talks to her a lot. I get the impression that she lives far away, and they talk on the phone quite a bit. I thought that was quite touching. A lot of siblings don't even stay in touch so it's nice to hear of a brother and sister being so close."

"Did he say what they talk about?"

"Their childhood, mostly, and their mother. I got the impression she wasn't a nice woman."

"He spoke about her in the past tense? So she's passed away?"

Maureen frowned. "Well, I'm not sure. Sometimes, he talked about her as if she'd passed but at other times, I got the impression she was still alive. So I can't help you with that."

Dani looked at the scant information on her note-book page. It wasn't much to go on. Perhaps the crime scene where the mother and daughter had been abducted would offer more leads.

Battle must have been thinking the same thing because he handed Maureen his card and said, "If there's anything else you think of—anything at all—please get in touch with me immediately. Day or night." He turned to the door and said, "Enjoy your Christmas" as he walked out into the hall.

Dani followed. Neither Maureen nor her husband saw them out.

When they got to the cars, Battle looked up into the snow-filled sky and closed his eyes. Dani could sense his frustration.

"She's been in contact with the killer," he said. "I thought she'd have more to give us than just his first name and the name of his bloody sister."

"It's something," she said. "We can get someone to plug these names into the database and see if anything comes up." Even as she said the words, she knew that it would likely be an exercise in futility for whichever constable got handed the task.

He sighed in resignation. "Yeah, I'll call it in and get someone on it. Now, let's get over to that crime scene and hope the bastard has slipped up and left us some evidence we can use to get to him before he kills again."

"Okay, guv." She got into her Land Rover and waited while Battle got into his own car and talked to someone on the phone, probably phoning in the order for someone to trawl through the database searching for a "Samuel, last name unknown" with a sister named Ruth.

As Battle had said, hopefully the crime scene would yield more information than Maureen Williams had.

When the DCI finally started his car and drove off along the snowy street, Dani followed, hoping they'd break this case soon.

Because if they didn't, they'd have two more dead bodies on their hands.

CHAPTER TWENTY-SIX

Tarnby was a tiny village which had quadrupled in size thanks to a new housing project on its north side. As Dani followed Battle's car along one of the new streets, she couldn't help but notice the contrast between old and new.

The village itself consisted of stone cottages, all different in design and spaced at irregular intervals along the main street. The new estate, on the other hand, was made up of identical yellow brick houses arranged in neat rows with mathematical precision.

Battle's Range Rover came to a stop outside a house which stood out from all the others because its driveway and the pavement were ringed by blue and white police tape. A number of police vehicles were parked near the tape and a couple of News vans were also present on the street.

Dani got out of her car and she and Battle flashed their warrant cards at one of the uniform officers guarding the scene's perimeter. He lifted the tape to let them inside.

The front door was open, and DS Lorna Morgan stood in the hallway, inspecting a large cardboard box that leant against the wall.

"What have we got?" Battle asked as he and Dani stepped inside.

Morgan consulted her notebook. "Teresa Matthews, 39, and her daughter Gemma Matthews, 16, both missing. Teresa's mother, Sandra Cole, arrived here at nine o' clock this morning. She was supposed to be spending Christmas with her daughter and granddaughter. When she got here, she used her key to enter the property after no one answered the door and found it empty. There are signs of a struggle in the living room and blood on the carpet. She called the police."

"Have the SOCOs been?" Battle asked.

"Been and gone, guv. They took samples of the blood and lifted prints from the house, including this box." She indicated the large cardboard box that was leaning against the wall. According to the picture and writing printed on it, the box contained a Panasonic TV.

Battle looked at Dani. "Looks like he delivered this and then decided to take more than just a signature."

"We're trying to find out which firm delivered the TV," DS Morgan said. "We've taken electronic devices from the house to see if there's an online order for it. If we can find the store it was ordered from, we can track which delivery firms the store uses to deliver their goods."

"Is there anything else?" Battle asked. "Something that might help us find him sooner rather than later?"

"Unless Forensics get a hit from the blood or the prints, there isn't much to go on, guv. Some neighbours remember seeing a white van on the street yesterday, but nobody thought anything of it at the time, so no one had a good look at the driver or got a number plate."

Dani sighed. She used plenty of online stores herself, and found them convenient, but she also knew that because of the proliferation of delivery vans driving around housing estates—most of them unmarked—it was easier for criminals' vehicles to go unnoticed by the residents. If they saw a strange van parked outside their neighbour's house, they assumed their neighbour was receiving a delivery, not being burgled.

And now the same thing had happened here; the killer had driven into this estate and out again without anyone taking so much as a second glance at his van.

Battle pointed into the kitchen. "Why is there a makeup bag on the floor?"

Dani followed his gaze and saw the bag lying on the kitchen floor, its contents of lipsticks, eyeliner pencils, and mascara brushes spilled out on the tiles.

"We think that Teresa and Gemma were getting ready to go out when the intruder forced his way into the house," Morgan said. "Apparently, they were going to attend a Christmas Eve service at the local church."

"And they never made it," Battle surmised.

"No, guv."

"So he's had them a while already. I don't think we're going to have a three-week time frame like we did with Abigail."

"Definitely not," said a voice from outside.

Dani turned to see Tony Sheridan standing there, his face almost in the space between the collar of his oversize jacket and the blue beanie pulled low over his head. He was stamping his boots on the driveway, as if to keep the blood circulating in his legs.

"Tony," Battle said. "Come and see what you make of this."

Tony entered the house, his eyes wandering around the hallway and into the kitchen. "Why is there a makeup bag on the floor?"

"We think Teresa and her daughter were getting ready to go out when our man arrived," Battle said. "He's a delivery driver. He was delivering this TV."

Sheridan stepped past them and made his way to the kitchen, crouching over the makeup bag and its spilled contents. "How old is the girl?"

"Sixteen," Battle told him.

The psychologist nodded and stood up straight, inspecting the kitchen. "And they both have dark hair? The girl and the mother?"

Battle looked at Morgan for help.

The DS nodded. "Yes," she said to Sheridan.

"It's his mother," Sheridan said under his breath.

"What do you mean?" Dani asked.

"He killed Tanya Ward in front of Abigail, telling her that he was doing what she wanted. Not Abigail, of course; she didn't want Tanya dead. In his mind, he was talking to his sister. Ruth. We know that Abigail played the role of Ruth in his fantasy, but I was never sure who Tanya Ward represented to him. Now it's clear. He wants to kill his mother. For Ruth."

"I'm not sure I follow," Battle said. "If he wants to kill his mother, then why did he kill Tanya Ward instead?"

"Because he can't kill his actual mother. Something is stopping him. It's one thing to kill a stranger but quite another to kill the person who brought you into the world. Ed Kemper, the Co-ed Killer, wanted to kill his mother but ended up murdering nine young women before he got around to achieving his actual goal."

"So you think his mother is still alive?" Dani asked. "We just spoke to someone who said she wasn't sure. Samuel sometimes speaks about her as if she's alive and sometimes as if she's passed away."

"Samuel," the psychologist said. "Is that his name?"

Dani nodded.

"Samuel. Samuel." Sheridan seemed to be rolling the name around his mouth, as if tasting it. "Why not Sam? Or Sammy? Samuel seems a very grandiose way of using that name. Most people would shorten it to Sam." He held out his hand to an imaginary stranger and shook the air as if greeting them. "Hi, I'm Sam. Hey, I'm Sammy. Hello, I'm Samuel."

Battle cocked an eyebrow.

"*She* calls him by that name," Sheridan said. "His mother, I mean."

"So she *is* still alive?" Dani asked.

"Oh yes, she's alive. He wants her dead. Ruth wants her dead. But she's still here and that bothers him for some reason. That's why he sometimes talks about her as if she's dead; in his ideal world, she is."

"Why?" Battle asked. "Why does he want her dead? Why does his sister want her dead? Have they suffered some sort of abuse at her hands?"

"I don't know," Sheridan admitted. "But I think there's another question hidden in all of this. I can see why he's getting a substitute for his mother; he can't bring himself to kill the actual target of his rage. But why a substitute for Ruth? Why take Abigail to play his sister? He wants to show Ruth that he can "do what she wants him to do" so why the substitute?"

"Perhaps for the same reason he substitutes the mother," Dani said. "He can't bring himself to perform the act of murder in front of his sister. She might turn him in."

Sheridan shook his head. "I don't think so. They have a deep relationship, these two. He said that murdering the mother is what she wants him to do, so they have discussed it, probably in detail. She wanted him to do it with a knife, though, not a hammer."

Dani wasn't sure how much of this Sheridan was extrapolating from psychological insights and how much he was making up off the top of his head. "Why do you say that?"

"He killed Tanya with a hammer from behind because he couldn't face her as he murdered her. Abigail said she never saw him use a knife. But Tanya's body was lacerated with cuts. He did it post-mortem. I think that was how he was supposed to kill her—how he and Ruth had planned it—with a knife."

He paced about the kitchen for a couple of minutes, head down, thinking.

When he raised his face to the people in the hallway, his eyes were slightly wider, as if he'd just made a realisation about something. "Ruth is dead," he said.

"What?" Battle seemed unconvinced.

Sheridan nodded. "That's why he has to get a substitute for her. It isn't that he can't show her the murder because he's afraid she'll turn him in; he can't show her because she isn't here. This is about revenge. Killing the mother is revenge for what happened to Ruth."

"What happened to Ruth?" Battle asked.

"She died," Sheridan said, looking down at the floor again and clicking his fingers over and over as if doing so would provide him with an insight. "At the mother's hand. Somehow. And now Samuel wants revenge. Or he blames himself for Ruth's death and wants to make amends."

"So Ruth wanted him to kill the mother, but he didn't, and now Ruth is dead," Dani said.

Sheridan nodded.

She supposed it made sense, but they had no proof that it was even remotely close to the truth.

"How does it help us find him?" Battle asked. "How does it help us save Teresa and Gemma Matthews?"

"The family might be in the system," Dani suggested. "There had to be some reason Samuel and his sister both hated their mother. If it was due to abuse, an incident might have been reported at some point."

"And if it wasn't?" Battle asked. "Let's face it, a lot of these things go unreported."

"They might still be in the system," Sheridan said. "If my theory about how this family unit has split apart is correct, there would have been arguments, incidents of violence. A neighbour might have reported a distur-bance." He thought some more and then added, "I wouldn't be surprised if there's some form of psychosis shared by the family members. It could be that one or more of them spent some time under psychiatric care, if not as a resident in a place like Larkmoor."

"Probably Larkmoor itself," Dani suggested. "That place is the link between Samuel and Tanya. Perhaps he was a resident there before he became a delivery driver."

"Surely Maureen Williams would have remem-bered him if he'd been a patient," Battle said. "She would have mentioned it." He pursed his lips, seeming to consider if he could be so sure of his words. Then he fished his phone out of his pocket and jabbed at the screen. He held it to his ear and said, in what was prob-ably the most pleasant tone he could muster at the moment, "Mr Williams, may I speak with your wife, please? It's DCI Battle. No, it will only take a moment. Thank you."

There was a slight pause and then he said cheerily, "Ah, Mrs Williams. Sorry to bother you. DCI Battle here. Yes, that's right, we did leave your house just a short time ago but something has come up and I have a simple question to ask you, if I may. Was Samuel a former patient at Larkmoor House? Mmm, I see. How long? Thank you very much, Mrs Williams. Have a nice day."

He ended the call and said, "She's only been working there a few months. If he'd been a patient before that, she wouldn't know about it."

"The rest of the staff would have recognised him," Dani said. "But we've only asked Maureen."

"You need to get back there," Battle said. "Take Sheridan with you. Morgan, come with me. We're going to bang on the doors of some delivery firms."

"They'll be closed, guv. It's Christmas Day."

"Then we'll find the home addresses of the managers and visit them there, won't we?"

She nodded. "Yes, guv."

Dani stepped outside into the snow, followed by Sheridan. There were more reporters at the crime scene perimeter now. Most of them were sheltering from the weather in their vehicles, but when they saw Dani and Sheridan emerge from the house, they braved the elements to get to the crime scene tape and shout questions.

Dani ignored them. "You follow me," she said to

Sheridan as he quickly strode to his old, blue Mini. She climbed into the Land Rover, ignoring the reporters gathering around her car with microphones and digital recorders.

Gallow had said the members of Murder Force had to be media-friendly but she wasn't technically a member of the team yet, so she was giving herself some allowances. When they saw Battle emerge from the house, the journalists all made a bee line for him, anyway, recognising his higher rank and hoping he might provide the answers to their questions.

She turned the Land Rover around so that she was facing the other way and waited for Sheridan to start his car. She didn't want to race off and leave him behind. His car looked like it might have enough trouble on a day like today without her pushing it to its limit as he tried to follow her.

The Mini didn't start.

"Come on," Dani said under her breath, watching the car in her rearview mirror. "Let's go."

After a couple of seconds, the driver's door opened, and Sheridan got out. He half-walked and half-slid up to Dani's passenger door and tapped on the window.

Dani buzzed it down. "What's wrong?"

"Erm, instead of following you, can I come in your car? Mine seems to have broken down."

She laughed at that, a welcome relief of the tension she felt after listening to Sheridan's theories about the dysfunctional family that had produced Samuel. "Of course, get in."

He climbed into the passenger seat and unzipped the huge jacket before putting on the seat belt. He removed the beanie and put it on his lap.

He saw her watching him and gave her a smile. "I know these clothes are too big for me. I've lost a lot of weight since I bought them. I'll get some new ones in the January sales."

She pulled away from the kerb. In the rearview mirror, she could see the reporters harassing Battle and —Murder Force or not—he was having none of it.

"So you think this guy's family life is as bad as you said back there?" she asked Sheridan.

"Oh, yes," he said, looking out of the window thoughtfully. "Probably even worse."

CHAPTER TWENTY-SEVEN

Samuel stood up and wiped snow off his jeans. Even though he'd uncovered the rock with his sister's name on it earlier, the new snowfall was burying it again. He bent down to clear its surface and reveal Ruth's name, but his freezing fingers were useless.

He folded his arms against his body in an effort to warm them up. He hopped from one foot to the other in an attempt to generate some warmth. Despite the fact that he was wearing a jacket, he felt as if his heartbeat had slowed down so much that it was barely pumping blood around his body. Maybe it would freeze completely, and he'd die here, on Ruth's grave. He supposed that would be a fitting end for him. There was a sort of poetic justice to it.

He couldn't leave this world yet, though. Not while his mother was still in it. She had to go first.

When he finally felt feeling returning to his fingers —pins and needles that pricked his nerves—he leaned against the back of the barn and looked down at the gravestone which was rapidly disappearing beneath the snow.

"I'm sorry, Ruth," he whispered. "I'm sorry I didn't save you."

He knew the exact moment he'd betrayed her. Christmas Eve ten years ago. In fact—he checked the time on his watch—it was about this time that she'd called him into her room and asked for his help.

She was no longer talking in vague terms about him protecting her from their mother; she had a deadly plan for him to carry out.

———

DECEMBER 24TH, ten years ago

"MICHAEL!" she whispered as he walked past her bedroom door, "Come here."

The door was open a crack. He pushed it open fully and went inside.

Ruth was sitting on the bed in her white night-gown, her eyes and cheeks wet with tears.

"What's wrong?" He sat on the bed next to her and put an arm around her shoulder.

She leaned against him, sniffing. "She's going to kill me, Michael, I just know it. I can see it in her eyes. The other day, she said there's no way this baby is coming into the world."

"I didn't hear her say that."

"You weren't here. She only says things like that when you aren't here to protect me."

"She shouldn't have said that; it's a terrible thing to say."

"I know what we can do," Ruth said. She pushed herself off the bed and went to the chest of drawers where she kept her underwear. She reached in and took out a hunting knife. As she held it up, the blade glinted in the sunlight suffusing through the net curtains on the window.

"What are you doing with that?" he asked. "That's grandad's knife." The last time he'd seen the knife, it had been in a box in the attic, along with their grandad's war medals and some old, faded photos. He and Ruth had discovered it a few years ago when they'd been looking for a quiet place away from their mother's attention. A secret place.

He'd forgotten all about the box and knife until now.

"This is how we're going to solve all of our problems," she said, reaching for his hand and opening the fingers. She pressed the handle of the knife against his palm. It felt cold.

"Take it," Ruth said.

Michael closed his fingers around the handle. "How is this going to solve our problems?"

She lowered her voice. "You've got to use it on her."

"On Mum?"

She nodded solemnly. "It's the only way."

He looked down at the weapon in his hand. Could he actually stab another person with it? Not just any person, but his own mother? He didn't think he had the stomach for it. "Ruth, I don't—"

She pressed a finger to his lips, quieting him. "Listen carefully. If you don't do this, she's going to kill me and the baby. There is no future where all of us live under this roof together."

Lowering herself onto the bed next to him, she snaked an arm around his waist. "You need to decide which future you want; the one where I'm dead and you're left here with her, or the one where *she's* gone, and this becomes our house."

Given such a choice, he'd always choose the latter option, but did he really have to kill their mother? Why couldn't things go on as they were now? He was sure his sister was being paranoid; he'd never seen their mother aim so much as an antagonistic glance in Ruth's direction.

He gazed at the sunlight reflecting off the blade. Ruth had obviously polished the weapon with great care. "Do I really have to do this?" he asked.

"If you want a future with me and the baby, yes."

He sighed. "I don't know, Ruth."

"You don't know what you want?"

"I know what I want but I don't know if I can do this."

"Of course you can. I'm putting my faith in you."

———

PUSHING away from the back of the barn, he wiped cold tears from his cheeks with the sleeve of his jacket. His sister had put her faith in him and where had that got her? In a grave behind the barn.

She'd lost everything, thanks to him.

———

HE'D HIDDEN the knife in the top drawer of his bedside table and tried to summon up the courage to use it. Around midnight on Christmas Eve, he'd even taken it out of the drawer and—holding it unsteadily in his hand—had entered his mother's bedroom.

She'd been sound asleep—or unconscious might be a more apt term, given the almost-empty bottle of vodka on the floor next to her bed—not stirring even when he'd stood over her, brandishing the knife. It would be so easy to do it now. All he had to do was plunge the blade into her body a couple of times. She'd never even know about it. She just wouldn't wake up ever again.

But he stood there in the shadows, listening to her breathing deeply, for almost half an hour and still didn't have the guts to go through with it.

Eventually, he left her room and went back to his own, squirrelling the knife back into the drawer and lying on his bed wondering how he was going to explain to Ruth that he couldn't do as she'd asked.

The next day, he'd found himself unable to say anything to Ruth about his failed attempt to kill their mother. He couldn't bring himself to do it anymore than he could bring himself to use the knife the night before. He couldn't bear to see her disappointed, especially disappointed in him.

So he'd kept quiet and sullen and mostly ignored both his sister and mother by driving out to the cliffs at Whitby and spent almost all of Christmas Day there, staring at the sea. He hadn't gone to his and Ruth's spot on the East Cliff; that place was for them and he didn't deserve to go there right now, considering how he'd let his sister down.

Instead, he'd spent the day on the West Cliff, telling himself over and over that he had to man up and perform the deed Ruth had requested. He'd once told her that he'd do anything for her and now he was hesitating to do this one simple thing?

After almost an entire day of berating himself, he got back into the car and headed for home, determined to do what he considered to be his duty. He'd go straight upstairs, grab the knife, and use it before he had a chance to even think about what he was doing.

He drove home as quickly as he dared without breaking the speed limit. The police seemed to be everywhere at this time of year, looking out for drunk drivers. He didn't want to draw attention to himself.

When parked outside the farmhouse and got out of the car, he heard shouting inside. The voices were his mother's and Ruth's. If they were arguing, now would be a perfect time to rush upstairs and get the knife.

As he pushed the front door open, he realised that his mother and sister were at the top of the stairs. They weren't just arguing; they were physically fighting. His mother had her arms on Ruth's shoulders and seemed to be trying to push her down the stairs. Ruth was struggling, clawing at her mother's face and neck.

"This baby must not be born," their mother was shouting. "It's an abomination."

Samuel could see that his sister's bare feet were perilously close to the top step. If he didn't stop this right now, Ruth would fall.

"Hey!" he shouted. "Stop it!"

His sudden shout caught the attention of both women and they paused in their struggle to look down at him.

"Michael!" Ruth shouted. "See what she's doing? I told you!"

His mother seized that moment of distraction to shove Ruth with all her might.

What happened next seemed to happen in slow motion. Ruth's feet stayed on the landing, but her upper body pivoted backwards over the staircase. Her arms scrambled for purchase but there was nothing to grasp, and her hands clawed desperately at the air. The sleeves of her white nightgown billowed out around her like angel's wings.

When her feet left the landing, Ruth's body seemed to be floating above the steps. It looked, to Michael, like one of those magician's tricks where he levitates his glamorous assistant into the air and passes a hoop over her body to prove there are no wires.

This was no illusion, though. Ruth wasn't being

suspended by anything and, finally, gravity grabbed her and pulled her down.

Her back hit the steps first, and Michael cringed as a sickening *crack* reached his ears. It wasn't the hard wood of the stairs that had broken; it was his sister's body.

Ruth's head hit the steps and this time, the noise was a heavy thud. She slid down the stairs headfirst, on her back, until she came to rest in the hallway, at Michael's feet. Her eyes stared up at him accusingly.

But they couldn't see him. Those beautiful, dark eyes wouldn't see anything ever again.

He stepped back from her dead body, unable to face those accusing eyes, and heard an angry animal-like sound rip from his throat. His back hit the wall and he slid down it, his legs no longer able to support him.

"Michael! Michael!" His mother was running down the stairs. She stepped over Ruth's body and rushed to him, crouching in front of him and pulling him to her chest, hugging him so hard that he had trouble breathing.

"You saw what happened," she whispered. "I was defending myself and she fell. It was an accident."

He tried to shake his head, but she held his face too tightly against her chest for him to move.

"It was an accident," she repeated, stroking the back of his head. "Now, listen to me closely, Michael. We have to deal with this ourselves. There's no point calling an ambulance; it's too late for that. And we can't have the police coming in here and snooping around.

She's gone and nothing can bring her back. So we have to sort this out. You and me."

She pushed his face away from her body and held it between her hands, gazing firmly into his eyes. "Do you hear me? We need to do what's right."

His eyes wandered across the floor to where Ruth lay, motionless.

"Listen to me," his mother said, turning his head away from the sight of his dead sister. "Go and get the shovel and dig a hole behind the barn. Make it deep. Do you understand me?"

He nodded. He understood. They were going to bury Ruth behind the barn.

"You're a good boy," she said. "Now go and get that shovel."

He got to his feet, leaning against the wall for support. Taking a deep breath, he walked shakily to the back door, keeping his eyes averted from the body at the foot of the stairs.

The shovel was leaning against the wall in the outbuilding. He'd put it there a couple of days ago after using it to clean out the hen coop.

Ruth had been alive then. Until a few minutes ago, his sister had been a part of his life. Now, she was gone.

He took the shovel to the area behind the barn and started digging. It was a cold day but at least the earth wasn't frozen as he dug the shovel's blade into it with powerful strokes born of anger. He was furious with himself. If he'd been man enough to go through with his plan last night when he stood over his mother's bed, Ruth would still be alive. It was all his fault.

It took him over an hour to dig the grave deep enough for his sister's body. By the time he was done, the hole was at least six feet deep. He could barely see over the edges when he stood inside it.

Clambering out and brushing dirt from his clothes, he leaned the shovel against the back of the barn and sauntered to the house. He wasn't in any hurry to put Ruth in that hole. There was a cold finality to it that he didn't want to face.

When he got inside the house, his mother was sitting at the kitchen table with a bottle of vodka. That seemed to be her answer to everything these days. Your daughter tells you she's pregnant? Drink a bottle of vodka. Pushed your daughter down the stairs and killed her? Well, just take a few swigs of that potato liquor and forget everything.

She'd at least had the decency to cover Ruth's body before she'd embarked on her journey into the bottle; a white sheet lay over the floor at the foot of the stairs, his sister beneath it.

"I didn't mean for that to happen, Michael," she said. Her words were already slurred, and he wondered if she'd started drinking the moment he'd left the house.

Ignoring her, he went to Ruth and tucked the sheet beneath her lifeless body. There was no use asking his mother for help; he was going to have to do this all by himself. Ruth would have preferred it that way, anyway, he supposed.

"I read somewhere about women falling downstairs and losing their baby," she said. "Or I saw it on TV. I can't remember. Anyway, I thought that if she just took a little tumble, everything would be all right again."

He hefted Ruth's body over his shoulder and took her outside, ignoring his mother, who was now crying softly.

He managed to get Ruth all the way to the grave without stopping. Once he was there, he laid her on the ground carefully and got into the grave himself before reaching over the edge for Ruth and gently pulling her in with him. He laid her across the bottom of the hole and eased himself out of the grave.

He supposed he should say a few words, so he looked down solemnly at his sister's sheet-covered form and said, "I'll avenge you, Ruth. I didn't do what you wanted me to do and I'm sorry for that. But I'll make it better. I'll make sure justice is done. I swear it."

―――――

"AND I NEVER KEPT MY OATH," he said, looking down at the snow-covered grave. Here he was, ten years later, standing over the grave, and his mother was still alive. Despite his impassioned oath all those years ago, he'd become depressed and listless after Ruth's death, barely able to get out of bed in the morning, much less kill anyone.

Then his mother had suffered a nervous breakdown in a shop and had been taken to hospital. He'd thought that God was doing what he'd sworn to do himself, taking the burden from him.

But his mother hadn't died; she'd merely convalesced in a mental hospital for a while. And the funny thing was that when she came out, she was even worse than when she went in. She'd found religion—or her own brand of it, anyway—and it had dug its claws into her even deeper than the drink had. She came home and changed their names to Mary and Samuel.

Ruth's name became taboo.

He turned away from the grave and trudged through the snow back to the house.

He found his mother in front of the TV, watching one of the morning chat shows she liked. At least she wasn't lying there with a bottle of vodka like in days gone by; she was sitting there attentively, watching the screen.

He glanced at the TV and half-recognised the hosts. The grey-haired dude was Martin-something and the plump blonde woman was Joanna Rose.

Martin was looking at the camera, saying, "Yesterday we spoke to Chief Superintendent Ian Gallow about the new police initiative called Murder Force. It seems that the case involving Tanya Ward, a nurse from York, and Abigail Newton, a schoolgirl from Derbyshire, has been developing. Police believe that the disappearance of Teresa and Gemma Matthews, a mother and daughter from North Yorkshire, could be linked to the ongoing Ward and Newton case."

"Unfortunately, Chief Superintendent Gallow isn't

here in the studio today," Joanna said, looking into the camera with her smoky blue eyes, "but we can replay our interview with him yesterday."

The screen changed to what was obviously a pre-recorded piece with a uniformed policeman talking to the hosts. He mentioned a new team called Murder Force, which was trying to solve the case. Two news-paper headlines appeared on the TV, showing the two star detectives in the team; DCI Battle and DI Summers.

So this old bloke and his bimbo sidekick were after him, were they? Well, they'd have a job. He'd made sure to cover his tracks. Let them try their best; they'd never find him.

He looked up at the clock on the wall. It was almost twelve noon. When he'd come home from Whitby ten years ago and seen his mother push Ruth down the stairs, it had been four o' clock in the evening. So it seemed only fitting that he go out to the bunker at four and do what must be done with the mother and daughter he'd locked in there.

Four hours. Not too long to wait.

After that, the old DCI and his pretty sidekick could search all of Yorkshire if they wanted.

All they'd find would be two dead bodies.

CHAPTER TWENTY-EIGHT

Christmas Day, 1:04 p.m.

HALF AN HOUR AFTER LEAVING TARNBY, Battle was driving across the moors, squinting to see clearly through the snow that the wind whipped against his windscreen. He checked the rearview mirror to make sure DS Morgan was following. He could barely see her cherry red Yaris through the swirling snow, but it was there.

His phone rang. He answered it with the hands-free controls. "Battle."

"It's Chris Toombs," the voice that filled the car said. "We met earlier. I've been looking at a laptop that belongs to Teresa Matthews. I was asked to find an order for a TV."

"What have you found?" Battle asked.

"Yeah, I got the order no problem. The laptop

wasn't even password-protected and the online store was in her history. The receipt for the purchase was in her emails, which I simply clicked into. Terrible security."

"Never mind that. Where was the TV ordered from?"

"I can do better than that; I can tell you which firm the store uses to deliver its goods. Anytime Deliveries. They're based in an industrial unit just outside York."

"What's the address?" Battle asked. Then he remembered that it was Christmas Day and there wouldn't be anyone there. "Shit."

"You've just realised what day it is and that no one will be at the industrial unit," Toombs guessed. "Luckily I pulled the depot manager's mobile number. His name is Simon Beale." He listed off a string of numbers, which Battle asked him to repeat and then committed to memory.

"Good work," he said.

"You're welcome, boss." The line clicked as Toombs hung up.

Battle slowed down gradually and pulled over to the side of the road. Behind him, Morgan's car did the same. She put her hazard lights on as she came to a stop.

He got out of the Range Rover and walked over to her Yaris, holding his hand up in front of his face as the snow lashed at him.

When he got to Morgan's car, her window was down. "Everything all right, guv?"

"I just got a call from a tech at the station. He's found the delivery firm. I've got the depot manager's mobile number. I'm going to ring him and see if he knows who delivered that television."

"Come in out of the wind, guv." She hit the central locking and unlocked the car.

Battle got his phone out of his pocket and climbed in. The Yaris was much smaller than his Range Rover and he felt like his bulk filled the entire car. He dialled the number Toombs had given him and waited while the call connected.

The man that answered sounded tired, as if he'd just woken up. "Hello?"

"Is that Simon Beale?"

"Yes, it is. Look, if this is about a delivery you were expecting yesterday, the weather—"

"It isn't about that, Mr Beale. This is DCI Stewart Battle of..." He paused. He used to say Derbyshire Police at this point of his introduction, but that wasn't right. North Yorkshire Police wasn't right either. "Murder Force," he said finally.

"Murder Force?" Beale sounded perkier now. "I've heard about you guys from the telly." He paused and then said, "Why are you ringing me?"

"I need to know the details of one of your employees. First name Samuel."

There was a pause and then Beale said, "I don't have any drivers with that name."

"He may go by Sam, or Sammy. Anything like that."

"No, sorry. I don't have any employees by that name. You must have the wrong—"

"I need to know who delivered a television to an address in Tarnby yesterday. If his name isn't Samuel, then it's something else. But I need to know who made that delivery."

Now, Beale sounded confused. "What? A television? What's this all about?"

"Would you have that information, sir?" Battle asked impatiently.

"Yes, of course, if we delivered it. The records are at the office, though."

"Mr Beale, I need to see those records right away."

"What, today? Can't this wait until tomorrow? The weather—"

"This is a matter of grave importance," Battle said. "Lives are at stake."

A note of curiosity entered Beale's voice as he said, "Is this something to do with that woman and girl that are missing?"

"What's the address of your office?" Battle said, losing his patience. His mimed a writing motion to DS Morgan. She got her notebook and pen ready.

Beale recited the address. Battle repeated it to Morgan, who wrote it down. She was already typing it into her SatNav when Battle asked Beale, "How soon can you meet us there?"

"I can be there in about an hour," the depot manager said.

Battle   checked   Morgan's   SatNav   display.

According to its calculations, they should be there at two o' clock, an hour from now. "We'll be there at about the same time," he told Beale. "If you get there before us, check the records for a delivery of a television set to 24 Lime Avenue, Tarnby. I want to know which driver made that delivery."

"Okay," Beale said. "See you later."

Battle hung up. He turned to Morgan and said, "Right, we need to get to that address as soon as possible."

"It'll take us more than an hour in this weather," Morgan said. "I don't think the SatNav accounts for that."

"Well, like I said, as soon as possible. And Beale had better wait for us." He climbed out of the Yaris and said, "I'll follow you," before he closed the door.

Climbing back into his Range Rover, he waited for Morgan to drive past and then followed her car through the snowstorm. If they lost Teresa and Gemma because of the weather, he'd never forgive himself. That was irrational, of course; he had no control over the snow. But he also knew that a lack of control over the weather wouldn't stop him from taking the blame personally if this case ended tragically.

He'd blamed himself in the past when things had gone wrong, even when the reason for failure had been out of his hands. Like the Daisy Riddle case. Daisy had gone missing fifteen years ago and he'd promised her parents he'd find her. That had been a mistake; all these years later, nobody had any idea what had happened to her.

And he took every ounce of blame for that on his own shoulders.

There had been parts of the investigation that he'd had no control over, like the fact that Powers had denied him some resources that might have helped in the search for the girl. But, at the end of the day, Battle had been in charge of the investigation and its failure was, ultimately, his fault. He'd made a foolish promise to Daisy's parents; a promise he'd been unable to keep.

As he followed DS Morgan's cherry red Toyota Yaris across the moors, he made a silent promise to himself.

We'll find them and we'll bring them back.

CHAPTER TWENTY-NINE

Christmas Day, 1:49 p.m.

SHERIDAN HAD REMAINED MOSTLY quiet in the passenger seat, which suited Dani fine since she had to concentrate on keeping the Land Rover on the road, which was all but invisible in the snow. They were moving at a snail's pace but she daren't go any faster. According to the SatNav, they'd be at Larkmoor House in five minutes. She only hoped the psychologist sitting next to her was right and that Samuel's name would be somewhere in their records.

She looked over at Sheridan. He looked pale and his right hand was gripping his seatbelt with fingers and knuckles that had turned white. She didn't think her driving was that bad.

"You okay?" she asked him.

"Yeah," he said, his eyes fixed on the whiteness beyond the windscreen. "I'm fine."

"No offence, but you don't look it. Do you want me to pull over for a few minutes?"

He shook his head. "I'm not car sick or anything like that."

"Are you sure?"

"I'm sure." He let out a breath between his lips and said, "I've got a thing about hospitals, that's all. I spent quite a lot of time in one a couple of years ago and I have some bad memories."

"You were involved in the Lake Erie Ripper case, weren't you?" she asked gently.

Sheridan nodded. "I can see you've done your homework."

"It was on breakfast TV yesterday."

"Was it?" He seemed genuinely surprised. "I didn't see that."

"So you were the psychologist who went into the Ripper's house and saved those girls."

"That was me," he said.

"If you want to stay in the car when we get to the hospital—"

"No, really, I don't. That's not going to help anyone, is it? I just need to face my fear, or aversion, or whatever it is, and get on with it."

She remembered something and frowned. "You interviewed Abigail Newton in the hospital at Whitby, didn't you?" If he'd managed to go into the hospital and all the way to Abigail's room, his phobia couldn't be that bad, could it?

"Yes, I did. Believe it or not, I was helped by DC Tom Ryan."

"Oh, I see. If there's anything you want me to do to help you, just ask."

"Well, that's the thing; I didn't ask Ryan to help me. I didn't even tell him about my fear. He just seemed to know somehow."

"So what did he do that helped you?"

"He distracted me. Told me he was going to stand in the corner and watch my interview with Abigail. I couldn't have that; I was trying to look non-threatening to her, and Ryan looks anything but. So we argued and the next thing I knew, I was in Abigail's room."

"So you want me to argue with you? Distract you?"

"No, really, it's fine. I'll be fine."

She wanted to tell him that he didn't look fine but held her tongue. He'd acquired this psychological wound—whatever it was—because he'd saved two lives. Two women would be dead if not for Sheridan saving them from one of Canada's worst serial killers. He deserved some respect.

"We're here," she said when she saw the driveway that led up to the large Victorian house. Putting the Land Rover into low gear so it wouldn't slip on the incline, she followed the driveway up to the car park.

There were only half a dozen cars here. Dani supposed that relatives who might be otherwise visiting loved ones in Larkmoor today had been put off by the weather.

She killed the engine and turned to Sheridan. "Are you sure you're okay, Tony?"

He nodded. "It doesn't even look like a hospital. It just looks like a house."

"Great." She got out of the car and was immediately battered by the wind and snow.

Sheridan got out of the other side and together, they rushed to the entrance door and into the reception area.

The same nurse who had been behind the reception desk earlier was still there. When she saw Dani, her eyebrows knitted together. "You again. Did you speak to Maureen?"

"We did," Dani said. "And now we're back."

"Yes, I can see that."

"We need to talk to you about past patients," Sheridan said. "It's very important and could save lives."

She turned to face him, her demeanour changing from hostile to cooperative. "Oh, all right. What do you want to know?"

Dani had no idea how Sheridan had seemingly charmed the nurse, but she stepped back slightly and let him do his thing.

"How about the name Samuel?" he asked. "Does that mean anything to you?"

The nurse chewed her lip for a few seconds and

seemed to be thinking. Finally, she shook her head. "No, that doesn't ring any bells."

"How long have you worked here?" Dani asked, remembering Maureen's admission that she'd only been at Larkmoor a few months.

The taciturn demeanour returned as the nurse regarded her. "I've been here three years, although I can't see what's that got to do with anything."

"The thing is, Patricia. May I call you Patricia?" Sheridan asked, leaning his elbows on the desk and giving the nurse his full attention.

Dani wondered if she'd have had a better response from the nurse if she'd also called her by the name on her badge. Probably not.

"It's Trish, actually," the nurse said, smiling.

"Trish," Sheridan said, returning her smile. "The thing is, the patient we're interested in might have been here some time ago. We don't know that for sure, but it's a possibility. Is there anyone working here today who's been at Larkmoor a long time?"

She thought for a moment and then nodded, "Sheila Hopkins. She's been here donkey's years."

"Could we possibly speak to Sheila?" Sheridan asked. "Thank you."

Trish picked up the telephone and dialled a short number. "John, could you bring Sheila to Reception, please? The police want to talk to her. Thanks."

She put the receiver down and turned her attention back to Sheridan. "She'll be here in a moment. The security guard is just going to fetch her."

Dani remembered the name Sheila Hopkins from the interviews she and Matt had conducted. Sheila had seen Tanya Ward drive away in her Beetle for the last time. She'd said in her interview that she'd worked here for almost twenty years. If anyone was going to remember a past patient, it would be her.

The phone on the desk rang and Trish answered it. After listening for a few seconds, she nodded and said, "Okay, thanks, John, I'll tell them." She replaced the receiver and said, "Sheila is dealing with a patient at the moment. She'll be down in fifteen minutes." She pointed at a row of vinyl-covered chairs lined up against the wall. "Have a seat while you wait."

Dani took a seat and Sheridan joined her.

"If our man was ever here, I'm sure Sheila will know," he said.

"And if he wasn't?"

He shrugged. "Then we have to hope the tech guys can find out who delivered that TV."

Dani nodded and checked her phone. No word from Battle. She wondered how he was doing tracking down that delivery.

———

———

———

THE INDUSTRIAL PARK where Anytime Deliveries

was based consisted of a number of identical warehouses. The only thing that set them apart from each other were the name and logos of various companies. Battle parked next to DS Morgan's car outside a unit that bore the name Anytime Deliveries.

A grey BMW was parked nearby, and Battle hoped it belonged to Simon Beale and that the depot manager was still waiting for them. It was 2:34 p.m., exactly half an hour after Battle had said he'd be here.

The door to the warehouse was opened by a slight man with collar-length greasy hair and gold-rimmed glasses. He nodded to Battle and Morgan as they approached him. "DCI Battle, I presume?"

"Yes," Battle said, "And this is DS Morgan. Have you had time to check those records?"

Beale nodded. "Yes, I have. Come in and I'll show you what I've found." He led them into the warehouse, which was lined with metal racks upon which hundreds of packages waited to be delivered to their final destinations. The air smelled of dust.

Beale opened a plain wooden door that led into a walled-off section of the warehouse that served as an office. Inside, an old computer sat on a scarred desk. Apart from a chair, there weren't any other furnishings.

"Here," Beale said, handing Battle a sheet of paper. "I printed this off for you. This is our driver who was supposed to make that delivery."

"Supposed to?" Morgan asked.

"Yeah, he never made it there. If he had, he'd have scanned the bar code on the box and got a signature.

That would show on my computer. There's no record of the delivery. I checked."

"That's because he was too busy abducting the occupants of the house to get a signature," Battle said. He looked down at the sheet of paper in his hands. It was a photocopy of a driving licence belonging to a Michael Stokes.

The photo on the licence showed a dark-haired young man looking emotionlessly into the camera. Battle checked the date of birth and a quick mental calculation told him that Stokes was now 28 years old, although he'd looked a lot younger when this photo had been taken. According to the licence issue date, he'd been 17. The photo had expired last year.

"And this is the definitely the guy who delivered that TV to Lime Avenue?" he asked Beale.

"I told you, he didn't deliver it. There's no electronic record. But it was on his van, yes. It was the next delivery on his route before I called him off the job."

"Was he in Derbyshire three weeks ago?"

Beale nodded. "Yeah, he was. We had a fridge freezer sent here by accident. It should have gone to a delivery hub in Derby. Michael volunteered to drive it down there."

"And that's when he saw Abigail Newton," Battle said. He handed the photocopy to DS Morgan. "Michael Stokes. Not Samuel. His middle name isn't even Samuel, it's Jonathan. Maureen Williams was wrong."

"Or he gave her a false name," Morgan suggested,

looking over the paper. "At least we've got an address. Grantham Farm, Cold Kirby, North Yorkshire."

"We need to get over there right away. And we need arrest and search warrants." He turned to the depot manager. "Mr Beale, thanks for your time. Do not contact Michael Stokes in any way. And if he contacts you, do not tell him we've been here or that we're looking for him. Is that understood?"

Beale shrugged. "I have no intention of contacting him. I'm going home to my turkey dinner."

Battle remembered the Christmas dinner he'd arranged with his wife and DI Summers. The DI obviously realised those plans had been cancelled but he hadn't contacted Rowena.

He left the office and strode through the warehouse towards the exit but stopped before he reached it.

"Everything okay, guv?" Morgan asked.

"I've got to call DI Summers," he said. "She's gone to that hospital to find a patient called Samuel. She's got the wrong name."

He dialled Summers' number. When she answered, he said, "Are you still at Larkmoor House?"

"Yes, guv, we're waiting to speak to one of the nurses."

"Listen, his name isn't Samuel. It's Michael Stokes, 28 years old. We've got his address and I'm going to sort out a warrant."

"That's great news. Do you want us to assist with the arrest?"

"No, you might as well stay there. No need to drive

down here in this weather. Find out if Stokes was a patient there."

"Will do, guv."

He ended the call and stepped out into the wind, shielding his face against the swirling snow. "You get those warrants sorted out," he said to Morgan as she went to her car. "I need to call my wife. Otherwise, I'll be in the doghouse."

As he got into the Range Rover, he rang Rowena.

"Where are you?" she asked as soon as she picked up. Her voice held notes of anger and fear.

"Sorry, love," Battle said. "Something's come up and we might be close to cracking this case. Christmas dinner is going to have to wait."

He heard her sigh. "I don't care about our dinner arrangements, Stewart. I'm worried about *you*. This snowstorm is closing in. I can barely see anything beyond the window. Are you all right out there?"

"I'm fine," he told her. "We've discovered a lead and I've got to follow it."

"Of course you have," she said, understandingly. "You do whatever you have to, but just check in with me every now and then if you can, just so I know you're okay."

"I will," he said. He almost added, "I promise," but he knew that he was going to be as busy as hell trying to secure the arrest of Michael Stokes, and he didn't make a promise he might not be able to keep.

"I'll see you when you get back," Rowena said.

"Okay, love." He ended the call and rested his head

back against the headrest, watching the snow whirl and dance around his car. He finally had a name and an address. If all went well, Michael Stokes would soon be in custody and Teresa and Gemma Matthews would hopefully be found safe and well.

The next couple of hours would be crucial to ensuring that outcome.

He picked up his phone again and opened the recent calls list. Finding Chris Toombs' number, he pressed it and waited for the call to connect.

"Toombs," the tech said as he answered.

"It's Battle again. I want you to look into something for me. A property near Cold Kirby."

"Thinking of moving there?" Toombs asked.

"No, I have an address of interest and I want to know anything you can find out about it. Particularly who lives there and if there are any licensed firearms at the property. I don't want any nasty surprises when we raid the place later."

"I can do that," Toombs said. "What's the address?"

"Grantham Farm, Cold Kirby."

"Got it. I'll get back to you if I find anything interesting."

"Thanks." Battle hung up.

He called the Murder Force incident room. The phone was answered by DC Tom Ryan.

"Ryan," Battle said, "get a team together. We're carrying out a search warrant. Grantham Farm, Cold Kirby."

"Yes, guv," the DC said. "How big a team do you want?"

"I want as many people as you can get hold of. And an ambulance.

The passenger side door opened, and DS Morgan climbed in, bringing a flurry of snow with her. She was carrying a laptop. She closed the door against the elements and said, "The warrants are being applied for, guv. We should hear back soon."

Battle nodded. "We need to get a team together to carry out the raid and the search. I just hope Teresa and Gemma are at the property and he's not keeping them somewhere else."

"That's something I wanted to talk to you about, guv," she said, opening the laptop. "Yesterday, you asked me to look into the cold war shelters. I found something that might be useful." She tapped on the keyboard and a map appeared on the screen, covered with red dots.

"It turns out the Ministry of Defence built over a thousand underground bunkers in the fifties and sixties. They're called ROC Posts and were supposed to be shelters for members of the Royal Observation Corps if Britain came under nuclear attack. They were closed down in the early nineties. A lot of them were demolished by landowners but some are still intact. There's a group trying to preserve the ones that are left, and I got a list of locations from their website."

She pointed at the map. "These are the bunkers that haven't been demolished." Placing her finger on the touchpad, she deftly zoomed in. "There's a bunker near Cold Kirby."

Battle looked at the village of Cold Kirby on the map and the red dot north of it. Teresa and Gemma could be in there, locked in the darkness, fearing for their lives.

"Let's get over there," he said. "The team can meet us at Grantham Farm. I want to have a look at that bunker."

"Yes, guv." She closed the laptop and opened the door. A blast of cold air chilled the interior of the Range Rover and Battle shivered. After Morgan had closed the door, he waited for the heating to kick in before typing Cold Kirby into the SatNav.

The display told him it would take 45 minutes to get there. That probably meant well over an hour in this weather.

At least if he made a move now, he had a better of chance of getting to the farm before the roads became impassable, which was certain to happen fairly soon.

He needed to make sure he got to Grantham Farm before the snowstorm cut it off from the rest of civilisation.

If the storm closed in and no one was at the farm to save Teresa and Gemma, they had no chance.

CHAPTER THIRTY

Christmas Day, 2:48 p.m.

"THAT'S GREAT NEWS," Dani said, feeling a rush of exhilaration now that they had a name and address for their suspect. "Do you want us to assist with the arrest?"

"No, you might as well stay there," Battle told her. "No need to drive down here in this weather. Find out if Stokes was a patient there."

"Will do, guv."

Battle hung up and Dani slipped her phone back into her pocket.

She looked at Sheridan, who was literally sitting on the edge of his seat. "His name isn't Samuel; it's Michael Stokes. He's 28. They've got an address, so I think an arrest is imminent."

Sheridan nodded. "I just hope Teresa and her daughter are all right."

"So do I," Dani said. She hoped that the fact Stokes hadn't had the women for long might mean they were unharmed. If Battle could get to the address in time, he could avert another tragedy.

The door to the inner part of Larkmoor House opened and Sheila Hopkins came through it, looking harried. She saw Dani and walked over to her. "You wanted to see me?"

Dani stood up. "Yes, I'd like to ask you about someone who may have been a patient here in the past."

Sheila nodded. "All right."

"Does the name Michael Stokes mean anything to you?"

"No, I don't believe so." Sheila frowned. "How long ago was he here?"

"We're not sure he was here at all," Sheridan said. "It's a possibility we're looking into."

"Michael Stokes," Sheila said under her breath, as if trying to jog her memory. "Michael Stokes." Realisation seemed to suddenly dawn on her face. "We had a Vera Stokes here a long time ago. I think her son's name was Michael. Yes, I'm sure of it. He visited her once or twice while she was here."

"How long ago was this?" Dani asked.

"It must have been nine or ten years ago."

"Was Tanya Ward working here when Vera was a patient?"

Sheila thought about that and then said, "Yes, she was. In fact, I'm sure Vera was under Tanya's care."

"Why was Vera a patient here?" Sheridan asked.

"If I remember rightly, she had some sort of break-down," Sheila said. "She'd been a patient at Larkmoor before, so she was brought here for a second time.'

Sheridan nodded. "I see. Did you remember her from her previous stay?"

"No, it was the first time I'd seen her."

"And how long have you worked here?"

"Nineteen years."

Sheridan looked up towards the ceiling and narrowed his eyes. "So she was here nine years ago, and at least ten years before that. She's obviously had mental issues for most of her life."

He turned to Dani and said, "We should probably pay her a visit. She might know what her son's been up to."

"Do you know her address?" Dani asked Sheila.

"I can get it from the records. Everything is on the computer." She paused. "Although I'm not really allowed to give that kind of information out."

"Listen," Dani said. "I think I know the address anyway. Grantham Farm, Cold Kirby. Could you just confirm that for me?"

"All right," Sheila said, nodding. "I'll check that."

As the nurse walked back through the door that led to the inner part of the hospital, Dani said to Sheridan, "If Michael has some sort of issue with his mother, it stands to reason that they might live together. If Sheila confirms it, I can let Battle know that Vera is at the address he's going to be raiding later. He'll probably want to take a mental health professional with him when he arrests Michael. It's bound to be a stressful situation for Vera."

Sheridan nodded.

Dani stared out through the glass doors at the driving snow. "If Michael met Tanya ten years ago, why did he wait all this time before he took her?"

"A trigger," the psychologist said. "He might have had conflicting emotions regarding Tanya all that time ago, confused her with his mother in some way, but he didn't do anything because his rage towards his mother hadn't grown to uncontrollable levels then. It lay dormant inside him until something triggered its awakening. Whatever that trigger was, it probably happened three weeks ago when he took Abigail, perhaps a short time before that. It built up inside him and the result was Tanya's murder and Abigail's abduction."

"Maybe his mother can shed some light on it," Dani suggested. "She might know what's been going on in Michael's life recently."

"Especially if they live in the same house," Sheridan said.

Sheila returned with a sheet of notepaper. "Vera doesn't live at Grantham Farm anymore. That was her address when she was admitted here the first time, when she was sectioned by her husband twenty years ago."

"Her husband?" Dani asked.

Sheila nodded. "Jonathan Stokes. Vera was here for almost a year."

"So when she was here the second time," Sheridan asked, "Did Jonathan visit her as well as Michael?"

Sheila shook her head slowly. "I don't think so, but I really can't remember."

"Did a girl called Ruth ever visit her?" Sheridan asked.

"No, I don't think so. I don't remember any girl."

"Is that Vera's new address?" Dani asked, motioning to the piece of paper in Sheila's hands.

"I'm not sure I can give that out."

"Sheila, this is important."

Sheila hesitated. "This is about that mother and daughter who went missing, isn't it?"

Dani nodded.

The nurse handed the paper over. "This is where she was living when she came here nine years ago."

Dani read the address and pulled her phone out of her pocket. She rang Battle and got his voicemail. "We've got the address of Michael Stokes' mother and we're going to interview her," she said. "We'll be at Wild Row Farm, Sleddale Road, Westerdale." She hung up and muttered, "Bloody voicemail."

"He's probably got no signal," Sheridan said. "I'm surprised the entire network hasn't gone down in this weather."

She nodded. "If we're going to get over to Westerdale, we'd better get a move on. Thanks, Sheila, you've been a great help."

The nurse nodded. "Be careful on those roads. God knows how I'm going to get home when my shift finishes."

Pocketing the piece of paper, Dani stepped through the main door and into the windswept car park. The falling snow was so thick that she could barely see her Land Rover. When she climbed in behind the wheel, she placed the paper on the dashboard entered the address into the SatNav.

While the car heated up, she rang the incident room. Her call was answered by DC Ryan.

"Ryan, it's DI Summers."

"Hello, guv. We're all just about to leave. The arrest warrant has just been granted for Michael Stokes and we're just gearing up to get over to his gaff. I assume you know about all of that."

"Yes," she said. "I need someone to do some background checks for me."

"Oh. Well, like I said, Battle has told us to get up to Grantham Farm ASAP."

"All right. Put me through to..." she searched her brain for the name of the tech she'd met earlier. "Chris Toombs."

"All right, guv, I'll just find his extension." She heard him tapping on a keyboard. "You're not getting in on the action, then?" he asked as he was typing.

"No, I've got something else to do."

"Putting you through now," he said. The line went dead for a few seconds, then she heard Toombs' voice.

"This is Chris Toombs; how may I be of service?"

"Chris, it's DI Summers. I need you to look into something for me."

"Okay, shoot."

"I need any information you can find on a Jonathan Stokes. He's the father of—"

"Whoa, *déjà vu!*"

"Sorry?"

"Jonathan Stokes' name just turned up in a search I did for DCI Battle. Jonathan and Vera Stokes are the registered owners of the farm where the arrest team is going. Grantham Farm."

"Okay. Well, I've just found out that Vera Stokes is now living at a different address. Or at least she was nine years ago."

"Wild Row Farm," he said.

"That came up in your search as well?"

"I did some digging. Vera inherited Wild Row Farm from her father fifteen years ago. I guess she owns both Grantham and Wild Row, since her husband, Jonathan Stokes, disappeared eighteen years ago."

"Wait a minute," she said. "I'm putting you on speaker. Tony Sheridan is here with me." She clicked the speaker button on her phone. "What do you mean he disappeared?"

"He left Vera and their two children, Michael and Ruth. Moved abroad, apparently."

"Eighteen years ago?" Sheridan asked.

"That's right."

"Two years after he had Vera sectioned," Sheridan said to Dani. "Maybe he couldn't stand living with her after she returned from the hospital. She'd been gone a year and he was the one who sent her away. That's bound to put a strain on any marriage."

"Maybe," Dani said.

Sheridan said, "Chris, do you know where Jonathan Stokes lives now?"

"No idea. Do you want me to look into it?"

"No, that's not necessary. I just thought he could throw some light onto what's been happening in that family."

"You're interested in Michael's background," Dani said.

He nodded. "Aren't you?"

"I'm more interested in seeing him behind bars."

Sheridan shrugged. "Fair enough."

"Thanks, Chris," Dani said. "I'll let you know if we need anything else."

"Okay, have a good one, and don't let the storm get ya." There was a click as he hung up.

Sheridan took out a notebook from an inner pocket in his voluminous jacket and scribbled something into it with a pencil.

"So the timeline looks like this," he said. "Twenty years ago, Jonathan Stokes had his wife Vera committed to Larkmoor House. Michael would have been eight years old. Two years later, Jonathan walks out. Michael was ten when that happened. Then, nine years ago, she had a mental breakdown and spent time in hospital again. So Michael would have been about nineteen. This may be where the resentment of his mother comes from. He feels she abandoned him."

"If he had abandonment issues, surely they'd be directed at his father," Dani said.

Sheridan shrugged. "The thing is, these events happened a long time ago, but his rage wasn't triggered until about three weeks ago. He frowned at the notebook in his lap. "There's something we're missing here."

"Well, while you think about that," Dani said, putting the Land Rover into gear, "We need to get over to Vera Stokes' house before all the roads close."

"Yeah, sure," the psychologist said, still staring at his notebook. He picked it up and examined the page of spidery writing. "Where is Ruth in all of this? I mean, I've theorised that she's dead, but when did she die? How? Sheila can't remember her coming to Larkmoor to visit Vera nine years ago. Was she already dead at that time? That long ago?"

"We can ask Michael those questions when he's in the interview room," Dani suggested, driving out of the car park and onto the main road. Visibility had been reduced to no more than a few feet beyond the Land Rover's bonnet, so she had to drive slowly and carefully to make sure they didn't come off the road.

It took them half an hour to get to Sleddale Road. The SatNav could only direct them to the general area of the farm, so while Dani drove the Land Rover slowly through the thick snowfall, she and Sheridan looked for a sign that might indicate where Wild Row Farm was located.

"There," Sheridan said, pointing at something in the trees by the roadside.

Dani followed his outstretched finger and saw a small wooden sign that had the name *Wild Row Farm* carved into its snow-blasted surface.

"I assume there's a road that leads to the farm," the psychologist said, "but I can't see one."

He was right. If there was a road or track that led to Wild Row Farm, it was covered with a blanket of snow.

"We'll have to go on foot," Dani said, pulling the Land Rover over to the side of the road and killing the engine. As the sound of the motor died away, along with the *whirr* of the windscreen wipers, the sound of the wind howling along the road became noticeable, along with the *pat pat* of snowflakes hitting the car roof and windscreen.

Dani realised how utterly alone they were out here.

She checked her phone. No signal.

"Right," she said, "let's see what Vera Stokes can tell us about her son."

Together, they exited the Land Rover. It was getting dark, so Dani went to the boot and retrieved two large torches. She handed one to Sheridan.

They found a gap in the trees that indicated where the hidden road was buried and trudged along it in the dark, their torch beams illuminating trees on either side of them and yet more snow.

After what seemed like an hour of walking but was probably a lot less, Dani thought she saw a light ahead.

She wiped melted snowflakes from her eyelashes and squinted.

"There's a light," she told Sheridan.

He nodded and they proceeded towards the farmhouse, which seemed to materialise out of the maelstrom. A red Nissan Micra was parked in front of the house, almost buried in the snow. It looked like Vera Stokes was at home.

Knowing that she'd need to put on her report what time she'd arrived at the house, Dani checked her watch.

It was almost four o' clock.

CHAPTER THIRTY-ONE

Christmas Day, 3:57 p.m.

DS MORGAN'S Yaris pulled over to the side of the road and Battle followed suit, parking next to a wooden sign that said *Grantham Farm*. He switched off his engine and headlights. As DS Morgan did the same, their cars seemed to be swallowed by darkness and the ever-present swirling snow.

He got out and zipped his coat up to his chin. His tweed hat wasn't going to stay on his head in this wind, so he tossed it into the boot and replaced it with a black woollen watchcap. He grabbed a torch and slammed the boot shut. He tested the torch, even though he checked it regularly. This kind of cold could drain the life from someone, so it wouldn't have much trouble draining a couple of batteries.

Morgan walked over to him, her own torch casting a wavering beam over the snow in front of her boots.

"I suppose it's that way," Battle said, pointing at a swath of deep snow that cut through the trees. "Come on, let's have a look."

"Shouldn't we wait for the team to arrive, guv?"

"I want to have a look at that bunker," he said. "If Teresa and Gemma are inside there, on a night like this, they don't stand a chance."

Having worked with Battle long enough to know that he valued saving lives over all else, including protocol, she merely nodded and followed him into the trees.

"I'll ring Ryan and tell him we've gone ahead," Battle said, pulling his phone out of his pocket with gloved fingers. A quick glance at the screen told him he had a voicemail. He listened to it while he and Morgan trudged through the snow.

It was DI Summers. "We've got the address of Michael Stokes' mother and we're going to interview her," she said. "We'll be at Wild Row Farm, Sleddale Road, Westerdale."

"They've found Michael Stokes' mother," he told Morgan. "They're going to interview her."

The DS nodded. She was looking at her phone with a frown on her face. "I was going to bring up the map of the bunker sites, but I've got no signal."

Battle looked down at his own phone and saw that the reception had dwindled to nothing. "Bloody hell," he muttered, slipping the phone back into his pocket.

"Well, I'm sure the team will realise we've gone ahead when they see our vehicles back there."

"They'll probably enter the farmhouse while we're at the bunker," she said.

"I don't have a problem with that," Battle said. "Not if it means we get Teresa and Gemma back safely. The team members know what they're doing. As long as Ryan doesn't try to abseil through the farmhouse windows SAS-style."

Morgan chuckled, the sound muffled by her scarf.

Up ahead, a blocky shape loomed in the snowfall.

"The farmhouse," Morgan said, pointing at the dark structure.

There were no lights on, no vehicles parked outside.

"Looks like he isn't here," Battle said, keeping his voice low, despite the empty appearance of the house.

"Shall we take a closer look?"

"No, our priority is the safety of those women. We need to find that bunker."

They skirted the house, which seemed, to all intents and purposes, to be unoccupied. Even so, Morgan and Battle turned off their torches and didn't speak as they moved towards the rear of the property.

When the dark house was a couple of hundred yards behind them, Morgan spoke. "The bunker should be somewhere in these trees to the north of the house."

They entered a small wood and turned the torches back on, pointing the beams of light at the ground.

"What are we looking for exactly?" Battle asked.

A waist-high shaft entrance made of stone with a hatch on top of it. "There it is." She pointed her light at a small structure that looked exactly as she'd described.

They went over to it and Battle inspected the metal hatch. It was unlocked. That wasn't a good sign. If Stokes had Teresa and Gemma in here, he'd have locked the hatch. If his prisoners were alive, anyway.

Battle's heart sank.

He flipped open the hatch, revealing a pitch-black shaft descending into the earth.

"Is there anyone down there?" he shouted. "Teresa? Gemma?"

His voice echoed in the space below but there was no answer.

"Hold this for a minute," he said, handing Morgan his torch.

As she took it, he climbed onto the top of the shaft and carefully lowered his legs into the darkness, finding the rungs of a ladder with his boots. "You wait here," he told Morgan. "I'll be back in a minute." He reached out for the torch and she put it into his gloved hand.

"Be careful, guv."

He nodded and made his way down the ladder. When he reached the floor, he cast his torch beam over the subterranean room. The place had been vandalised at some point. The walls were covered with graffiti and the floor was strewn with discarded beer cans and broken bottles. The air smelled of urine. A crack in one wall had let water in and a large puddle covered half of the floor.

Battle turned around and ascended the ladder. As he climbed out of the shaft and breathed in the sharp, fresh air of the evening, he glanced at Morgan and shook his head. "No one's been down there except yobs and drunks."

The DS turned to the farmhouse. "So they could be in there."

"Yes," Battle said, looking at the dark windows. "And if Stokes isn't home, this could be our best chance to get to them without any hassle."

Morgan nodded.

They trudged back through the snow to the house.

"Let's try the back door," Battle said. "That way, we won't make footprints around the front and alert Stokes to our presence if he comes back."

She looked at her watch. "Guv, the entry team should be here by now."

"They're probably stuck in the snow."

"How are we going to get in?"

"Shouldn't be too difficult," he said. "First, we see the door is unlocked." He tried the handle, but the door didn't budge. Two frosted glass strips ran from the of the door to the bottom. He used his torch to smash the one closest to the door handle and reached inside. His gloved fingers found a key in the lock. He turned it and tried the door again.

It opened.

He shouted, "Teresa? Gemma? Are you in here?"

There was no reply. The air that drifted out of the house had a sweet scent.

"You smell that?" he asked Morgan.

She nodded. "Flowers."

This wasn't the smell he'd have expected to come wafting out of a house occupied by Michael Stokes.

He stepped inside and found himself in a tidy kitchen. From the outside, the house had looked derelict and that, along with the state of the bunker out back, had made him wonder if no one lived here and the address on Stokes' driving licence was wrong.

But the kitchen indicated that someone had been here recently. A mug sat next to a kettle on the counter, along with a jar of coffee, pack of tea bags, and a bag of sugar.

He checked the fridge. There was fresh milk in there.

Morgan picked up the mug and showed it to Battle. "Not the sort of thing I'd expect Stokes to drink his daily cuppa from."

The mug bore the slogan *God Guides Me Every Day* beneath a simple drawing of a crucifix.

"Maybe that's where he got the inspiration to nail Tanya Ward to that barn wall," Battle said.

The smell of fresh flowers bothered him. Now that he was inside the house, he recognised the cloying smell. Lilies. He looked around the kitchen for a vase but couldn't see one. The flowers must be elsewhere in the house.

The living room was sparsely furnished, with just one armchair, a coffee table, and nothing else, but it was clean and tidy. No lilies in here, either.

"It doesn't look like anyone lives here," Morgan said, looking around the room. "If they do, they live a very spartan existence."

"Maybe he doesn't spend a lot of time at home," he suggested. "He's out in his van most of the time. Probably just lays his head here. Let's check out the bedroom."

"There's another door in the hall," Morgan pointed out. "I think it might lead to a cellar."

He'd been so busy thinking about the elusive flowers that he'd walked past a door beneath the stairs and not even noticed it.

He went to it and tried the handle. The door opened and the smell of lilies became overpowering. A set of wooden steps descended into darkness.

Morgan flicked a light switch on the wall and a dim bulb hanging over the stairs flickered to life. The other bulbs in the cellar below were equally as dim, judging by the faint light at the foot of the stairs.

Leading the way, Battle went down to the cellar, trying to ignore the heady scent of lilies that hung in the air. The cellar had a dirt floor and an old-fashioned wood-burning boiler sat against one wall but other than that, the only thing down here was flowers. Dozens and dozens of flowers.

Glass vases had been arranged along the walls and each held half a dozen or so white lilies. More flowers lay on the dirt floor. Some were fresher than others but none of them were dead or wilted.

"What the hell is going on down here?" he asked.

His question wasn't directed at Morgan; it was simply an expression of his bewilderment.

Morgan pointed at an area of the floor in the far corner. "Guv, look at that."

Battle narrowed his eyes and nodded. The cellar floor was even except for in that one area, where a depression could be seen.

He'd been taught to recognise clandestine graves and knew that a depression in the earth was a telltale sign of a body buried beneath. As the body decayed over time, the dirt above it sank into the grave.

That explained the flowers; somebody was visiting the grave and leaving the lilies on and around it. They might even be a measure to counter the smell of what lay beneath the dirt.

"It can't be Teresa or Gemma," he said. "The earth wouldn't have sunk like that so quickly. Whoever is under there has been there for some time."

He walked over to the depression and knelt down next to it, running a gloved hand over the dirt. Was this another of Stokes' victims? One they didn't know about?

Tentatively, he dug his fingers into the ground and pulled a handful of earth away.

"Should you be doing that, guv?" Morgan asked from behind him.

"We need to know if there actually is a body under here before we call in Forensics."

"The team is on its way here, anyway."

He was well aware of that, of course, but he had to

know what was buried here, in Stokes' cellar. He continued to dig, and it didn't take long before he'd cleared enough dirt away to reveal an almost skeletal hand and the cuff of a red and black flannel shirt.

"Looks like a man, judging by the clothing," he told Morgan.

He noticed something on the wall, almost at ground level. It looked like a word on the bricks, but the light cast by the bulbs was so dim that he couldn't see it clearly.

He shone his torch at the wall. The single word, painted in black, came into focus.

Jonathan.

Battle stood up and turned to Morgan.

"I think we've just found Jonathan Stokes."

CHAPTER THIRTY-TWO

Christmas Day, 4:00 p.m.

DANI KNOCKED on the farmhouse door as she and Sheridan sheltered from the snow beneath the porch roof.

There was no answer.

"Maybe she's gone away," Sheridan suggested, peering at the lit, curtained windows. "She might have left the lights on to deter burglars."

"You can't see the house from the road," Dani said. "Any potential burglar would have to be coming up the drive to see that the lights are on." The red Nissan wasn't proof that Vera Stokes was at home—she could have left the house in a different vehicle—but Dani was sure there was someone in the house. She could sense it.

She knocked again, louder this time.

The wind picked up, howling through the trees and whipping sheets of snow across the porch. Dani lifted the collars of her jacket and lowered her head against the onslaught.

The door opened, spilling light and warmth onto the porch. A dark-haired woman who looked like she was in her fifties stood in the doorway. She wore a long white robe that made Dani think she might be a member of a church choir. Perhaps she was, and she'd sung at a Christmas service today. Or maybe she wore the robe around the house because it was comfortable. It was clear by the slight bump in the front of the robe that she was pregnant.

"Come in, come in," the woman said. "We can't have you standing outside in this weather." She stepped back to give them room and ushered them inside. When Dani and Sheridan were in the hallway, the white-robed woman shut the door, and the howling wind quietened.

"Mrs Stokes?" Dani asked, reaching for her warrant card. "Vera Stokes?"

"Yes, that's me," Vera said. "What can I do for you?"

Dani showed her the card. "I'm DI Summers from the North Yorkshire police—"

"Yes, I know who you are," Vera said. "I saw you on *Live with Jo and Martin*. Well, a picture of you, anyway." She turned her attention to Sheridan. "I'm not sure I know your name, though."

"Tony Sheridan," the psychologist said, with a charming smile. "It's lovely to meet you, Vera. My colleague and I thought we might freeze to death out there."

Vera's eyes widened, as if she'd just remembered something. "Come in, you poor things. I'll put the kettle on." She pushed a door open and entered a living room where a television was showing one of the *Home Alone* movies.

"Thank you very much," Sheridan said, following Vera into the room. "That would be great."

Dani had the distinct impression that the psychologist had just got them into the house by using the power of suggestion.

She entered the living room and unzipped her jacket slightly. The heat in here was stifling.

"I'll be back in a minute," Vera said, disappearing through an archway that led to a spacious kitchen.

"She didn't even ask us why we're here," Dani whispered to Sheridan.

"She's probably glad to see anyone, especially today," he said in a low voice. "I bet she's been sitting in front of this TV on her own all Christmas."

Dani checked her phone. She'd expected to hear from Battle that Michael Stokes had been arrested. Maybe the DCI still didn't have a signal or was too busy getting Stokes to the station.

An arrangement of three framed photographs on the wall caught her attention, and she went over to inspect them. One of them showed a young boy and

298 ADAM J. WRIGHT

girl playing outside a farmhouse. The house didn't look like Wild Row farmhouse, so she assumed the photo had been taken at Grantham Farm, where Battle was at the moment, and where Vera used to live.

She gestured Sheridan over. He squinted at the picture and said, "Must be Michael and Ruth."

The next photo showed two men grinning at the camera. They wore hard hats, lumberjack shirts, and had safety goggles hanging around their necks. At their feet lay two chainsaws. A number of stumps could be seen in the picture, as well as a pile of felled trees.

The boy and girl from the first picture could be seen in this photograph as well, only here, they looked younger. Dani guessed Michael to be around eight and Ruth six. They sat on a small concrete structure in the distance, behind the two men, with the moors stretching away to the horizon beyond.

"Jonathan Stokes?" Sheridan speculated, pointing to the younger of the two men.

Dani shrugged. "It could be. He left eighteen years ago, when Michael would have been ten years old. This was taken a few years before."

The third photo was a snap of Michael sitting on the cliff near Whitby Abbey. He was maybe sixteen or seventeen and he looked like any lad of that age; grinning at the camera inanely.

"He looks happy in this picture," Sheridan said.

Dani nodded. "No sign of what he was to become later."

"There usually isn't."

Vera came back into the room with a tray of china cups and a matching teapot. She set it on the table.

"Your son looks very happy here," Sheridan said, pointing to the photo of Michael on the cliff. "Did you take this photo?"

Her face darkened. "No, someone else did. They were always going to that cliff and leaving me here on my own. Sometimes, I thought they only went there to get away from me."

"They?" Sheridan asked casually.

She ignored him and focused her attention on the tray. "Now, who would like a nice cup of tea?"

"Is this your son Michael?" Dani asked.

"Samuel," Vera said. "He has a new name, as do I. I'm Mary now. It's only right to have a new name when you're reborn."

"Reborn?" Sheridan asked. "You mean in a religious sense?"

She nodded. "That's right. Samuel and I live by the commandments of God. We do as He tells us."

"I see," Sheridan said. "And what does He tell you to do?"

"To atone for our sins."

Dani felt the conversation was starting off on the wrong foot. She wanted to ask about Michael, not get a religious sermon. She opened her mouth to ask Vera about Michael, but Sheridan raised a hand, stopping her.

He looked at the photos on the wall and then at Vera. "Who's the little girl in these pictures? Is she your daughter?"

Vera pursed her lips and made a "Hmmmm" sound before busying herself with the tea.

"And I assume one of these two strapping gentlemen is your husband."

"Oh, yes," she said. "That's Jonathan on the left. The other man is my father, God rest his soul. They were clearing trees at the back of the property that day. Pleased as punch, they were, when they finished the job. I took that photograph of them."

"Jonathan moved away, didn't he?" the psychologist asked. "I think I heard that he went abroad somewhere."

She let out a short laugh. "Jonathan? Abroad? No, he loves this area too much. He'd never move away."

Sheridan looked surprised. "Oh, so he lives locally?"

"Of course," she said, pouring tea from the pot into the cups. "He's at our other farm."

"Grantham Farm?" Dani asked. If Jonathan was at the other farm, he was probably being questioned by Battle right now.

Vera looked up and nodded. "Yes, that's right."

"So you and he are separated?" Sheridan asked.

She laughed again. "No, nothing like that. It's just that Jonathan is there, and I live here. It works better that way. But I visit him all the time. Samuel thinks I go out gallivanting with other men but that's not true at all. I'm faithful to Jonathan. We sit and talk for hours, long into the night. We reminisce about the good old days, you know, that sort of thing."

Dani felt her blood turn icy. "You said Samuel thinks you go out with other men when you go to Grantham Farm. So he doesn't live there with his father?"

Vera frowned at Dani, as if the answer to that question was obvious. "No, of course not. We used to live there, all of us did. But now, Samuel lives here with me."

"Is he here now?" Dani tried to keep the tension she felt in her body out of her voice. Battle and his team had gone to the wrong bloody house.

"No, he's left me on my own again," Vera said. "That's all he ever does these days. I've barely seen him all day. You wouldn't think it's Christmas, a time you're supposed to spend with your family."

"Mrs Stokes, where is he?"

Vera waved her hand towards the rear of the house. "Out there somewhere. Feeding the hens, or so he tells me. They must be the best fed hens in all of Yorkshire, the amount of time he spends with them. Or perhaps he's on that bike he likes to ride around in all weathers." She nodded. "Yes, I'm sure I heard the engine just after he went outside."

"When was this?" Dani asked.

"A couple of minutes before you arrived."

Dani resisted the urge to sprint out of the back door and look for Michael. If he was on a vehicle, she'd have no chance, especially in this weather. "Mrs Stokes, this is very important. Do you know where he goes on the bike?"

Vera picked up one of the cups and blew on the tea before taking a sip. "I have no idea what he gets up to or where he goes. If he was younger, I'd know exactly where he'd be. The bunker. He used to go there all time whenever we visited his grandad here. Can I go to the bunker? he'd ask over and over. His grandad never refused him, so off they'd go, traipsing to the bunker. I never saw the appeal, myself. There's nothing there except an empty room."

Dani's adrenaline kicked in. She tried to keep her voice steady as she asked, "Where exactly is the bunker?"

"At the back of the property," Vera said. "That's it, in that photograph. That's what he's sitting on top of. His precious bunker."

Her phone rang. She pulled it out of her pocket and saw Battle's name. Thrusting the phone at Sheridan, she said, "Tell him what's happened and where we are. The team needs to get over here now."

She rushed through the archway and into the kitchen, searching for the back door. She flung it open and stepped out into a snowy yard. A white van was parked out here, next to a cluster of outbuildings.

The snow was relentless, but she could see the faint impressions of tyre tracks that reminded her of the track she and Matt had found in the frozen stream bed.

The snow hadn't completely wiped them out, but they'd soon vanish.

She hurried out of the yard and onto open land, keeping her head down against the onslaught of wind and snow as she followed the rapidly disappearing tracks.

CHAPTER THIRTY-THREE

Tony answered the call from Battle with a quick, "Just give me a second, boss." He looked over at Vera and said, "Could I possibly use your bathroom?"

"Yes," she said, sipping her tea. "It's just upstairs on the right. Is our friend coming back for a cuppa?"

"Perhaps in a bit," Tony said. He ascended the steep wooden staircase that led to the next level and turned right. But the door he opened didn't lead to a bathroom. The room beyond was a bedroom. It didn't matter; he only wanted to get out of earshot of Vera while he told Battle to send the cavalry. Vera was under some sort of psychological stress and he didn't want to make it worse by letting her know a rabble of coppers was coming to the house.

"I'm here, boss," he told Battle.

"Where's DI Summers?" the DCI asked gruffly.

"She's gone after Stokes," Tony said. "He's here,

living with his mother. You need to get everyone over here right away."

"Right, we're on our way. I can't say when we'll be there though. This bloody weather is closing off the roads." There was a pause and then he said, "Is Vera Stokes there?"

"She is."

"Don't let her go anywhere. We found Jonathan Stokes' body buried in the cellar here. According to the SOCOs' initial assessment, he's been under the earth at least fifteen years. We're going to be taking Vera in for questioning."

Tony had known that the woman downstairs had psychological issues, but Battle's news made it abundantly clear just how deeply they were embedded in her mind. She'd said that she visited Jonathan at Grantham Farm regularly and spoke with him long into the night. That was obviously a delusion. But the fact that she knew her husband was in that house suggested she had some part in his death and burial there.

"Just to warn you, she might need to be handled with a gentle touch," he told Battle. And not only because of her mental issues; she's pregnant." He wandered around the room, which seemed to be Vera's bedroom, judging by the makeup on the dresser and clothes hanging in the open wardrobe.

"Just make sure she doesn't do a runner," Battle said, before hanging up.

Frustration filled Tony. He wanted to go out back

and help Dani, but if he did that, a murderer —Vera Stokes—might get away.

He slid the DI's phone into his pocket and was about to leave the room when something in the wardrobe caught his eye. He slid aside a white robe on its hanger and revealed the two items that had looked out of place among the dresses and tops.

He stroked his chin as he considered the implications of what he'd just found. Hanging from the rail were two latex, fake baby bumps, one larger than the other. Both were larger than the bump Vera currently sported beneath her robe.

So the pregnancy was fake. She was obviously planning to move to the larger fake bumps as time went on.

But why?

Had she lost a child? If his hypothesis was correct, then yes, she had lost one. She'd lost Ruth. But Ruth couldn't have been a baby when she died; Tony himself had just seen a photograph in which she was at least six years old.

A mother faking a pregnancy because she'd lost a baby was something Tony had encountered before, but not someone faking a pregnancy after the loss of an older child. He supposed it was possible, but there seemed to be something else at play here.

He went back downstairs and into the living room, where Vera was sitting on the sofa, watching the *Home Alone* movie.

Tony sat next to her. "I'd love that cup of tea now, if

that's okay."

"Of course," she said, smiling. "Did you find the bathroom?"

"I did."

She handed him one of the full china cups and said, "Merry Christmas."

"Merry Christmas. Thank you."

He took a sip of the tea and said, "Are you hoping for a boy or a girl?"

Her hand went to the bump beneath her robe. "I really don't mind."

"That's probably the best way to look at it," he said, nodding. "You don't want to set your heart on a particular outcome and then be disappointed when it doesn't happen. Children are like that, though, aren't they? You have hopes and dreams for them, hoping they won't make the mistakes you made when they grow up, and then they go ahead and make those same mistakes, anyway."

"Yes, I suppose so," she said.

"Girls are the worst." Tony took a sip of tea, taking time for his words sink in and then added, "They sometimes turn away from their mothers once they reach a certain age. It isn't right, really; they should remember who brought them up. Who nourished and cherished them."

"Yes, you're right," Vera said. "My daughter was just like that. Rebellious. Willful. She wouldn't listen to a word I said."

Tony didn't say anything further. It hadn't escaped

308 ADAM J. WRIGHT

his attention that Vera was talking about her daughter in the past tense. He sipped his tea slowly. If he was right, Vera had a lot more to say on this subject and, given a little time, she would tell him more than she probably intended.

"She was always going off to that cliff," she said, finally. "And she just had to snap her fingers and Samuel would follow her there like a lapdog. He didn't have any friends. He was always an odd child and I think the other children could sense that. Ruth was the only one who understood him, I think." Her hand flew to her mouth, as if she'd said something she shouldn't have.

"What's wrong?" he asked her gently.

"We don't speak her name in this house. I don't allow it."

He nodded slowly, as if he understood. "I can see why. Some things—and people—are best forgotten, aren't they?"

"Yes," she said, nodding along with him. "They are."

He gestured at the bump beneath her robe and lowered his voice to a conspiratorial whisper. "I bet you're hoping it's not a girl. I don't envy you, having to go through all those kinds of problems a second time around."

She looked down at the bump as if seeing it for the first time. "This? Oh, no, this isn't real. Silly me for keeping up the pretence in front of you. I only wear this for Samuel."

"For your son? I don't understand."

Her face darkened. "He's been getting steadily more and more depressed over the years. I can recognise the symptoms of a breakdown, having had some first-hand experience, and I thought he was heading for one. I had to do something to help him. I thought back to the time in his life when he was happiest. It was when his sister was pregnant. He just seemed so optimistic and full of life at that time. So, I thought that if I told him I was pregnant, he'd get that happy smile back again and avoid a mental breakdown."

"Was his sister pregnant when she...went away?"

"Yes," Vera said, "She was."

Tony realised he'd found the trigger that had eluded him for so long. Michael had internalised his rage over Ruth's death for years, letting it build up inside him. But he had controlled it. Then, his mother had told him that she was pregnant and that had brought the emotions to the surface until they boiled over. Vera had been trying to help her son, but she'd inadvertently triggered his rage.

And Tanya Ward had died as a result.

"When I told him," Vera said, "it had the opposite effect of what I'd wanted. He looked at me with a glare that would have slain me on the spot if looks could kill. I was going to tell him that I was lying and show him the bump I'm wearing, but his mood had turned so dark that I didn't dare say anything. I had the feeling that if he knew I wasn't pregnant, he'd...do something."

Tony finished his tea and set the cup back on the

tray. "Do you know what he's capable of?"

"Yes, I think so," she said, nodding slowly, her eyes unfocused. "It was when Tanya Ward went missing. Tanya had been my nurse in a hospital some years ago. Samuel would come to visit me and when he did, I saw the way he looked at her. Not in the way many men look at women, with lust in their eyes. No, this was something different. A cold, calculating stare. Like I could see something working behind his eyes; something dark."

She put her cup on the tray next to the teapot. "When it was on the News about Tanya, I had my suspicions. But I told myself I wasn't thinking straight. Then it was announced that there was a link between Tanya and a girl that went missing in Derbyshire. I remembered that Samuel had been in Derbyshire a few weeks earlier, delivering a fridge. As I said, I know what the darkness of the soul looks like and I saw that in Samuel every time I looked at him. Every day since the day I told him I was pregnant."

Tony had no doubt that Vera did indeed recognise the darkness of the soul. She had probably murdered her own husband and daughter.

"Shall I pour us another cup?" he said, indicating the teapot.

"Oh, yes, that would be nice."

He poured the drinks and passed her a cup. As she took it from him, he said, "We'll just wait here a while and enjoy the movie, shall we?"

She smiled at him. "Yes, I'd like that."

CHAPTER THIRTY-FOUR

Dani had no idea how long she'd been wandering in the snowstorm. The tracks were almost completely gone now, nothing more than slight depressions in the snow, almost invisible in the beam of her torch.

She shielded her eyes and tried to make out movement or shapes in front of her but could only see the swirling whiteness of the storm. The wind screamed around her like a banshee announcing an impending tragedy.

Aware that she might stumble into Stokes blindly, she reached into her pocket and took out a canister of Captor spray. The spray only worked when sprayed directly into the eyes, which would be almost impossible to do accurately in this wind.

She wished she'd brought her baton from the car, but she hadn't had time to get it; Teresa and Gemma Matthews were out here somewhere, and they needed her help.

If she needed a handy weapon, and the Captor failed, the torch would have to do as a backup. Its casing was made of steel and she reckoned it was heavy enough to deal a painful blow, especially if she chose the target area carefully.

She moved as quickly as she could through the deepening snow. It soaked through her trousers, numbing her legs. Her face felt rigid and every breath she took into her lungs froze her insides.

She knew that even if Battle and the team had set off straight away from Grantham Farm, it would take them time to get here.

Time that Teresa and Gemma didn't have.

She was their only hope.

As she trudged on through the seemingly never-ending whiteness, she wondered if she'd actually fallen somewhere back on the trail and was dreaming all of this while she slowly froze to death. She felt discon-nected from the rest of the world, alone in a vast expanse of nothingness. Cold and snow were all there was. Even the tracks had disappeared now, buried beneath a white shroud.

Disoriented, she tried to continue in a straight line, but had no idea if she was achieving that goal. For all she knew, she might be going in circles.

Then she heard something. At first, she thought she'd imagined it, or it was the banshee wind playing tricks on her. But then she heard it again. A metallic *clank*.

Using the sound as a guide, she broke into a jog, pushing through the snow with powerful strides. She needed to get to Teresa and Gemma as soon as possible.

A dark shape became discernible through the falling snow and she realised, as she approached it, that it was the concrete structure she'd seen in the photograph on the farmhouse wall. The bunker.

A quad bike was parked a short distance away but there was no sign of Stokes.

Dani moved quickly to the concrete shaft. The hatch was open. A ladder descended into the pitch-black room below.

"This is Detective Inspector Summers of the North Yorkshire police," she called into the shaft while her eyes scanned the area around her. "Is there anyone down there?"

Two female voices floated up to her, one younger than the other.

"Yes! We're down here!"

"Please help us!"

"Is he down there with you?" she called.

"No," the older voice answered.

"Please help us," the younger voice pleaded.

Dani couldn't go down there. If Stokes slammed the hatch shut, she'd be trapped with Teresa and Gemma. "Can you get to the ladder?"

"No, we're tied up. We need you to untie us."

"You're going to have to wait a little longer," Dani said. "I need to find him." She moved away from the hatch and over to the quad bike. A canvas bag on the back of the bike held everything a kidnapper needed to restrain victims: duct tape, rope, cable ties, strips of cloth that could be used as bindings or gags, and a long-bladed knife.

"Step away from the bike," a voice shouted over the howling wind.

Dani turned to face Stokes. He held a shotgun in his hands, and it was levelled at her chest.

"Michael, you don't want to do this," she said.

"Don't I?" he said. "What you mean is that *you* don't want me to do this. *I* want to do it. I *need* to do it."

"Need to do what? Kill a woman and a young girl? What will that achieve?"

"Don't try to confuse me," he said, raising the gun slightly. "I need to kill my mother for what she did to my sister."

"And then what?"

"Then I take the girl to the cliff and she doesn't come back."

"Is that where you were taking Abigail Newton when she jumped from your van? You were taking her to the cliff to end her life?"

"Shut up! You don't understand. It's where Ruth would have wanted to spend her last moments, not lying at the foot of the stairs. I need to put it right. She was relying on me. She had faith in me."

Dani took a step closer to him. If she had even an outside chance of getting the Captor in his eyes, she had to be as close as possible, otherwise the wind would simply snatch the spray away before it got anywhere near Stokes' face.

"Help me to understand, then. You said your mother did something to your sister—"

"She killed her." The hard expression he'd been wearing on his face slipped away and was replaced by tears and a quivering lip. "She killed Ruth."

"Okay, I understand why you're angry, but this isn't going to achieve anything. You're killing people who have nothing to do with what your mother did."

"Well, I can't very well kill *her*, can I? Not while there's an innocent life inside her."

"Michael, you don't have to kill anyone. If your mother has committed a crime, then let the police handle it. We're here to help you."

"No, you're here to stop me."

"I can't let you hurt those women."

Dani lunged forward, depressing the button on the Captor and flinging her arm out in front of her to get the canister as close to Stokes' face as possible.

He instinctively flinched, bringing a hand up to his face.

The wind blew the stream of liquid away before it got anywhere near him.

Dani followed up with a downward blow of the torch across his arm, hoping to make him drop the shotgun.

He didn't. Instead, he pulled the trigger.

The blast didn't sound loud at all, which surprised Dani. She would barely have known the weapon had been discharged at all if not for the white-hot pain she suddenly felt on her right side. She didn't dare look down to see what the damage was; while she was still able, she had to stop Stokes.

She whipped her arm up at his face, as if slapping him with the back of her hand. But it was steel, not flesh that contacted the bridge of his nose. The torch slammed into his face and sent him reeling, his hands going to his bloody nose.

He dropped the shotgun in the snow.

Dani stepped over it. She didn't have time to stop and pick it up. She didn't know how much time she had before she lost consciousness. Black dots swum in her vision and her legs felt unsteady.

She reached Stokes, who was leaning forward and trying to control his bleeding nose. Dani brought the torch down hard onto the base of his skull. He let out a *whuff* sound and collapsed onto the snow.

Dani angled away from him and now she went for the shotgun. Picking it up, she hurled it into the maelstrom. With one hand pressed against her side, she staggered to the quad bike. She felt as if she had a thousand stinging hornets in her rib cage. She knew she was about to pass out from shock, or maybe even blood loss.

Grabbing a roll of duct tape from the canvas bag, she began to make her way back to Stokes. She had to restrain him before she lost consciousness.

The world suddenly began to spin crazily around her. She dropped the tape and fell to her knees.

Don't black out. Not yet.

Despite the amount of will she exerted to stay conscious, the black spots bloomed in her vision, blotting out everything.

CHAPTER THIRTY-FIVE

Samuel woke with a groan. He had the worst headache of his life; the back of his head pulsed with angry pain. He got to his knees and surveyed the scene around him.

The detective was crumpled on the ground some distance away, a roll of duct tape lying next to her. She was already partly covered with snow and that made him wonder how long he'd been out of it.

It didn't really matter.

The knock on his head, although painful, had brought him clarity. He now knew what he needed to do.

Climbing to his feet gingerly, he put a hand to the back of his head. Even through his glove, he could feel the swelling there. His nose also felt swollen, as if it was a tight balloon attached to his face. It had stopped bleeding, probably due to the cold temperature, and the blood had crusted over his mouth. He could taste its coppery tang on his lips.

He took a few tentative steps forward. The pain flared in his head but, despite that, he felt all right. No, better than all right; he felt good. He knew where he was going and what he had to do. His path was clear. He'd ignored it for too long, made excuses to avoid doing what had to be done, but no more.

He walked over to the detective. The snow beneath her body was tinged red but she was still breathing. He could see the front of her jacket rising and falling with each breath.

He'd known, when he saw her picture on TV, that she was pretty but she was even prettier in the flesh. She was also clever. He had no idea how she'd found him. But one thing he did know was that if one cop was here, then there were sure to be plenty more on their way.

He had to act quickly.

If all went as he planned, then it didn't matter how many members of the Murder Force, or whatever it was called, came here. All they'd find would be a dead body and he would be long gone, on his way to be with Ruth forever.

Leaving the detective in the snow, he climbed onto the quad bike and started the engine. The machine rumbled beneath him, powerful and purposeful.

The woman and the girl in the bunker started shouting again but he ignored them. He'd wasted too much time avoiding the one thing he should be doing. Killing Tanya Ward hadn't brought him any relief from the torment that tortured his mind; the knowledge that he'd let Ruth down by not killing their mother in time.

The woman and her daughter were distractions, sent by the Devil to mislead him, just as Tanya and the girl who'd jumped from his van had been.

He took the knife out of the canvas bag and held it in front of his face. His grandad's knife. The knife Ruth had pressed into his hand and begged him to use. The blade reflected his bloodied face.

Stowing the knife inside his coat, he turned the quad bike around and headed towards the house. The wind was at his back, as if speeding him to his destination. Even the snow, which had blown into his face on the way to the bunker, now seemed to be dancing in the air around him, creating patterns that he couldn't decipher but that he knew were telling him to hurry up and complete his task.

Whether she had a baby inside her or not, his mother had to die. The knife that Ruth had given to him would now be used exactly as she had asked.

Their mother would pay for what she had done to his sister and then Samuel would go to the cliff where he'd spent so much time with Ruth and end his own life with the same blade. He would be with Ruth forever.

Maybe, after it was all done, the police would find her grave behind the barn and dig her up so she could be buried properly. Maybe they'd even bury her with him in a cemetery. A shared grave. That sounded perfect.

He saw the farmhouse lights through the swirling patterns of snow and grinned.

Soon, everything would be put right.

CHAPTER THIRTY-SIX

Tony checked his watch. Dani had been gone ages. He'd thought that a woman as capable as she obviously was, would find Michael and take him down quickly. He hadn't even considered any other possibility, and Battle's order to keep an eye on Vera had kept him here in the house.

Now he was thinking that he should have gone with his colleague. Vera wasn't going anywhere. She had no idea that the same Murder Force she'd seen on TV was, at this moment, headed for her front door.

And Tony wasn't sure how many more cups of tea he could manage. He was already dying to go to the loo. "Do you mind if I use the bathroom again?" he asked.

Vera tore her eyes away from the TV and nodded. "Of course. You know where it is."

In fact, he didn't know where it was, since the last time he'd ventured upstairs, he'd wandered into Vera's bedroom, but he was sure he could find it. He got up off the sofa and went upstairs, taking his phone out of his pocket. He was about to call Dani when he realised he had her phone.

He reached the landing and found the bathroom. It was indeed on the right, but Vera hadn't mentioned that it was the *second* door on the right.

After he'd rid himself of five cups of tea and was washing his hands, he made the decision that when he got back downstairs, he was going out to find Dani. He'd find Vera's car keys and take them with him to keep Battle happy, but he was sure she wasn't going to budge from the sofa.

Besides, the team would be here soon, surely. Even with the bad weather, they'd had plenty of time to travel the few miles between Grantham Farm and here.

Looking at his reflection in the mirror and nodding to it as if confirming his own decision, he left the bathroom and crossed the landing. He was going to find Dani. He'd thought she'd deal with Michael Stokes no problem but he, more than anyone, should know that it was a terrible mistake to underestimate killers.

When he got to the top of the stairs, he froze for a second. The air felt colder, as if someone had opened a door to the outside. He peered down at the sofa. Vera wasn't there.

"Shit!" She'd done a runner after all.

He vaulted down the stairs and called, "Vera? Are you there?" Opening the door that led to the hallway, he was surprised to find the front door closed. Returning to the living room, he peeked out through the window. Vera's red Nissan Micra was still parked where it had been when he and Dani had arrived, and it was still half-buried in the snow.

Tony went into the kitchen. She'd gone out of the back door and left it open. Why? She wasn't going to get very far on foot.

He heard an engine start and rushed outside in time to see a white van parked at the side of the house, engine running. Vera was in the passenger seat and, behind the wheel, Tony could see a young man wearing a New York Yankees baseball cap.

Vera saw Tony through her window and stared at him with worried eyes. She mouthed the word "help" before the van pulled away, ploughing through the snow and heading for the front of the house and the road that led away from the farmhouse.

"Michael!" Tony shouted. "Stop!"

But the van kept moving, driving away into the snowy night.

Tony sprinted back into the house and searched frantically for Vera's car keys. "Where would she keep them?" he asked himself over and over as he opened drawers and cast his eyes over every surface in the kitchen and living room.

"The front door," he told himself. "A lot of patients who suffered from mental issues could be forgetful, and one of their coping strategies was to keep items in a place where they'd be found when needed. Vera would need her keys if she was going out the front door.

He strode to the hallway and found a blue, ceramic ashtray sitting on a small table by the front door. A selection of keys lay inside, including a black fob with the Nissan logo embossed on it in silver plastic.

Tony snatched it up and returned to the living room to grab his coat. Putting it on, he left the house and ran through the snow to the half-buried car. Opening the driver's door, he started the engine and put the heater on full blast. Closing the door again, he swept the snow from the windscreen and the headlights.

Michael had come back to the house, so did that mean Dani hadn't found him? Or was the truth something much worse?

He dragged his phone from his pocket and called Battle.

When the DCI answered, Tony said, "We need an ambulance. I think DI Summers is down. Stokes has escaped in his van. He's taken his mother."

"We've got an ambulance with us and we should be there in a couple of minutes," Battle said. "Which way is Stokes headed?"

Tony looked towards the road, but he couldn't see it because of the trees. "I don't know." Then he remembered the photo of Michael on the cliff near Whitby Abbey. If Michael knew he'd been found out, he was probably carrying out some sort of end game. He'd most likely choose somewhere he knew well to do that.

"Whitby Abbey," he told Battle. "He's probably going to Whitby Abbey."

"All right. I'll send some of the team there while the ambulance attends DI Summers. What condition is she in?"

"I don't know. I'm not sure where she is. I shouldn't have let her go out there alone. I should have gone with her."

"Calm down, Tony, we'll be there in a minute. Just wait there."

"No, I'm going after him." He ended the call and got into the Micra. He had to push the driver's seat back to fit inside. As he reversed away from the house, the snow that had been on the roof slid over the windscreen. Tony found the wipers and switched them on.

The car skidded as he spun the wheel so that he was facing the road that led through the trees. Even though he wanted to gun the engine and get the car up to speed, he applied pressure to the accelerator pedal gently. There was no point in spinning the wheels and going nowhere.

The Micra set off down the road at a steady pace. The van's tracks were clearly visible in the headlight beam, but Tony was sure he knew where Michael was going. When the farmhouse road intersected with the main road, he realised he didn't know the way to Whitby from here.

He dug into his pocket and retrieved his phone, stabbing at the screen until he got the GPS app. As he typed his destination into the app, he realised how much his hands were shaking. Images of the Lake Erie Ripper's house, the front door open and waiting, flashed into his mind.

Trying to ignore them, he managed to get the destination into the phone and turned up the volume before tossing the phone onto the passenger seat. A woman's voice told him to turn left.

He did so, and noticed that the van tracks also led in that direction.

He pressed the accelerator as much as he dared. He'd be no good to anyone if he skidded off the road and ended up in a ditch.

Peering through the windscreen, he tried to pick out the rear lights of the van that was somewhere ahead of him, but the snow was too thick to see much of anything.

If he didn't catch up to Michael soon, he had no doubt that by the time he arrived at Whitby Abbey, both Vera and Michael would be dead.

———

DANI CAME to when she heard an engine start up somewhere nearby. Her eyes fluttered open and she winced at the pain in her side, which felt like she had white hot coals burning under her skin. As the engine noise receded, she sat upright in time to see Michael riding away into the storm.

Her heart sank as she realised he might have Teresa and Gemma with him.

Getting to her knees, she took a moment to orientate herself. She must have passed out from the shock of being shot. Her body had chosen the worst time to shut down.

The snow where she'd been lying was stained with blood and more was leaking from a ragged tear in her jacket. She picked up the roll of duct tape and wound it around herself tightly. She didn't have time to inspect the wound in her side. She had to find out if Teresa and Gemma were still in the bunker and get them to safety.

If they weren't, she had to get back to the farmhouse, anyway. She couldn't stay out here; she'd die of exposure before too long.

With the duct tape cinching her ribs, she picked up her torch, got to her feet, and made her way to the open hatch. "Are you still down there?" Her voice echoed in the darkness below.

"Yes, please help us," Teresa's voice replied.

Gritting her teeth against the pain in her side, Dani lowered herself through the hatch and found the ladder with her feet. When she got to the bottom, she had to lean against the wall as she shone her torch around the room.

Teresa and Gemma were tied to a bed by the far wall. They both had wide-eyed expressions of fear on their faces that Dani had seen many times. At least they were fully clothed in winter gear; Stokes must have made them put their coats and hats on before taking them from their house. It wouldn't fit his plans if they died of exposure down here in the cold and dark.

"My name's Dani," she told them as she pushed away from the wall and approached the bed. "I'm going to get you out of here."

"Where is he?" Teresa asked.

"He's gone. He's not here." She thought of Sheridan at the farmhouse. She had no way of warning him that Stokes was probably on his way there. She shouldn't have given the psychologist her phone before coming out here, but she hadn't been thinking straight at the time. All she could think of was saving Teresa and Gemma.

Holding the torch in her mouth, she worked at the knots in the rope that secured the women to the bed. It took a while, but she finally untied them and stepped back, leaning on the wall for support again while they clambered off the bed.

"Thank you," Teresa said, shaking her arms as if trying to get the blood flowing into them. "I didn't think we'd ever get out of here."

"We're not out of the woods yet," Dani told her. "We're in the middle of nowhere and it's a long way back to safety. Are you both able to walk?"

They nodded quickly. There was no way they were going to spend any longer down here than they had to.

"All right, let's go," Dani said, shining the torch at the ladder.

They climbed out one by one, and when they were all out and standing by the hatch, Dani pointed at the quad bike tracks in the snow. "We follow those," she said, raising her voice so she could be heard above the wind.

Teresa and Gemma nodded their understanding and all three of them set off into the swirling storm, their eyes fixed on the tracks at their feet.

We're going to make it, Dani told herself. *Just stay conscious. Ignore the pain.* With every step, a sharp stabbing pain flared in her ribs. She couldn't remember ever being in this much agony; not even when she'd given birth to Charlotte.

After taking a couple more steps, her legs gave out and she tumbled into the snow. Teresa and Gemma knelt next to her with concern in their eyes.

"Are you all right?" Teresa asked.

"Just give me a minute," Dani said through gritted teeth. "I'll be okay." Even as she said the words, she knew they weren't true. Something inside her was broken; probably one or two of her ribs.

Gemma looked into the storm with a worried expression. "Did you hear that? There's someone out there."

Dani listened. She heard a shout. The sound was snatched away by the wind. Then it came again. Distant but recognisable. Someone was calling her name.

"Dani!"

She tried to call back but taking a breath was too painful.

"Can you call back?" she asked Teresa and Gemma. "Get his attention."

"Are you sure?" Teresa asked, holding her daughter closely. "Is it safe? Do you know who it is?"

Dani nodded. "It's my boss."

CHAPTER THIRTY-SEVEN

Tony steered the Micra onto the road that led to Whitby Abbey. He could see the van now, its red taillights glowing in the darkness ahead, and he pushed the Micra's speed up a fraction to get closer.

The taillights ahead suddenly flared as Michael applied the brakes and the van stopped. The doors opened and Michael got out. He went around to the passenger side and dragged Vera out of the vehicle before heading off toward the cliff with her.

"No!" Tony shouted. He was too far away to talk to Michael, to try to reason with him. If he didn't get to Michael now, Vera was as good as dead. There was no time for caution, He pressed the Micra's accelerator to the floor. The car's tyres spun uselessly for a couple of seconds, then found traction. The Nissan shot forward.

It only took a couple of seconds to reach the parked van, which suddenly loomed in the windscreen. Tony applied the brakes. The Micra fishtailed, spraying snow into the air as it skidded across the road. Its bonnet clipped the van and Tony was slammed against his seatbelt before the car came to a dead stop.

Releasing the seatbelt and pulling it off, he opened the door and scrambled out of the car, looking for Michael and Vera.

He saw them, moving towards the cliff edge, Vera struggling against her son as he pulled her along over the slippery snow.

"Michael!" Tony shouted, breaking into a jog. "Wait!"

"Don't try to stop me," Michael shouted back. He had one arm around his mother's throat, while his knife-wielding hand hovered over her chest, the blade pointed at her heart. His voice sounded calm and that worried Tony. Michael was playing his endgame here and seemed accepting of the bitter end his plan entailed.

His face was bloody, and he looked like he was in pain. That probably meant Dani had found him after all, and some sort of scuffle had ensued. The fact that Michael had returned to the farmhouse and Dani hadn't, made Tony's gut feel hollow.

"Listen to me," he said, slowing his pace as he got closer. "This isn't going to change anything." He cast a worried glance at the cliff edge. Michael and Vera were dangerously close to it.

Two hundred feet below, the sea crashed against rocks, tumultuous and wild.

"It's going to change everything," Michael said.

"She'll die for what she did to Ruth, and I'll be with my sister forever, the way it should have been all along."

"And what about the baby she's carrying? Does that deserve to die as well?"

Michael faltered. His eyes flickered down to the protrusion beneath his mother's robe. He had no idea it was nothing more than a silicon bump and a few straps holding it in place.

"Do you think Ruth would want you to kill an innocent child?" Tony said. "What would she say if she could see you now?"

"She can see me." Michael held the knife at his mother's throat. "This is what she wanted me to do ten years ago and now, I'm finally doing it."

"Really?" Tony asked. "She wanted you to kill an innocent baby? I don't think so. What kind of person would she be if she wanted that?"

"She was a beautiful person. A kind and loving person."

Tony could hear vehicles coming along the road behind him. The team had arrived. But instead of feeling glad that he had backup, he was fearful that their presence might send Michael over the edge, literally as well as figuratively.

"That's not how she'll be remembered, though, is it?" he said to Michael, trying to keep the young man's attention. Despite the fact that every nerve in his body felt wound up so tightly that it might break, he tried to keep his voice casual. "I can see the headlines now. They'll all say you killed a pregnant woman for your dead sister. It's going to stain Ruth's memory, Michael. She'll be remembered as an evil girl who wanted you to kill a baby."

"She didn't want me to kill a baby!"

"No, she didn't. In fact, this was all about protecting a baby, wasn't it? The baby that was growing inside her."

Michael nodded.

"But the papers won't see it that way," Tony said. He could hear car doors being slammed shut behind him. Footsteps approaching. "I mean, if you think Ruth would be okay with you killing a baby, that says a lot about what kind of person she must have been. The media will have a field day with it. Ruth's will become known as a child-killer."

"That isn't true!" Tears started to run from Michael's eyes, mingling with the blood around his nose and mouth.

"It doesn't matter if it's true," Tony said matter-of-factly. "They print stuff that isn't true all the time to sell newspapers. Do you think the general public will believe Ruth was a lovely girl and that you've got it all wrong by thinking she'd want you to kill a pregnant woman? Or will they believe Ruth was evil and has been manipulating you from beyond the grave?"

Michael shook his head. "No, this is all wrong."

The footsteps were getting closer. Tony turned his head towards the dozen or so uniformed police officers behind him and held up a hand. They stopped in their tracks and waited.

"It *is* all wrong," Tony said, turning back to Michael. "The only thing you'll achieve by carrying out your plan is to drag Ruth's name through the dirt."

Michael glanced at the cliff edge. "I just want to be with her."

"Michael," Tony said, sensing that this conversation was about to come to an end one way or another, "If Ruth was the wonderful sister you say she was, she wouldn't want you to die. Not like this. She'd want you to live your life. Put the knife down and let your mother go. Then you can tell me all about Ruth and I'll make sure the papers get it right."

Michael hesitated, his eyes flickering to the cliff edge and then his mother, and then the cliff edge again. Tony could see the tension increase in the young man's face. He wondered if he would have time to rush forward and pull Vera and Michael back from the edge.

"You're right," Michael said, finally. "I can't have people believing bad things about Ruth. I won't hurt an innocent baby." He pushed his mother away from the cliff edge roughly. She stumbled and slipped on the snow.

Michael turned towards the cliff edge. "But I want to be with her. I need to be with Ruth."

Tony's heart leapt into his mouth as he realised Michael was about to rush over the edge of the cliff but the young man's features, which had become accepting of his fate suddenly changed to anger and he turned back towards his mother.

Vera was lying on the ground. The fake bump

beneath her robe had become dislodged when she'd been pushed and was now lying at an unnatural angle. It was obvious to everyone, and, most importantly, to her son, that she wasn't pregnant at all.

Suddenly realising that an innocent child played no part in the equation at all, Michael approached his mother with the knife. "You liar! How could you lie to me?"

"I only wanted you to be happy," Vera cried. "I only ever wanted you to be happy."

Michael raised the knife above his head, his features twisted into a mixture of hate, misery, and anger.

Tony sprinted forwards towards the mother and son, but even as he did so, he knew he wasn't going to get there in time to save Vera.

A shape came barrelling out of the swirling snow, colliding with Michael and knocking him to the ground. The knife landed in the snow some distance away.

DC Ryan was on top of Michael, raising a fist to punch the young man in the face.

"Ryan, no!" Tony shouted. "We've got him. It's all right. We've got him."

Ryan resisted the urge to land his fist on Michael's face and, instead, rolled the young man over and cuffed him with a pair of handcuffs that had been hanging from his belt. He looked over at Tony. "You're right, doc, we've got him. But that was a bloody close one!" His trademark grin appeared on his face.

The uniformed officers moved forward to deal with Michael and his mother.

Tony walked away, back towards the Micra, ringing Battle as he did so. When the DCI answered, Tony said, "Is she okay?"

"Well she's not about to enter Strictly Come Dancing," Battle said, "but she'll live. She's in the ambulance now, along with Teresa and Gemma Matthews."

Tony closed his eyes and let out a long sigh of relief. "That's good news," he said.

"What's happening your end?" Battle asked.

"Vera and Michael Stokes have been arrested."

"Well, that's good news, as well. This sorry mess has finally come to an end."

"Yes," Tony said. He reached the vehicles. Half a dozen SOCOs, in white Tyvek suits, were examining the van and the Micra.

"Umm, I need that one to get home," Tony told the officer nearest to him.

"Sorry, it's evidence," she replied. "We've been told to bring it all in, including this car."

"Great," Tony said, turning away. How was he supposed to get home now?

"I'll give you a lift, doc." Ryan was standing a few feet away, hands thrust in the pockets of his jacket but otherwise seemingly unaffected by the cold.

"All right, thanks."

"I'm parked over here," Ryan said, nodding towards a car park where a number of police were parked, along with his Aston Martin.

The two of them walked towards the car.

"Good job talking him down," Ryan said. "At one point, I thought they were both going over that cliff."

"Good job yourself. That was some rugby tackle. You saved that woman's life."

Ryan nodded. "All in a day's work."

They reached the car and got in.

"Do you think every case is going to be like this?" Tony asked, looking through the windscreen at the uniformed officers leading Michael and Vera, in hand-cuffs, to the police vans. "Now that we're part of Murder Force, I mean. Is it all going to be so dangerous and desperate?"

Ryan started the engine and pulled out of the parking space. "It had better be," he said with a grin.

CHAPTER THIRTY-EIGHT

Dani sat in her hospital bed, watching the television in her room but not taking in any of what she was looking at. Her thoughts kept returning to the events of the day. The pain in her side, dulled by morphine, felt like nothing more than a dull ache now but the doctors who operated on her had told her that she had two cracked ribs.

According to the SOCOs who had taken Michael Stokes' gun from the van and examined it, the weapon looked like it had been sitting on a shelf in damp conditions for years and, as a result, the gunpowder in the cartridges had degraded.

That, along with the facts that the cartridges had been lightly loaded with bird shot—which was lighter and less damaging than buckshot—and Dani had been wearing layers of thick clothing when she'd been shot meant the outcome of her encounter with Stokes had ended much less seriously than it might have otherwise.

The surgeons had removed the shot and bound Dani's torso to let the ribs heal.

The door to her room opened and Charlotte entered, her face a mask of concern.

"Charlie!" Dani said, sitting up. "What are you doing here?"

"What do you mean what am I doing here?" Charlotte bent over her and gave her a gentle hug. "You're in hospital so of course I'm going to come!"

"I meant how did you know I was here?"

"Tony Sheridan rang me from your phone. He explained what had happened and said he thought I should know. He's very nice."

"He is," Dani said. "But I wasn't going to worry you until tomorrow. I didn't want you spending your first Christmas away from home worrying about me."

"Don't be ridiculous." Her daughter dropped into an armchair next to the bed. "I always worry about you. You know that."

"Well, you shouldn't. I don't want you to. How did you get here?"

"Elliot drove me. He's downstairs in the cafeteria. The nurse at the desk said you can't have too many visitors in the room."

"I'm sure two is fine."

Charlotte smiled. "There are a lot more people than that here to see you, Mum."

As if on cue, Sheridan's head appeared around the door. "Can we come in?"

"Yes, of course," Dani said.

The psychologist entered the room, followed by Tom Ryan and Matt Flowers. "I thought I'd better return this," he said, showing Dani her phone and placing it on the bedside locker.

"Thank you. How are things going at the station?"

"Vera had admitted to killing her husband," he said. "It seems she wasn't too happy about being committed and soon after she got out of Larkmoor, she bludgeoned Jonathan to death and buried him in the cellar. Michael and Ruth didn't know anything about it and, soon after, they moved to Wild Row Farm. But Vera kept returning to that cellar to speak to Jonathan. She'd convinced herself that he was alive. I don't think she could face the fact that she'd killed him."

"We'll get more out of them tomorrow morning, after they've spent a night in the cells," Battle said, appearing at the door. "How are you feeling?"

"Not too bad," Dani said. "I think the drugs are keeping most of the pain away."

"Well, you take as much time as you need before you come back to work. Murder Force isn't going anywhere. We'll be waiting for you when you're ready."

"Thanks." She turned her face to the window, tears welling in her eyes. She wasn't even sure why she felt like crying.

Reading the situation, Battle said, "Right, everybody out. Let's leave DI Summers to have some time with her daughter."

He ushered everyone out of the door and gave Dani a short wave before leaving himself.

"It's okay, Mum," Charlotte said, taking Dani's hand. "You can cry all you want; you've had a tough day."

"I'm okay," Dani said, patting her daughter's hand. She looked at the night and the snow beyond the window.

Last winter, it had been the Snow Killer. This winter, Michael Stokes. She turned to her daughter and said, "I just really hate this time of year."

―――――

GET the next book in the series now!

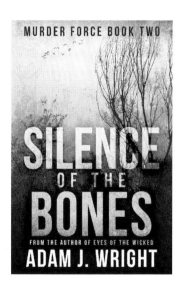

A WICKED MERCY - Harriet Quinn Book One

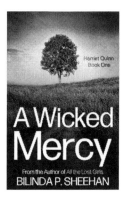

A new series starring Yorkshire profiler Harriett Quinn.

Printed in Great Britain
by Amazon